Nina Bawden was born in London in 1925 and educated at Ilford County High School for Girls and Somerville College, Oxford. Her acclaimed career spans twenty adult novels, ten of which are published by Virago, and seventeen for children. For ten years she served as a magistrate, both in her local court and in the Crown Court. She has also sat on the councils of various literary bodies, including the Royal Society of Literature – of which she is a Fellow – PEN, the Society of Authors, and the ALCS. She is the President of the Society of Women Writers and Journalists. In addition she has lectured at conferences and universities, on Arts Council tours and in schools. Nina Bawden is married to Austen Kark, formerly Managing Director of the External Services of the BBC. They live in London and Greece. Nina Bawden was created a CBE in 1995.

THE WORKS OF NINA BAWDEN

NOVELS

Who Calls the Tune (1953)
The Odd Flamingo (1954)
Change Here for Babylon (1955)
The Solitary Child (1956)
Devil by the Sea (1958)
Just Like a Lady (1960)
In Honour Bound (1961)
Tortoise by Candlelight (1963)
Under the Skin (1964)
A Little Love, A Little Learning (1965)
A Woman of My Age (1967)
The Grain of Truth (1969)
The Birds on the Trees (1970)
Anna Apparent (1972)
George Beneath a Paper Moon (1974)
Afternoon of a Good Woman (1976)
Familiar Passions (1979)
Walking Naked (1981)
The Ice House (1983)
Circles of Deceit (1987)
Family Money (1991)

CHILDREN'S BOOKS

The Secret Passage (1963)
On the Run (1964)
The White Horse Gang (1966)
The Witch's Daughter (1966)
A Handful of Thieves (1967)
The Runaway Summer (1969)
Squib (1971)
Carrie's War (1973)
The Peppermint Pig (1975)
Rebel on a Rock (1978)
The Robbers (1979)
Kept in the Dark (1982)
The Finding (1985)
Keeping Henry (1988)
The Outside Child (1989)
Humbug (1992)
The Real Plato Jones (1994)
Granny the Pag (1995)

PICTURE BOOKS
Princess Alice (1986)

AUTOBIOGRAPHY
In My Own Time (1995)

A
NICE
CHANGE

Nina Bawden

A *Virago* Book

Published by Virago Press 1998

First published by Virago Press 1997
Reprinted 1998

A CIP catalogue record for this book is available
from the British Library

ISBN 1 86049 405 6

Typeset in Berkeley by M Rules
Printed and bound in Great Britain by
Clays Ltd, St Ives plc

Virago
A Division of
Little, Brown and Company (UK)
Brettenham House
Lancaster Place
London WC2E 7EN

For Austen

You see, one thing is, I can live with doubt and uncertainty and not knowing. I think it's more interesting to live not knowing than to have answers which might be wrong.

I have approximate answers and possible beliefs and different degrees of certainty about different things but I'm not absolutely sure of anything and there are many things I don't know anything about, such as whether it means anything to ask why we're here . . .

Richard Feynman (1918–1988), Joint Nobel Prize for Physics 1965

1

THE LAST THING TOM JONES HAD expected was to run into Portia on holiday. An embarrassing encounter in London was all he had ever envisaged – and dreaded. They both live (that is, he assumes Portia still does) in the same square mile of the city, a proximity once blissfully convenient that after they ceased to be lovers had deeply alarmed him. For a long time he had feared they might run across each other by chance, bracing himself whenever he and Amy went to a theatre, an art gallery, a neighbourhood party.

His fears (he told himself fairly truthfully) were for Amy. Although she knew he had had an affair and had forgiven him, put it behind her, she had never met Portia, had no idea what she looked like, had not once asked her name. The thought of the two women in the same room together, his innocent Amy unknowing, appalled him. (The thought of enlightening her, as he would honourably have to do should this disagreeable situation arise, had appalled him

1

even more.) But as the years passed (four by now) he had worried progressively less; lately, he realises now, hardly at all. Foolishly . . .

Never let your guard slip, that's the lesson, he thinks gloomily, watching the small, neatly plump figure (still surprisingly and immediately familiar) trundling her wheeled suitcase out of the airport into the agreeably hot Aegean sunshine, advancing towards a smartly polished green minibus. Deciphering the name of the hotel, painted in flowing gold script on the side, Tom's last, faint hope dies.

Christ, he thinks, feeling sweat breaking out at his hairline, around his shirt collar. What the hell is she doing here? What the hell can *he* do? Amy has booked (a package deal, paid in advance) this reportedly comfortable hotel entirely for his benefit. She hates lying around pools, or on beaches, is bored by rich food as she is bored by rich people, likes to keep on the move when she travels. But he has just had a small but humiliating operation that made bicycling around Brittany, their earlier, energetic plan for this summer fortnight, out of the question. Amy pretended (again for his sake) that she was not disappointed. An idly luxurious holiday would make a nice change, she had said. She had even gone shopping for what she considered suitable clothes with quite convincing enjoyment. This, too, was to please him.

She is wearing one of her purchases now, a full-skirted black dress rampant with purple roses that accentuates her height and dark, bony looks, making her appear unnaturally exotic and foreign, a handsome gypsy rather than a respectable lawyer. Better if she had stuck to her white blouses, her neat suits and trousers, Tom thinks, watching

2

her point out their bags to a porter. He hobbles (walking is still sometimes shockingly painful) towards her. 'Why don't we get a taxi?'

She looks at him, frowning. 'Do you really want to? It's a long way and we've already paid for the bus.'

Now was the moment. *Darling, I'm sorry, this is so ridiculous*. He says, 'Oh, well, then. Never mind,' feeling the usual irritation – presumably, if you'd been born rich like Amy, taking care of the pennies was an indulgence, a luxury.

She says swiftly, 'Oh, I'm sorry. Of course, if you're tired.'

'I'm fine.' He widens his eyes – a good campaign trick, producing the open and honest expression that goes down well with the kind of voters who long to believe that not all politicians are venal. 'I was thinking of you. I'm such a bloody useless sod at the moment, you've had to do everything, I thought you might be more comfortable.'

This is overdoing it, even for Amy. She raises her dark eyebrows with an amused (though fond) incredulity.

'I do sometimes think of you,' he says haughtily.

'I know, darling.' A contrite, though still amused, smile. 'Look – we will take a taxi.'

'No. You're quite right. Waste of money.'

Covertly, he looks beyond her. Portia is watching her suitcase being loaded into the luggage compartment of the minibus. When it is stowed to her satisfaction (she has always been fussy about her possessions, insisting her coat is hung where she can see it in restaurants, keeping her purse on her lap), she turns and stares in his direction. Has she *seen* him? She is wearing large, very dark glasses. Oh, God. At least she isn't clacking towards him on those silly heels, gold bangles tinkling, uttering shrill squeaks of

3

welcome. Has he changed so much? *Aged*? Perhaps he has put on a little weight, turned a mite grey at the temples. He stands erect, tucks in his belly, stretches his jaw line. Ah, now she *is* looking at him. Head on one side like an inquisitive bird. Pretty hair – still the same auburny red, flaming orange where the sun strikes it. Dyed, probably. That she dyed her hair had not struck him before.

'Why don't you get in the bus?' Amy says. 'I need to go to the loo.'

'Why didn't you go on the plane?' He hears himself ask this boorish question and shudders. 'Oh, God. Sorry. I only meant, you won't be long, will you? I'll wait. Run along, there's a good girl.'

She runs, full skirt catching between her legs, impeding her normal long, loping stride. There is no hurry. Why does she take him so *literally*?

Portia is getting into the minibus. *Of course*, he remembers, she is short-sighted. At this distance, he will be just a blurred figure. Unless her sunglasses are made to prescription. Or she has already spotted him on the plane.

He ought to warn Amy. It will ruin her holiday. (His is ruined already, but never mind that!) Surely Portia can be relied on? She had always been sensibly discreet, understood he loved Amy, had no intention of leaving her. Though one can never be certain. Portia has a malicious streak. Several times she had rung him at home, putting on a peculiar, guttural accent, pretending she thought she was speaking to a laundry to complain about sheets and towels, articles of clothing that had been returned soiled or damaged. Perhaps he should get in the minibus while Amy is safe in the lavatory and warn Portia not to make trouble. But even if he could bring himself to do that (and a

4

dreadful paralysis of will seizes him at the mere thought) it would be a grotesque kind of betrayal, a conspiracy against Amy. That is how Amy would see it, certainly. If she finds out, she might leave him. She had nearly left him in the beginning, when he had told her. (Found himself telling her without having meant to, blurting it out on her *birthday*, for Christ's sake.)

Maybe honesty is the safest policy now. Or maybe not.

He begins sweating again. Amy might pretend to believe he had been taken by surprise but at the back of her mind she might wonder if he were still cheating her. Worse – that he had arranged this absurd assignation. However much he might deny it, protest the affair was over, that Portia had, long since, consoled herself elsewhere, why should Amy trust him? The worm of doubt must always be there in her mind. No, that is unfair. It is he who feels he is no longer trustworthy, that in lying to Amy he has compromised himself irretrievably. He can never again think of himself as an honest man. (There is a certain enjoyment in this self-abasement that he acknowledges occasionally, even though most of the time he prefers to see it as a decent humility.)

The sunlight shimmers liquidly between the open doors of the airport and the minibus. Other people are getting in. Perhaps, with luck, there won't be room for them after all. The hotel is a couple of hours away, he thinks Amy has told him. Alone, in a taxi, he would have time to explain to her, gently and ruefully, making a wry joke of it. How would *he* take it if the boot were on the other foot? If it had been an ex-lover of Amy's who had turned up so unfortunately? Amy has no lovers, ex or current, as far as he knows. But, for the sake of supposition, would she tell *him*? Probably not, he decides. Women are more brazen than men, better liars, more *practical*. Amy wouldn't see this situation as presenting the kind of moral difficulties he feels he is faced with. In fact she might get quite a kick out of it, a romantic excitement, sexually stimulating. If she were to become more eager in bed, would he guess she was deceiving him?

He ponders darkly as he watches her coming towards him. She has brushed her thick brown hair; it bounces on her broad shoulders, on her benign forehead. She says, 'Come on, poor old love,' and tucks her hand under his elbow in what seems an unnecessarily proprietary gesture. On the other hand, it is a good thing that Portia should observe them behaving so obviously as a *couple*, stop her getting any silly ideas. He says, 'Let me take that bag, darling,' and freeing his arm, slings the canvas holdall on his shoulder, between them.

The only vehicles immediately outside the airport building are the minibus and a vast, grey, army tank with two sleepy young soldiers on guard beside it. There is a long line of yellow taxis a couple of hundred yards away, but an even longer line of prospective passengers shuffling along in the heavy heat. Amy says – fatuously, it seems to him – 'See what I've saved you from!'

There are several vacant seats in the minibus. Tom and Amy sit immediately behind the driver. Portia is at the back of the bus, on a bench seat with two other people, smiling and talking and waving her lit cigarette in its ebony holder. *Bloody smoking*, Tom thinks, sitting down after one furtive, unreturned glance, eyes front, neck rigid. Amy had never smoked and he had given up when the children were small. He must have come home with the smell in his hair, on his breath. When the balloon went up finally, when he

6

had stupidly *sent* it up, wanting to make love to her after a celebratory dinner and suddenly ashamed of this falsehood lying between them, Amy had said, 'So that's why you stank of tobacco!'

Why the hell hadn't she said something before, he thinks sourly, sitting in the hotel minibus with Portia smoking and chattering behind him. It would have come to an end a lot sooner if Amy had been more suspicious. 'She can't have loved you all that much or she would have known,' Portia had cried angrily, and he had been fool enough to repeat this to Amy, either resentfully half-believing it or seizing upon it as a fatally feeble defence, laying himself open to the obvious answer, 'I suppose I trusted you.'

Amy offers him her hand now, trustingly, and he holds it on his knee. She laces her fingers in his and he squeezes them gently. She sighs and snuggles against him. Nestles. Amy is big and angular but it seems she has a touching image of herself as little and feminine. That is, it seems touching sometimes. Tom fears that Portia, gazing at them as she must surely be doing by now, she isn't *that* blind, will find Amy comical.

Amy says, 'Relax, darling, you feel terribly *tense*,' in her loudest, most cheerful voice, and Tom grits his teeth. The driver had started the bus when Amy spoke. Could Portia have heard her above the noisy grind of the engine? He looks at his wife and sees she is smiling, her upper lip caught between her large, white teeth. He is seized with a horrible sudden fear that Amy's remark was deliberate, that she knows Portia is there, and is teasing him.

Utter rot, he thinks, only a madman would think that of Amy. A paranoid lunatic.

*

'Ha! What are you up to? I've got my eye on you, Jones, don't think I haven't!'

The tone of the voice is familiar. It rings in Tom's ears so clearly that he almost turns round to see if old Clack-Teeth is in the bus with them. Loathsome man, made two years of his schooldays a misery, but safely dead now of cancer. Tom answers him silently. 'Nothing, Sir. What did you think, Sir?'

'I asked the question, devious fellow. Come on now, out with it, don't keep me waiting.'

Tom breathes deeply and slowly, steadying himself against this sepulchral attack, this voice from the tomb. *Devious fellow*! Sarky bugger. Always springing up out of the ground like a genie when you least expected it, sneering dark nostrils, thin, crooked mouth, eyes bright as torches. It only needed one figure like that to ruin a childhood, blacken the bright day, destroy innocence.

'Get back in your box, you old fool.'

Amy says, 'What did you say?'

'Nothing.'

She looks at him doubtfully. Has she seen his lips moving? *Had* his lips moved?

'Talking to yourself,' Amy says, shaking her head playfully. 'First sign of madness.'

Amy also hears voices. (Not really a sign of madness, in her view, just a common human condition.) One speaks inside her head now. 'Silly cow, can't you speak naturally?' But Amy cannot always speak to Tom naturally. She is sometimes afraid of him, her fear manifesting itself in this unnatural, bright voice that grates on her inner ear. Why can't she shut up? But she knows when something is wrong, scents danger in his brooding look, and her treacherous tongue wags with a life of its own, turning her into the fool she is sure at these times he thinks her. Trying to ingratiate herself with him makes her despise herself. It is like cracking a joke with the dentist to put off the moment when the needle goes into the gum.

She thinks of a better analogy.

Amy is a solicitor. Once, in a magistrates' court, she had watched while the police applied for a Care and Protection Order for an eight-year-old girl whose mother had, on several occasions, threatened to kill her. The mother said to the Bench, 'She's always been difficult, not like the others. Even in the womb. She never moved in my womb.'

The child was in court. This was some years ago, before the Children Act put an end to these poignant appearances. The little girl had wept and clung to her mother. She had asked to go into the witness box. 'So you'll all know it's true what I say.' The tiny creature had stood there on tiptoe, clutching the ledge, swearing she loved her mother, that her mother had never hurt her and she wanted to stay with her.

Amy had understood this child absolutely. The only safety for a victim lies in appeasement. Not that she can honestly apply this lesson directly to her own life. But she does apply it.

She says, 'It's a wretched drive until Corinth. Hideous suburbs. And then all the industrial blight. Factories and oil refineries. That's the cause of the dreadful pollution.'

Tom doesn't answer. Has he really not heard her? Or is he pretending? Her father used to play the same trick, sitting at the table at mealtimes in a contemptuous silence into which words fell as if into a furnace, shrivelling in torment as soon as spoken. 'Not his fault,' her mother used to say to her daughter. 'He has suffered so much. More than we can ever know.'

Amy's father had spent the Second World War in a Japanese prison camp. 'Not *my* fault,' Amy had thought – and still thinks. Why should a man take it out on his child for something that happened before she was born?

'Mmm.' Tom speaks at last. He is clearly not interested in industrial blight. Nor, though he has started to wheeze, in the pollution of Athens. But at least he has answered her. And, even if his smile is distant, as if he were thinking about something else, it is still a smile.

Poor pet, Amy thinks, he must be miserably uncomfortable. If only he had let her put the rubber ring in their hand baggage! But men are so self-conscious about that sort of thing. She must be quietly sympathetic, try not to keep up a stream of relentless, bright chatter. And she is sympathetic. It is just that when he puts on that brooding, bored look she grows nervous, relating it partly to certain guilty velleities she hopes he is unaware of, partly to her own clumsiness. She knows she is awkward. When she was adolescent, her large limbs, her prominent teeth, her loud laugh, had made her despair. She was aware that when her father looked at her, which was seldom, he sighed. Now it is only with Tom that she feels these physical characteristics to be shameful, disabling. With other people (more often with women than men) she is unself-conscious, competent, kindly, a good listener, even a good talker, on rare occasions quite witty.

Well, cheery, anyway, she corrects herself. Cling on to that, she thinks, turning and smiling at the two old ladies in the double seat just behind her. Since they are all apparently going to the same hotel (stuck in the same boring place, is how Amy thinks of it) she might as well try to be friendly.

The couple she smiles at respond. It would be hard not to respond to Amy's sweet smile, her long, eager face. They are both withered beauties with lined, pretty faces and soft hair that is coloured and waved with such elusive art that even Amy, who normally notices only expressions, the life of the eyes and the mouth, receives the notion that these are two very rich old parties indeed. Equally subliminally, without conscious effort, she understands that the clothes they are wearing, though as seemingly simple as those that she wears in the normal way, at home, in the office, in court, are mysteriously different. Of course, they are both tall, slender, long-necked and straight-backed; remarkably alike, she thinks suddenly. Sisters. Twin sisters, perhaps. One bolder than the other as if she always takes the initiative.

The bold one says, 'Hot enough for you? I thought I was going to melt back there at the airport. Like stepping off the plane into an oven.'

There is something about her vowel sounds that doesn't fit with the elegantly discreet clothes, the expensive hair. Amy, who has a legal practice in the East End of London, thinks that she recognises the local tongue; the strong, lively cockney that is only thinly disguised by elocution lessons or even by years of careful mimicry.

Amy is neither a snob nor a philologist. She is more concerned with what people say than with how they say it. But she is interested, when the other old lady speaks, to hear how different quite similar voices can be. 'It will be

11

cool by the sea,' this old lady says. 'Edie darling, I did tell you it would be hot this time of year, why do you never believe me?' She has a clear, beautifully modulated, distinctly upper-class voice; the giggle, young, clear and girlish, that follows is unexpected. But it reminds Amy of something. Something – or someone.

She stretches her hand over the back of her seat. 'Amy Jones,' she says. 'And my husband, Tom.'

Tom turns, nods, and smiles with adequate grace, then glances beyond them (a bit slyly it seems to Amy) at the other passengers: a middle-aged couple, a woman with red hair and sunglasses, a pretty girl, a tall, clean-shaven man with rimless spectacles who is holding an open book on his knee that he is not reading. Apart from the glasses, this man is a bit like James Stewart, Amy thinks: that soft-lipped mouth, the narrow, gentle, intelligent face.

Amy often sees people as film stars, not of her own youth, but her mother's. When Amy was growing up, her mother's passion for films was the only thing she had been able to share with her that allowed them both to escape from the house (and the sad, broken man whose misery and rage filled it) for afternoons or evenings at film clubs, any cinema within reach that advertised films from the forties and fifties. For her heroes, Amy lived in a time warp. When she first met Tom he had reminded her of Spencer Tracy. Though Tom was taller, he had the same square, strong, open face; a good man, honest-eyed. She had even had a fanciful dream of herself as Katharine Hepburn, her gawkiness transformed into coltish grace, her toothy grin into an appealing, wide smile.

Edie takes her hand. 'Edith Farrell,' she says, 'that's what . . .' Before she can finish her sentence the other

woman breaks in, quickly and lightly. 'And I am Jane
Farrell.' She substitutes her hand for Edith's; it is lighter
and cooler, a quite different sensation from her compan-
ion's.

Amy wondered why they were pretending to be sisters.
She had thought they might be, but that was before Jane
Farrell had spoken.

Amy says, 'I think we are going to be lucky with the
weather. When we landed, I could hardly believe it. It was
so grey in London.'

Edie and Jane look at each other and then smile at Amy,
a glint in their eyes like children with a mischievous secret.
She wonders what it is, whether she should ask, tease it out
of them and decides, since Tom is sitting beside her, against
it. Tom is cautious with strangers, a cautiousness learned
from his mother who had always behaved as if the world
around her was peopled with natural enemies – as if she
were a small field mouse, or shrew. And politics is a factor.
Amy suspects that Edie and Jane are dyed-in-the-wool Tory
ladies (their age and their sex make it almost certain) and
they would almost certainly want to put their point of view
should they discover Tom is a Labour Member of
Parliament. That would be the last thing Tom could cope
with just at this moment. So Amy simply smiles back and
turns to the window to look at the marvellous deep cleft of
the Corinth Canal, and for the rest of the journey sits
silent, unaware of the presence, the unexploded bomb
three seats behind her.

2

PORTIA, IN FACT, IS FEELING MORE amused than explosive. The lurch of discomfort she had felt at London airport, recognising Tom just ahead of her in the queue at Security, and seeing (for the first time in the flesh instead of in a smudgy newspaper photograph) his agreeably plain, horse-faced wife, had been replaced during the flight by the anticipation of the spectator waiting for the curtain to rise on what promised to be a good play. Putting on her darkest glasses, she signalled to herself her position as a member of the audience, not one of the actors. She had briefly wished that her current lover was sitting beside her. Dave was younger, and had more hair than Tom. But she had dismissed this crude thought very quickly and not just as being unworthy. Being alone made the situation more interesting for her if not for poor Tom.

What a turn-up for the books, Portia thinks, what a *lark*! Oh, she is a bit sorry for Tom who is not the sort of man to take this really quite minor bit of embarrassment in his stride.

She isn't in the least sorry for Amy. Horse-Face is Tom's problem. She can barely remember the murderous rage she used to feel when he had to rush home because a child was ill, or for a family visit to Horsey's old mother. Or was it Tom's mother?

It was difficult now to believe there had been a time when she had loved Tom enough to wish his wife dead. He had known that she wished it, been shocked on one level and flattered on another, but in the end it had been the violence of her feelings that had made him run for cover. If she had played Tom's game, never mentioning Amy, just letting him keep Horsey locked up in her stable, they might have staggered through to a blissful old age together.

Was that what she had wanted? Hard to remember. Certainly Tom didn't have the stamina for a double life. Not a natural philanderer, he had needed to justify himself in a moral, or at least social, way. As long as no absolute harm was done, people should be free to explore and develop themselves through different relationships, allow their personalities to burgeon and flower instead of wither on the stalk as Tom felt his was in danger of doing, stuck as he then was on the back benches, an undistinguished member of Her Majesty's Loyal Opposition. He was a better and more effective person because he was in love with Portia had been Tom's theory, implying (though not of course saying) that their affair was making him nicer to Amy, or at least better able to sustain what he had also implied (again without saying so, merely with the occasional silence, or sigh) was a tedious marriage, an old shoe he continued to wear out of kindness and duty.

15

Liar, Portia thinks now (fairly dispassionately, if with rather more heat than she had felt on the aeroplane), lucky escape she'd had, really. It was the old paradox. If he had left Amy for her she could never have trusted him afterwards, knowing how virtuously he had deceived Amy. Nor could she have coped with his morose moral struggles, his need to see himself, always, in a good light. She had understood his moods once, even admired him for them in the beginning when she had been crazy about him. She can see, observing the droop of his shoulders, his attitude of histrionic dejection, that he is going through one of his bad times at the moment. No need for *her* to be sorry for him, he is quite sorry enough for himself!

Portia sits up straight, fishes in her voluminous bag for cigarettes and smiles radiantly at the woman beside her, a chubby small person in a pale blue silky suit, obviously new, as is her matching blouse and handbag. Beneath woolly permed hair, her soft, small-featured face is marshmallow pink with excitement. Though Portia has already learned, in the first hour of this interminable, cramped, bumpy journey, rather more than she wants to know about this lady and her elderly gnome of a husband sitting on her other side, there is no obvious alternative diversion.

The lady's name is Beryl Boot and this is her first trip abroad, her first holiday for seven years. Mr Boot (whose name Portia has not discovered since Beryl refers to him only as 'Daddy') has told her that it seemed a good moment to get away, business being slack at the moment and Mother (Daddy's mother, apparently, not Beryl's) being a 'bit more perky than usual'. It is their twentieth wedding anniversary, they have five children, three girls married and living away, two sons in the business, and only Mother living next door to care for. 'Beryl needs a break,' Mr Boot had said, a remark (patronising, to Portia's mind) that had made Beryl blush with pleasure. Portia wonders what the 'business' is. Nothing about them, neither clothes nor conversation, suggests any project much more ambitious than a corner shop. On the other hand, the hotel they are going to is expensive and they are not on a package deal, they have flown first class on the plane and booked a suite with a sea view and a balcony. The only reason they have taken the bus is the difficulty of negotiating with a Greek taxi driver.

All this 'Daddy' Boot has already told Portia with the aim, so it seemed to her, not of establishing his own status, about which he seems perfectly confident, but of making it clear to her how much he values his wife. It is Portia's habit, when speaking to married couples, to address her remarks to the man unless the woman is exceptionally beautiful or has some other obvious distinction, but Mr Boot is a man who makes his position clear from the beginning. 'Make no mistake, don't flirt with me, woman,' is the message he sends, ice-blue eyes twinkling, and Portia receives it without offence, wishing all men were so straightforward. A bit of a cheek, of course, since Daddy is hardly the kind of man she would bother to send the slightest of sexual signals, but the only rebuke she allows herself is the delicate one of setting herself out to be fulsomely charming to his wife.

Portia says, 'I believe the hotel is in a lovely position. High over the town and the harbour, but there is a lift down through the cliff and it's only a short walk to the centre. Peace and bright lights as well, just what you need for a really good holiday.' She tries to imagine what Beryl's idea of a really good holiday is. 'Waited on hand and foot. Nice for a change.'

Beryl gives a short, nervous shriek, followed by a little sigh. 'The trouble is, I can't help feeling selfish. There's Gavin, of course, but Sharon's so casual. And Ida's all right in her way but she has her bad days.' Another little shriek, accompanied by a jerky lift of the elbow. 'You know?'

Portia nods. Ida is a drunk, presumably, but who are Gavin and Sharon?

Beryl continues confidently, 'We've got good neighbours but it's not the same, is it?'

'Mother's all right,' Mr Boot says.

Beryl is reproachful. 'You can say that, Daddy, but you can't know, can you? She said she was feeling funny when I popped in this morning.'

'Always feels funny, even if we're only out for the evening. She'd tie you to the bedpost if she could, Beryl.' He pats his wife's knee. 'Do me a favour, let me do the worrying. We're not going to the Gobi desert. Gavin can always reach us by telephone.'

Daddy Boot looks at Portia and says, with a slight rising of colour – it pains him, perhaps, to acknowledge that his wife's method of conversation can be confusing – 'Gavin's my brother. He and his wife are staying with our mother while we're away, and good luck to them. She's ninety-seven and she's had her own way all her life. It's been hard on Beryl.'

'Oh, Daddy, don't say that, she's a lovely old lady.'

'And you're a lovely young one,' Mr Boot says, indulgently jocular, producing another shriek, louder this time, that makes the man sitting on the single seat one row in

18

front of them turn around, perhaps startled. He looks from Beryl, to Portia.

Portia grins at him. Although getting on a bit, late fifties, even into his sixties, he is good-looking in a slightly epicene way: a sweet, curving mouth, a soft, double chin. Is he gay? He shows no sign of being attached to, or even acquainted with, any of the other people in the minibus. Not that Portia is looking for an involvement. She has Dave (or to be more accurate she has as much of Dave as she cares for, the rest belonging to a wife and two children living in Birmingham) and Dave will turn up at the end of the week if his film is going to schedule, and even if it doesn't she is happy to be alone.

Being *seen* alone she might mind rather more. How frightful if Tom should start pitying her, poor lonely lady, though worse if it started him thinking she must be missing him still! That would be *unendurable*. As is his behaviour! After all, she had done some research for him in the House of Commons before (as well as during) her time as his lover. They had things in common besides carnal knowledge! To ignore her like this was *uncivilised* – as well as uncivil. Stupid, too; he knew her well enough to know it would anger her. Why on earth had he not simply come up to her at the airport and introduced her to Horsey?

Unexpectedly, Portia begins to enjoy the healthy rage burning up in her. She smiles at the man on his own rather more openly, inviting him to join her in laughing (silently, kindly) at Beryl. The man smiles back, but only politely, and returns to the uncorrected proof of the British novel that is open on his lap.

*

19

He thinks, pretty woman, with a stir of sexual interest, liking the generosity of her smile, her slightly slanting, wide-set, amber eyes, her red hair. But Philip intends to remain alone on this trip which for him is not a holiday but a wake.

In part of his mind what has happened seems a bad dream that will be forgotten by morning. Throughout the week he has just spent in London, seeing other publishers, agents, some of his British authors, he has constantly expected Matilda to walk through a door, materialise beside him, be in his bed when he wakes. He understands that this belief is normal, part of the process of bereavement, but it doesn't feel normal. He can't believe it will pass and, indeed, doesn't want it to because once it has passed she will be truly dead, gone for ever, and that will be quite unbearable. Or, rather (Philip often edits his own thoughts as he is used to editing other people's words) he is not yet ready to bear that eerie emptiness, that total loss. So he yields to the temptation of imagining she has gone ahead of him to the hotel and that when he arrives she will be there, waiting for him at the entrance.

Why should she have gone ahead? Philip, a scrupulous man even in daydreams, ponders this problem, gazing out of the window at the passing landscape which has now become mountainous; bare-boned, angular ridges, silvery olive trees on the lower slopes. Suppose there hadn't been room for everyone in the minibus and she had volunteered to take a taxi. Assuming the taxi to be a more comfortable ride, he would naturally have persuaded the two old ladies to go with Matilda and remained, himself, in the minibus. She will be waiting for him at the entrance to the hotel. He will get out of the minibus and she will run to him, smiling.

20

No, not smiling. The last time he saw her alive, she was smiling. Playing the memory back as he does obsessively, he can see nothing that could have warned him. It was her usual lop-sided smile, anxiously sweet as if half afraid of rejection and it made him feel protective and tender as he picked up his overnight bag, as he kissed her goodbye. He had rung from the airport and, hearing the answerphone, assumed she was out, caught the plane to San Francisco, attended the library conference, rung late in the evening and been irritated because she could at least have left a message on the machine.

He had not been alarmed. Matilda had friends with whom she acted quite normally. Hating being alone, she had probably gone to a theatre, perhaps spent the night with a friend. But she might have told him!

He had not telephoned the next morning, partly out of pique, partly because his flight was so early, and arrived home, unwarned, unsuspecting, to be met by the distraught daily maid, the police, the horror that has been with him for a month now, four weeks of aching grief and guilt. He should never have left her.

She had been so afraid he was going to leave her for ever. Every evening he was ten minutes late coming home confirmed her belief in his final departure. He would find his suitcase packed, his books cleared from the shelves. She yelled at him to get out. 'Then it will be over and I shall have peace! It's the waiting for you to go I can't bear.'

Philip had wondered if in some part of herself she really did want to be rid of him. That she had stopped loving him. Or that she loved someone else. And then saw that she was goading him in this way out of some inexplicable but true despair, a deep, unavoidable suffering; that she

21

hated herself for it, hated the person she was becoming, hated what she was doing to him, to them both. It seemed to him at these dreadful times that there were two Matildas. Even while the harridan was screaming abuse, the frightened eyes of the real Matilda were begging him to help her. *That* Matilda lay in his arms at night, often happily, but he could never be sure which one's head would be there on the pillow when he woke in the morning.

He was bewildered. He was also ashamed. This was his upbringing. From two years old, when he had arrived in New York, a small refugee from Hitler's Germany, he had been brought up by a Quaker couple from Philadelphia, the brother and sister-in-law of an American diplomat in Berlin who was a friend of his father's. These people were strict in manners and morals, reserved in behaviour, careful with money (though moderately wealthy, their principles made them live modestly), always kind, always reasonable. All the years they had cared for him he had never heard a voice raised in anger, listened to a discussion that was not conducted in a temperate fashion, and ever since, as far as he could, he had lived within the disciplines they had taught him. When his sweet, bright Matilda became so mysteriously wild and irrational he was shocked and ashamed by her lack of control. He assumed that, deep down, she must be ashamed too, and so became her accomplice, helping her to hide her distracted condition from everyone.

The thought that she might be clinically ill was something he almost refused to consider. Although he had, in the end, consulted a doctor: a man who was writing a medical book for his firm, bringing up the subject over a routine lunch, his shame had made him reduce the severity of her symptoms to silly storms of tears about nothing, and as a result the advice he was given was anodyne. Women went through these phases. Matilda was feeling the recent departure of her grown children as well as the loss of her parents, both of whom had died recently, within a month of each other. She was in mourning for part of her life that was over, her role as mother, as daughter. She should be encouraged to take up other interests. Perhaps she should think about hormone replacement therapy. 'I take it,' this doctor had said, 'that all's well between you?'

And Philip had nodded. How could he have said to this stranger – to anyone – *She believes I am going to leave her.*

Now he blames himself, naturally. She was in pain for so long, and he had only provided the mildest of palliative measures; his love rationed to the time he could spare to be with her. She had told him what to do only a few days before she had left him for ever.

'Take me away, somewhere we can be by ourselves. If we could be alone, I think I'd get better.'

He had felt a sudden choking annoyance. For God's sake, they *had been* going away. This European trip had already been planned to include a few days in the pleasant hotel she remembered so happily. He would have to make one professional call (on an irritatingly reclusive woman writer who lived in the Peloponnese) otherwise they would have nothing to do except be together! Lazing in the sun, swimming, talking – or, indeed, moaning and wailing if that was what she felt she needed to do. 'Though I hope you won't want to,' he had said, laughing to disguise his impatience, and she had turned away from him.

It was as if she had been sweating with the agony of a

23

burst appendix and he had only offered her aspirin. He should have taken six months off, nine months, a year. It would not have been easy. Although he was a vice-president, on the board of the company, things being as fluid as they were in American publishing, he might have come back to find his desk occupied. Not that this possibility scared him. He could find another job. Even if he didn't, he would have a handsome pension from his current firm and his adopted family had money and no other children. It was the Protestant work ethic that held him, that glum, grey imperative stiffening his mind and his heart against more important personal loyalties. 'She must have been desperate,' his old Quaker mother had said at the funeral. 'Didst thou not see it?' And he had felt rightly rebuked, although she had not meant to rebuke him, simply been asking an obvious question. He had put his wife, his first duty, *after* his work, after publishing ephemeral novels. (Well, not all ephemeral, he hoped, although that was irrelevant.) The trouble was, one was never presented with clear-cut issues until it was too late. 'I suppose I didn't,' he said to his mother, and was aware of the lie as a stone, flung against the clear blue glass of her gaze. She had blinked and answered, briskly forsaking the biblical pronoun as if this liar, her son, no longer deserved it, 'Well, how could you know, Philip? Only God knows what went through her poor mad mind. Let us pray He forgives her.'

Philip cannot believe Matilda was mad. He is not certain that she meant, or wanted, to die. Rosanna, their daily maid, had been due to arrive forty minutes after Philip had left. Like Philip, she had had no reply when she had telephoned to say she must go to the dentist and would not be in until the next day and, like Philip, she had assumed that Matilda was out. It was Wednesday, and Matilda often went to the hairdresser on Wednesdays.

It was the only day Rosanna had missed since she had come to work for them three years before. She had always arrived on the dot; as people say, you could set your watch by her. To think of Matilda lying in a bath of blood, his spare razor beside her, confidently waiting for the reliable Rosanna to come to her rescue, fills Philip with horrified pity and pain on one level, and on another with a dark confused anguish. There is a certain dignity about choosing your moment to die, to go bravely forth. The possibility that Matilda had not meant to go through with it seems to diminish and cheapen her, turns her from a tortured soul into a trickster, a blackmailer.

Philip cannot make up his mind what to think. He feels he will never make up his mind about anything, ever again. He cannot decide whether he wants to publish the novel by the young British author that lies open on his knee now; or, indeed, if he wants to publish anything at all in the future. He does not know why he is carrying on with this absurd 'holiday'. He could have visited the demanding old horror (which is how he thinks of the elderly woman whose bestselling historical novels pay his not inconsiderable salary as well as allowing him to publish literary works that barely creep into profit) in a day's trip from Athens.

He is sweating suddenly, though he feels chilly, too; a kind of flu-shiver. And his mouth is ominously dry. *Oh God, is he going to be sick?*

'Like a swig?'

The girl occupying the single seat in front of him has

25

turned round and is proffering a plastic bottle of water. Up to now, Philip has only been aware of the back of her head; her shaggy light brown hair, crimped Rossetti style, had reminded him of his daughter. Phyllis is twenty-two, working for her Master's in Education at Cornell University. This girl is older, Philip thinks, a judgement based on the poise with which she has approached him, a middle-aged stranger. She is frowning now in an almost motherly way, regarding him anxiously. She says, 'I'm sorry, I don't have a cup. I just thought you looked pale.'

She has spoken softly, no one else in the bus seems to be listening, but to Philip it is as if she has alerted the whole world to his misery. He responds quickly, baring his teeth in what he hopes is a cheerful grin, 'I certainly could use a drink.' For the first time in his life he tilts his head back to drink from a bottle that has just been drunk from by a stranger; his lips where her lips have been.

He imagines, *still warm from her mouth* – and is shocked by the ease with which this thought enters his mind and the flush of pleasure it gives him. He takes the clean handkerchief from his breast pocket, wipes the neck of the bottle carefully, and hands it back. He says, 'Wonderful. Thank you.'

'You're welcome,' the girl says. Her English voice delivers this American response with a smile; it is a shy little joke to convey that she knows where he comes from. Then, at once, she turns round to face the front of the minibus, leaving Philip both relieved and regretful. He doesn't want to talk to anyone, either at the moment or in the foreseeable future. But now she has turned away from him, he feels lonely.

*

26

Prudence Honey has turned away so abruptly, partly to hide a smile at this old man's hygienic fussiness, partly because she doesn't want to 'encourage' him. She inserts these mental quotation marks because it is the sort of thing her mother would say. 'I know you don't mean to encourage them, dear. You've just got such a nice, giving nature you want to befriend the whole world. The trouble is, *they* don't know that's all it is, do they?'

Prudence's mother is an innocent woman of fifty. She has a nice, giving nature herself and knows what it can lead to. In her case it made her a single mother in her twenties and an anxious one in her forties. Observing her daughter bounding up to strangers like a friendly puppy, ever eager to comfort the handicapped, the lonely, the lost, she fears for her. She wonders (Mrs Honey, as she has chosen to call herself, keeping her maiden name but changing the title, is not an uncritical or foolish woman) whether too strong an impulse to help the unfortunate might suggest a lack of self-confidence. Does her sweet Prudence feel safer with people who are less able, less pretty, less clever than she is? If so, she has failed her.

In fact Prudence is a strong, happy girl, at ease with mankind, loving towards her mother whose feelings she respects and indulges, and with a perfectly adequate conceit of herself. Her kindness to others is instinctive; a simple overflowing of health and good spirits. She will take care not to 'encourage' Philip, but only for his sake, in case the poor old chap should expect more than a reviving drink of cool water and be disappointed. It is as if her mother's love and concern for her has always been so unfailing, so rock-like and sheltering, that Prudence has never felt herself to be vulnerable.

Or not until now. Last week she broke with her lover, another junior doctor in her department at the London Hospital, and although (as she keeps telling herself) she is more worried about how Daniel is taking it, she is beginning to feel hollow inside.

She had left Daniel in tears at the airport. She had known he would cry (Daniel is a young man who cries rather easily) and she had begged him not to take her to Heathrow, but he had insisted. His life might be over, or at least, worthless to him at this moment, but taking her to catch her plane on this ridiculous excursion is one thing he can do for her, and do it he will, whatever it costs him.

Sometimes exasperation with Daniel makes Prudence grind her teeth, something she hasn't done since she was a very small girl on the rare occasions when her mother wouldn't let her do, or have, what she wanted. Daniel had not wanted her to go to Greece without him; ignoring his wishes had seemed to him a treacherous rebuff and (he has actually hinted) was partly the reason he was unfaithful with the pretty Sister in Casualty. The fact that Prudence is not flying off to please herself but is going to meet her grandmother (another, legitimate, Mrs Honey) who is on an expensive cruise in the Mediterranean and the Aegean and has summoned her granddaughter to meet her because she expects to be bored by the time the *Morning Tide* reaches the Peloponnese, does not alter the case, to his mind.

Daniel is one of a large, sprawling family; when his parents married they each had four children already, and since his mother left his father she has presented Daniel with two other half-brothers, neither of whom he likes, any more than he liked his stepsisters and stepbrothers. There were

28

always too many of them, great louts with heavy boots and angry girls in tears, and the little half-brothers, agreeable enough to begin with, have grown fat and whiney in the care of a mother too old and too weary to bring them up sensibly.

Daniel doesn't care if he never sees his mother, father, and stepfather, or his various siblings and grandparents and step-grandparents, again. Unsurprisingly, he finds it hard to understand Prudence's daughterly and grand-daughterly concerns. Not only does he love Prudence, but she is the first person he has felt safe with in his whole life. How can she trot off so meekly, leaving him at the crook of a finger, the moment her grandmother beckons her?

'You can come too,' Prudence had said. 'Granny would love it.' But dancing attendance on Mrs Honey is not Daniel's idea of a holiday. Greece would be fine if he and Prue could be alone there, swimming and snorkelling and eating and drinking and making love, no interference from anyone, no one else to consider, no old lady to cosset, fuss over, buy drinks for, make conversation with. Though perhaps that is precisely what Prudence wants! A distraction from his boring company. Anyone will do, even a tiresome old woman! Which means, of course, that Prudence doesn't love him, can never have loved him, as he loves her.

Hence (in what is now Daniel's version of events) the Sister in Casualty. He was so hurt, offended, dismayed and distraught by Prudence's refusal to listen to him that he had to console himself somehow. Besides the Sister is married, an older woman, therefore no threat. It was purely physi-cal, comfort for a crying child, and only three times. Well, four, perhaps – it was so *unimportant* he didn't notch up the occasions. In actual *time* probably only a couple of hours out of their relationship. His relationship with Prudence, that is. Whereas Prudence spends weekends with her mother when he is on duty, and is going off now to spend a week with her grandmother.

'But they're my family,' Prudence has said over and over again. 'My mother. My grandmother.'

She cannot understand why Daniel doesn't understand. It is so simple to her. Before she met Daniel, the two Mrs Honeys were the people she loved best in the world, and she still loves them as much as she loves Daniel, if differently. And Daniel must love the Sister in Casualty or he wouldn't have done what he did. She must be worth loving. Everyone is worth loving. And the Casualty Sister is certainly handsome and sexy even if she does have a moustache.

Sitting in the minibus Prudence wishes she had not mentioned the moustache to Daniel. It was crude. Perhaps Daniel finds moustaches attractive; some men like hirsute women. Not that he has ever complained *she* was not hairy enough. Well, he wouldn't, would he? Daniel is a courteous lover. Her *love*, not just a lover. Oh, how she is going to miss him.

Someone in the bus – a foreign voice, the driver presumably – is pointing out something to his passengers, a castle, the Palamides, the biggest castle in Europe. And everyone is trying to look where he points, craning their necks at the crenellated battlement above on the skyline. Obediently, Prudence turns round, straining to see through the back window, but although she sees the old walls tumbling down the steep mountain she sees them through a mist of tears.

And the old man behind her gives her his clean handkerchief.

3

The Hotel Parthenon was conceived (so Amy tells Tom, seeing it as her role to supply him with this kind of detail) during the time of the Colonels. Like all dictators, all Pharaohs, their megalomania cried out for grandiose monuments to sustain it. Marble was ordered from the finest quarries in Greece, stone from the Pelion, seasoned hardwoods from Scandinavia, bathrooms from Italy. Since the site of the hotel was halfway up the mountain (though below the great castle) an immense tunnel was blasted through the rock and lifts installed for the convenience of guests returning on foot from the little town, after a shopping trip, or at the end of the evening.

When the Colonels departed in the early 1970s, it was clear that the project was a vastly expensive mistake. It could reasonably have been abandoned, turned into an example of instant archaeology (a temple to a Greek Ozymandias, is Amy's suggestion) but the wood and the stone and the marble and the baths and the showers and the toilets had already either arrived, or were imminent, and inertia prevailed. The carpenters, the stonemasons, the marble craftsmen built nobly, but the puzzled Greek plumbers who installed the sophisticated Italian sanitary fittings had been less successful. Amy (who has stayed here before, with her mother) has already warned Tom that one of the quirkier features of the Hotel Parthenon is the diverting variety of the surprises awaiting guests in its bathrooms.

It strikes Tom that the marble-cool space of the monolithic entrance hall would have been more impressive if it had not been chock full of delegates to an international conference on psychology, most of them – *thousands* it seems to his horrified gaze – swarming like chattering ants round the noticeboards to discover bus and boat times, excursions and cultural activities as well as forthcoming discussions and presentations.

'*Transpersonal psychology, Problematic cannabis use, Satanic lyrics in hard rock/ heavy metal*,' he mutters to Amy. 'Which do you fancy for the pre-dinner slot? I thought you said this was a good, old-fashioned, grand hotel.'

'All grand hotels take conferences and package deals nowadays,' Amy says briskly – in what Tom gloomily recognises as her *no nonsense* tone. 'We're on a package deal. I expect they'll dispose of this conference lot in a separate dining room, different meal times, so you won't have to discuss satanic rituals with anyone.'

'Lyrics,' Tom says. 'Not rituals.'

But Amy is gone, insinuating herself through the milling ants with snake-like speed and grace, aiming to arrive at the reception desk before any of the other passengers from the minibus. Tom pushes his way after her, hoping for a cool room and a bed in – at the most – twenty minutes. He relies on Amy to fix it; she is good at getting people to do things for her expeditiously; she can even find porters at railway stations, taxis on rainy nights, persuade assistants in crowded supermarkets to open up a new till for her. And yet she is never loud-mouthed or bossy; she just has this way with her.

Money, he thinks now. That's the answer. Amy was brought up to give orders to servants, to anyone paid to take care of her comfort, without feeling self-conscious about it. He doesn't approve of this classy skill for a number of foolish and kept-to-himself snobbish reasons, but on this sort of occasion he is grateful for it.

He has never felt so exhausted. Leaving aside the hairy road from Ankara to Istanbul (remembered with horror from an all-party fact-finding mission in the 1970s to assess Turkish suitability for a Customs Union with the EEC) the road from Athens to Corinth must be the worst in the world. Amy *knew* what it was like, didn't she? God knows why she had thought it a suitable journey for a man getting over a dismal operation for piles.

He has reached the desk at last. Amy is waving a key at him, tossing her thick hair, grinning triumphantly. *Attracting attention*, he grumbles inwardly – and is suddenly amused by the way one of his dead mother's milder condemnatory phrases slips so effortlessly into his mind. *Showing off* would have been a more damning complaint in her book, but Amy is not guilty of that major crime. She can't help her height, nor the fact that all the psychologists in her proximity appear to be unusually small, as are the middle-aged couple from the minibus who are standing beside her. Neither the man nor his wife can be much above five feet tall. They make Amy look taller than ever; a gypsy goddess, a dramatic, dark Valkyrie.

If they hadn't been sitting next to Portia in the minibus, Tom would not have given the Boots a second glance. He sees now that the little woman has a sweet, artless face, like a pretty pug dog. As she smiles at him he is reminded again of his mother. Only this woman is younger, of course.

Beryl says merrily, 'More like Liverpool Station at rush hour than a posh hotel, isn't it? I'm lucky that Daddy is quick on his feet. Left to myself I'd always be stuck at the back of the queue.'

Amy says, laughing, 'Mr Boot certainly pipped me at the post.'

She makes this remark so that Tom should know the name of these fellow travellers. No blame attaches to ignorance on Tom's part, he has not spoken to the Boots before, but Amy has been a politician's wife long enough to cultivate the habit of feeding Tom with names, as well as with potted histories.

Mr Boot nods. He says, 'She's a sharp operator herself, your good lady, Mister . . .'

'Jones,' Tom says heartily. 'Tom Jones.'

'Pleased to meet you,' Beryl says, beaming. 'It'll be nice to recognise a few friendly faces in this busy old place. Our little lot will have to stick together, won't we?'

Tom nods and smiles, as if this prospect is the most delightful thing he can imagine instead of what he most fears.

Taking his arm, Amy rescues him. 'Come along, darling, we both need a wash and a rest, then we'll be ready for all sorts of jollity.' And she gives the Boots one of her most gracious smiles.

Getting into the lift with half a dozen youngish Japanese, Amy catches sight of herself and Tom in the orange-tinted mirrors, a blowsy giantess side by side with a doddery invalid, yellow with fatigue and pain, and wonders why on earth they have come here. An exhausting and tedious journey for a tired man, only to find the hotel infested with tiny psychologists at the end of it.

Oh, she knows why. She and Mummy had such a happy time here three years ago, celebrating (though of course neither of them would have quite put it that way) the merciful death of the husband and father whose misery had clouded both their lives for so long. For Amy it had been especially rewarding to watch her mother *unfold* – grow plumper and younger and happier as each peaceful day dawned. It was the only unathletic vacation Amy has ever enjoyed and when it was clear that poor Tom needed a sedentary respite instead of a bicycling holiday in Brittany, the large rooms and the shady balconies of the Hotel Parthenon sprang at once to her mind.

Now Amy sees that somewhere less traumatic to get to; the south of France, northern Italy – almost any destination that could be reached without going through Athens, through the hell of that notorious airport and the crowded fetid streets of the capital – would have been preferable. She had tried to talk to Tom about the wild beauty of the Peloponnese and the hotel in Nauplion that her mother had found so recuperative, but Tom had been feeling so miserable physically, so uncomfortable and defeated, that he had been unable to show any interest. 'You fix something, whatever you like. If you think that hotel will do, where you went with old Harriet, then go ahead and book it.'

And instead of warning him about the airport and telling him how long a drive it would be to the comfort of the Hotel Parthenon, she had protested that he really must *not* call her mother 'old Harriet' in that contemptuous, cruel tone, just because he was angry with her for marrying again, a husband not to his liking! Amy had known she sounded angrier than the apparently mild offence seemed to warrant and had half expected Tom to shout back at her. Instead, he had apologised instantly, with a sly, guilty grin, and said he called everyone 'old' at the moment, it was a silly habit he'd fallen into, he meant nothing unkind, indeed, he intended it as a kind of clumsy affection, *she* knew that, didn't she?

Amy knew exactly what he meant. Tom was *furious* with 'old Harriet' for marrying again '*at her age*'. Not, of course, openly. His official line was that he was delighted that his adored mother-in-law was happy at last with the man she should have married in the first place – and would have married, indeed, if Amy's father had not returned from the Japanese prison camp to snatch her practically from the church door.

He claimed – and Harriet never denied it – that she had engaged herself to him before he went to the war. He had carried her picture with him ever since, the photograph of a shy sixteen-year-old, in school uniform. He said it had kept him alive. And Harriet had married him. It was her duty, she told her weeping young lover, her horrified parents. He had sacrificed so much for his country. She had done nothing.

Well, high-mindedness, sacrifice, had been in the air at that time. But it is Tom's view that Harriet has not learned her lesson. She has continued to be too tender-hearted for her own good. The real trouble with this second marriage, with what seems on the surface a satisfying story of sweethearts united in their November days, is that Dick, the new husband, is quite spectacularly poor; a long-widowed, retired librarian whose small pension is mostly spent on helping to keep his dead wife's disabled son in a home for the handicapped, and supporting their middle-aged daughter who has two children but is apparently unable to hold down a job, or a marriage.

'Bang goes our kids' future security!' had been Tom's first reaction, and although he had drilled himself into a more acceptable response almost immediately, Amy was sure that he still felt her mother had cheated them. In the year between her first husband's death and her marriage to Dick, Tom had established Harriet in his private thoughts as a rich old lady whose money would eventually come to his children. (Delicacy prevented him from contemplating the benefit to Amy and himself should Harriet die before they did although that was, by and large, more likely than not.)

Amy knew how Tom had felt then, and she knew that he knew that she knew. Although they had not discussed it since, she was sure he must be ashamed of his feelings and, for his sake, she was ashamed to acknowledge them, let alone encourage him to express them. It would be unfair to Tom. He was too decent, simply too *good* a person to be allowed to devalue himself in this way. Besides, he not only loved Harriet, he admired and respected and valued her. Why, in that last terrible year, when Amy was spending most nights with her parents, helping the nurse to calm and restrain her raving father while her mother snatched an hour's rest, Tom had done his best to help. Whenever he could manage it, he had gone home early to be with the children who were too young to be abandoned and too old for a babysitter, and on the nights he had to stay at the House for an adjournment or a late division, he always telephoned to warn her.

As the lift clanks upward, Amy is reminded that he would have been free to do more for them all during that dreadful time, for their children if not for her mother and father, if he had not been caught up with 'that woman' – which is how Amy, in her old-fashioned way, thinks of Portia. She does not know her name, nor wishes to know it; to ask, to be told, would be to dignify the creature in some way, turn her into a sentient being with ordinary human characteristics some of which might not be wholly bad. She may, for instance, honestly have *loved* Tom – though Amy cannot really believe this. Amy can imagine falling in love with a man who has a wife and children, but renunciation would be her natural next step, not consummation and deceit. She could never wish anyone to suffer as she saw poor Tom suffer, from remorse and regret . . .

Amy remembers (entirely without satisfaction) Tom's white-faced panic when she had said she was thinking of leaving him. It had made her immediately ashamed of herself – giving in to her feelings in that incoherent, wild way when there were two children to be thinking of first, before her own foolish despairs. Bill and Kate were Tom's children as well as hers. How could she have contemplated taking them from him?

He had said, 'I'm the one who must go, if you say the

38

word. You hold all the aces. The house is yours, you bought most of the furniture, you bought both our cars. You earn more than me, you don't need me for anything.'

She should have slapped his face, she thinks sometimes. How could he think about who 'held the aces' at a moment like that? And it was so *unfair*: she had wanted to put the house in both their names. It was Tom who had refused. He was such a prude about money.

Amy's heart is thumping painfully in her throat. Of course, when she stayed here with Mummy *all this* was still fresh in her mind. When she had booked this holiday two weeks ago, it had not occurred to her that it might rouse up that past unhappiness, open the wound again.

The lift has stopped, the gate is open. The Japanese have left, a couple of them with concerned looks at Tom and mute enquiring glances at Amy. She has nodded reassurance, she doesn't need help, but now Tom is visibly sagging. He gives her a brave, shaky smile and Amy says, 'Come on, old love, two shakes of a lamb's tail and we'll have you tucked up in beddy-byes.'

Philip is disconcerted to find that he feels so surprisingly calm and relaxed. Although this is not the room he had shared with Matilda, the furniture is similar, and he had expected a rush of memories. He lies on the bed, his eyes closed, trying to recover her, bring her back, not the lost, weeping soul who tortures his conscience but the happy woman on holiday.

She had a blue cotton dress. She washed it and hung it on the balcony overnight and was pleased to find it dry in the morning. They had breakfasted on the balcony, sitting in broad wooden chairs with sagging but comfortable canvas seats, and watching the life of the wide sea in front of them: the little fishing boats, gulls swooping and crying behind them, the *Flying Dolphin* approaching the harbour, a huge, yellow insect stilted high on thin legs that collapsed as the hydrofoil slowed, settling its breast on the water.

In his mind, Philip places himself on the balcony and looks across at Matilda. He can't see her yet, the chair opposite remains empty, but if he concentrates he must surely be able to bring her back. She would not have dressed yet, so what would she be wearing? Some kind of white, fluffy robe? Matilda had always complained he didn't 'take any interest' in how she looked, what she wore. Perhaps she was right. He is not a man who notices women's clothes. All he can readily remember is the blue cotton shift she had washed in the basin and hung out to dry on the balcony.

He abandons his search for Matilda. Ghosts come when they want to, he tells himself, not when you beckon them. It is too late in the afternoon for a nap. If he drops off, he will sleep until midnight. He gets off the bed, fiddles with the key to open the minibar, takes a miniature bottle of whisky, pours it into a glass, carries it out to the balcony. Sitting in one of the chairs he remembers from that earlier time (much more clearly than he seems to be able to remember Matilda) he determines to settle to the British author's novel even though he has more or less decided it is a book he is unlikely to publish.

Instead, he finds himself thinking about the nice girl on the minibus who offered him her bottle of water. Sensible girl, thoughtful girl, pretty girl, same untidy hairstyle as Phyllis, his daughter. He wonders how Phyllis is. She had seemed composed when he said goodbye to her. Too composed? Well, she took after him, he'd never been one to show much emotion. Matthew was different. Matthew named for Matilda, Phyllis for him. *That* was a touch affected, he thinks now. Does Matthew think of himself as his mother's boy? Matthew had been the only family member to shed tears at the funeral.

Philip doesn't want to think about Matthew.

He wonders why the pretty girl on the minibus was crying. Perhaps, a bit later, when she has had a chance to rest, he will find her in the bar or by the pool. It would not be inappropriate to offer her a drink, surely? Or she might approach him to return his handkerchief.

Prudence Honey has washed out the handkerchief and put it on the side of the bath to dry. She has found the plumbing eccentric. Some taps turn on, others don't, and hot water comes out of the cold tap and cold water out of the hot tap. She stands under the lukewarm dribble of the shower and decides a swim in the pool would be more refreshing.

She has already telephoned her mother to say she has arrived safely, and she has written a letter to Daniel. She has written several letters to Daniel in her mind; this is the first that has been committed to paper. Every single word of it is blazoned on her mind; her lips move as she repeats it to herself. Suddenly, the blood rises, flushing her neck and her face; she moans, aloud and histrionically, turns off the shower and runs, naked and wet, to seize the white envelope she has left on the bed. She tears it across several times, and hurls it into the waste basket. Then frowns, and sighs. She fishes the small pieces of paper out of the basket,

41

puts them into the enormous glass ashtray that sits on the handsome desk (all the furniture in this hotel is important-looking and heavy), carries it to the balcony, and lights it with the book matches that have a picture of the original Parthenon stamped on the cover.

In one of the two suites on the floor above, Beryl Boot has settled in nicely. She has unpacked the suitcases and the hand luggage, hung up Daddy's clothes in one enormous wardrobe and hers in another and is now investigating the long double balcony with an eye to setting up the nylon washing line she has brought with her.

Daddy has taken his shoes off and is lying on one of the king-size beds with a whisky in one hand and the telephone in the other. Talking to one of the boys, Beryl assumes, though she never listens to what Daddy is saying when he is on the telephone, any more than he listens to her when she says things like, 'Goodness, we'll be clean with two bathrooms, won't we?' which is something she has said several times in the last twenty minutes without at any point expecting an answer.

Having arranged the washing line to her satisfaction, she sits in one of the generously sized wooden chairs on the balcony, puts her feet up on another, and contemplates the broad expanse of sea before her. On this hot, windless day, the water is colourless, flat, almost oily, and the mountains on the far side of the great bay are misty, fading into the sky. A couple of small boats chug slowly from the harbour on the right of Beryl's vision to the headland on the left. The old town lies below her, a jumble of red and grey roofs, painted houses, narrow, white streets that she finds romantic.

She sighs with pleasure. Tomorrow she will explore the town. Just to look. By herself. That is always the best way. Daddy won't mind if she goes on her own. He likes her to enjoy herself. Not like some husbands. He'll be all right, he's got his crossword puzzle books and they said at the travel agent you could get English papers even though they were a day late. And if he gets bored he can always ring the boys and shout at them. Not that he bullies them, or not really, but he likes them to know who's the boss.

A wind is getting up. Beryl watches the surface of the silken sea ruffling, and feels the cool air on her cheek. There is a smell of smoke, too; something burning. She gets to her feet to investigate, look over the edge of the balcony and watches the charred bits of paper dance and whirl just beneath her.

In the adjacent suite (two large rooms with communicating doors and two bathrooms and a double balcony) the two ancient beauties are lying side by side, on twin beds, their faces larded with white cream and their eyes hidden beneath plastic eye pads containing what looks like blue jelly. They are both wearing pale pink gowns made of light cotton, and are performing the same gentle exercise: flexing and relaxing their bare feet and their buttocks. At this moment they look like identical twins. Carved in stone on a tomb.

One says suddenly, 'Why did you have to put on that silly voice?'

And the other answers, 'We got away with it this time, didn't we?'

'So far.' This response appears to be given reluctantly, but perhaps it is their habit to sound grudging with each other. Then, 'Don't forget it's my turn!'

'Who d'you think is likely to recognise her? All too young. In that bus, anyway.'

'The man wasn't. The one on his own. Liked the look of him.'

They both giggle; each with the same light, girlish giggle. Like an echo of each other.

'Coarse cow!'

'Tish was always coarse under that innocent air. That's what hauled 'em in. The man's after the girl, anyway. Though if he has any sense he'll go for the redhead. Less trouble. More likely to be grateful, too.'

Silence for a while. Then Jane, or perhaps Edith, says with a pensive seriousness absent from earlier remarks, 'That colour is real, by the way.'

Portia, brushing her hair in the bathroom, turns from the glass, holding the hand mirror aloft so she can admire the shining mane tumbling down her naked back. The curve of her waist and the creamy hollow that runs from her shoulderblades to her buttocks gives her pleasure, too. In this inadequate and therefore kindly lighting, she looks consolingly pretty and young. Even if not quite a girl any longer. Dave says, *My lovely ripe plum*.

Portia frowns, puts down the hand mirror, and leans close to the bathroom glass, curling her lips back as she examines her mouth. *English teeth* is how Dave, the English-born son of a female American dentist, once described them.

'Bugger Dave,' Portia mutters aloud. 'A mite crooked but at least mine own.'

44

This makes her laugh. She wrinkles her nose at her reflection. She admires her straight, narrow nose, turning to look at her profile. She will go beaky eventually, but not until she is very much older, around fifty-nine, say. Her mother kept her looks into her mid-sixties, until her plump flesh fell away, and she died. Portia has inherited a round body and slanting, topaz eyes from her mother, her hair from her father. Her mother was Italian, from Genoa; her father, now living in an old people's home outside Dublin, was an Irish seaman, chief engineer on a passenger liner. Portia thinks 'was', not 'is'. Although her father is still alive, his wits have gone. The last time she saw him she thought 'There is no one there', and she has not visited since. He has relations nearby, a lively old sister, a younger brother who can be relied on to 'see to him'. Sometimes they send Portia a postcard. When he dies one of them will write her a letter.

Portia shivers, thinking of dying, and then wriggles into her black bathing suit, removing the detachable straps so the sun will not leave pale stripes on her shoulders. Round her waist she ties a sarong-like garment patterned in orange and purple that reaches below her knees, hiding her thighs which are beginning to sag. She gives her reflection a more considering look than before and sighs lightly. She really is too fat. Dave's ripe plum. Dave is too young for her; still in his early thirties. She is too old now to be a young man's voluptuous older woman. All right if she were still only forty, or forty-one or even forty-two. But forty-five is a watershed. A watershed she passed a couple of years ago.

Besides, Dave is married, and married men, as Tom Jones has just reminded her, are trouble and grief. Perhaps she will put Dave off. Send him a fax. She has work to do; she

45

can't afford to hang about waiting and wondering if and when he is likely to come. Though it had seemed a good idea when Dave had suggested it. She has to hire a car to explore the Peloponnese well enough to do her piece for the newspaper travel supplement she writes for, and Portia dislikes driving on what she considers the wrong side of the road, particularly when zigzagging up and down mountains. If Dave could have done the driving the second week, she could manage the local stuff, the town, the tavernas, the beaches, in the first. She had planned to lie by the pool and get a good tan while she read up the basics. There is a particularly good old *Guide to Southern Greece* by Brian de Jonge that she intends to plunder, not for up-to-date touristy chat but for the ruins – which is how Portia terms the great classical sites in her mind. The advantage of ruins is that they stay where they are and change little; if anything new has been found, dug up, some fresh historical perspective invented, there is usually someone around to give Portia the gist of it. She has found Scandinavians, the Swedes and the Finns, particularly useful in this regard. Unlike the Germans, the French and the British, they come to Greece for the antiquities, not for the beaches. And they are not likely to read any of Portia's articles so she can plagiarise as she pleases. In Portia's opinion, anyone who wastes time reading a travel supplement, or indeed anything in a newspaper apart from bare reporting of the main political and international news, cannot be a serious person.

Portia has a low opinion of journalism in general and finds her unexpected talent for writing enjoyably readable nonsense embarrassing. Convenient, though; she has to admit it. After she split up with Tom she had worked with (and slept with, and loved) an old Labour peer known as 'Bumpy' to everyone, famous for the generosity of his opinions, his cheerfulness and his simple honesty, and when he died twelve months ago (mercifully and suddenly, in her bed, in her arms) she had told herself she was 'finished' with politics.

She turned down a number of posts she was almost immediately offered, as well as a suggestion that she might put in for an *almost* safe seat at the next general election, and accepted a series of lunches with friends of Bumpy's in journalism who were all, by now, fairly old, but not too old to be useful. A couple of them turned out to be only interested in recruiting her as an assistant lobby correspondent but the editor of a popular (though right-wing) daily broadsheet asked her if she had thought of writing a biography of 'dear old Bumpy'. Someone should do it, such a long life in politics, he must be about the last to have really *known* Churchill in his great days. And so on.

Portia said she would think about it. In the meantime she needed a job. The next day, the woman who ran the monthly travel supplement of this editor's newspaper, telephoned and asked her if it would amuse her to go to Florida. The Florida tourist board was anxious to encourage British package-deal tourists to come in the summer, to fill the hotels vacated by the winter visitors, and would make sure Portia had an agreeable time, first-class travel, first-class hotels.

Portia had nothing better to do. She found Florida unpleasantly sticky in the summer heat, and full of small, stinging insects. She came home and wrote a solemn article on the conflict between the desire of the tourist industry to maximise profits and the right of their customers to honest information about the reason for cheap rates out of season; then, after a telephone call from the editor of the travel supplement, rewrote the piece craftily, so that it said much the same thing but in an elliptical manner and with a lighter touch. She expected it to be spiked all the same, and was amazed when the travel editor rang to congratulate her on 'getting the hang of it', and paid her more, for less work, than she had ever been paid in her life.

She thought, a little resentfully, *Bumpy would not have approved*. Perhaps one of the reasons she was shying off the biography was that it was hard to see how to write about someone so thoroughly good. Or was she just lazy? Shameful, when she knew Bumpy had meant her to do it. He had never discussed it with her but he had, in a sense, left his life in her hands.

He had nothing much else to leave. He had owned nothing except the small house in the Welsh mining town where he had been born and where his older brother lived now, and the furniture in his rented flat. He left the house to his brother and his furniture to his daughter along with a few pretty things, pictures and mirrors and china ornaments that had belonged to her mother who had died twenty years earlier. But he had left Portia his books and his papers.

A tedious legacy in some ways. Portia lived in a terraced house in a back street in Islington. She had books of her own and some spare shelf space but Bumpy's library, which had not seemed all that enormous in his large, gloomy, old-fashioned mansion flat in Victoria, loomed and threatened in her small, pretty rooms. A carpenter, called in to put up new shelving, advised her that she would have to strengthen the floors if she didn't want to bring the whole house tumbling down.

She had left most of the books in packing cases in the basement room next to the kitchen, standing safely on London clay, on a quarry-tiled floor. A few of Bumpy's 'papers' appeared to be filed neatly enough in old metal cabinets; rather more had been dumped into old cardboard boxes, some of them collapsing or bulging under the weight. A dusty, musty smell arose from them.

Portia told herself she was reluctant to pry into Bumpy's past. There might be things he hadn't told her. Things he had forgotten about and would not want her to know. Although it was hard to think what such things could be. Bumpy was the last man on earth to have shameful secrets.

Off and on he had kept a diary. These were in one of the cardboard boxes which had actually fallen apart, spilling the contents on the quarry floor. Portia had assumed they were merely for appointments until she picked up a couple of five-year diaries, plump leather books with decorative gilt clasps. There was a dedication in each, *To darling Daddy, from Mary.*

Bumpy had talked about his daughter, who was a doctor in Liverpool, but he had never mentioned her age to Portia. She had looked in *Who's Who* and found that Mary was three years younger than she was. This didn't bother Portia, who had never thought of Bumpy as a father figure, but she had sometimes wondered if it bothered Bumpy. Had he ever looked on *her* as a daughter? Lumped her together with Mary? And another thing. Mary wasn't married. Had Bumpy thought that when he died, she and Portia might comfort each other? Two single women the same age?

They had sat in the same front pew at the funeral. They had cleared the flat together. Portia had dealt with Bumpy's clothes, throwing hopelessly worn suits and shirts into bin bags and setting aside anything that might, mended and cleaned, be of use to the Salvation Army. There was much more to be thrown away than there was to be kept. Portia, who didn't cry easily, had found herself hoarse with tears. She had said, to Mary, 'He spent *nothing* on himself. Holes in his shoes, missing buttons . . .'

And Mary had said, 'Oh, he was always hopeless, don't *worry*, dear! He wouldn't have wanted you to look after him in that way. And, oh, I should have said *thank you*! I mean, thank you for making his last years so happy.'

She had gazed at Portia with enormous, sad, liquid eyes and Portia had felt a hot surge of pure hatred. How could Bumpy have fathered this utterly stupid middle-aged woman?

She had screamed at her, 'Bumpy was my *lover*. I would have sewn on his buttons if that's what he'd wanted, not that I'm much good at sewing. But he would much rather we went to bed. He made *me* happy, you ignorant cow.'

To her shame, she had wept. And, of course, Mary had forgiven her instantly. She would have embraced her if Portia had not stormed from the room, and locked herself in the bathroom where she thumped her fists on the tiled wall, bruising her knuckles and easing her pain. When she emerged, tactful Mary had prepared a tray with whisky, ice, glasses, and half a packet of stale cheese straws she had found in Bumpy's kitchen cupboard.

Although there has been some necessary correspondence between them, they have not seen each other since. Catching sight of Bumpy's last five-year diary, placed on the bedside table along with her reading glasses, two Elmore Leonard paperbacks and *A Guide to Southern Greece*, Portia recognises that if she does decide to write about Bumpy she will have to have some sort of contact with Mary. With *that bloody woman* is how she expresses it in her mind, determined to ignore what she knows is the real reason for her dislike of the innocent doctor in Liverpool, which is her very existence as *Bumpy's daughter*. Bumpy had no other close living relations and Portia has a jealous nature. And that is yet another reason why she is hesitant about the biography: having to admit to herself that Bumpy is not hers alone.

She had put off reading the five-year diaries, of which there were four altogether, all given him by his daughter and covering the last twenty years, in case they should point to other women, other love affairs. But when she did read them, she had to admit that there was nothing for even the most suspicious mind to feed on. And although, in the last years, the entries that related to herself were minimal and discreet, it was clear that she had been part of his life in a way that no one else had been after his wife died. (Even Portia cannot be jealous of Bumpy's long-dead wife. Or admit to it, anyway.)

There are enough blank pages in the diaries to suggest that Bumpy only wrote in them from time to time to please a daughter who had thought them a suitable present for a lonely widowed father. And there is barely any reference to his personal life; certainly no mention of illness or despair, no True Confessions. The entries are short and cryptic: who he had spoken to, lunched with, occasionally what he had heard. Since Bumpy's standing in the Party was so established as to be effectively monarchical, he had frequently been called on to advise or warn, but all his comments (on what may or may not have been that sort of occasion) were so prudently coded as to be practically

51

indecipherable, which was presumably what he had intended. Portia, more interested, anyway, in personalities, found the diaries dull. Until the fourth volume when Bumpy 'started in' – which is how she puts it to herself – on Tom.

Suddenly Portia chortles aloud in a stagey way though there is no one to admire her performance. The only reason she put this diary in her luggage was because it had struck her, at the very last moment, just as she was leaving the house, that it was unfair to Tom to leave it lying about where one of her nosy friends might pick it up and read it. (Portia has two spare rooms and is generous with her front door keys; she has been poor enough herself to appreciate the value of a free pad in the city.) If she had known Tom was going to be on the same aeroplane, flying to the same place, she might have chucked the bloody book in the bin instead of shoving it in her handbag.

Portia thinks – this is quite the silliest thing that has ever happened to me. Coincidences happen all the time but this is two coincidences rolled into one! How Bumpy would laugh! She starts to laugh herself, and then, suddenly, finds herself missing Bumpy so badly that she doubles up with the pain of it and falls on the bed where she lies for a minute or two, moaning softly until the worst is over. Then she gets up, puts the diary in the drawer of the bedside table and picks up her room key and *The Guide to Southern Greece*.

There is a covered bar at the side of the pool. The only customers are two of the other minibus passengers who are having a drink together: the nice-looking older man, and the much younger girl. She is wrapped in the white, towelling robe supplied by the management. Her mass of crimped hair is still sleekly wet, her feet bare. He is dressed in what Portia can see is an expensively cut linen jacket and has, she guesses, been lying in wait to intercept this young woman after her swim. You didn't waste any time there, my lad, Portia thinks, and goes to lie by the pool.

The two Misses Farrell have dinner served in their suite. The only other traveller in the minibus who does not appear in the dining room between eight and eight-thirty is Tom Jones, who after a purgatorial spell in the bathroom has gone peacefully to sleep. Amy, seated at her table for two with his vacant place opposite, plans to see what the meal is like before she decides what to do; whether to take him a tray from the dining room, or wait until later and order from the room service menu which wasn't all that good, she remembers. Being ravenously hungry herself, she finds it hard to imagine what kind of food a man in Tom's fragile state might be tempted by. She orders a pasta dish for her first course and tucks in like a navvy.

Portia hesitates when she enters the dining room, uncertain whether to let the waiter seat her at a table for one, or to catch someone's eye. Apart from a few Greek families who are making a cheerful amount of noise, the only other diners are some of the folk who travelled with her from Athens. The psychologists have either eaten earlier or are roistering elsewhere, in one of the dungeons, perhaps? Looking for the elevator on her way back from her swim, Portia has discovered that there is an extensive subterranean area behind the pool bar: conference rooms, hairdressers, beauty parlours, so why not a dining room?
     Observing Horsey stuffing her face on her own, Portia

decides on the sociable option. The man and the girl who were drinking in the bar are sitting at a round table with five or six vacant places but neither of them looks up as she passes. So she is left with the Boots. Beryl is beaming at her anyway. She says, 'Do come and join us.'

Beryl is wearing a pink chiffon dress with a stiff-looking underskirt and glittery beading on the bodice; Mr Boot, a white, open-necked shirt, a pair of baggy grey shorts that reach to his hairy knees, ankle socks and running shoes.

Beryl smiles as if she has read Portia's mind. 'I dress up when we go on holiday and Daddy dresses down. That way, it makes a change for both of us.'

It would be foolish to underestimate Beryl Boot, Portia realises. She says, 'That's a very pretty dress. Are you sure you don't mind if I join you?'

'Our pleasure,' Daddy Boot says. But he makes no move to leap to his feet and draw out a chair for her. Portia who has no feelings about this one way or the other is surprised all the same: she would have thought Daddy was a man to set some store by conventional gallantries. She seats herself hastily, hoping Beryl hasn't plucked this thought out of the ether, and smiles from one to the other.

Prudence Honey is having a better time dining with Philip than she had expected. He is easy to talk to. Rather to her own surprise she found herself telling him about Daniel and the Casualty Sister (leaving out the moustache) and instead of making light of her feelings he seemed to understand them and sympathise. There are other ways in which he is unlike other old men: he doesn't seem to be deaf, or fidgety about his food or his health, or have obvious trouble with his prostate. Not that Prudence has encountered all that many old men except as patients in hospital.

And since her grandmother is arriving tomorrow there is no need to worry about 'encouraging' him. Philip is clearly not the sort of man to make an unseemly grab at a girl the first evening. Indeed, thinking along those lines, it occurs to Prudence that it might be a good idea to introduce him to Mrs Honey, who is still interested in men in spite of the fact that she will be sixty-nine next birthday. Older than Philip, she guesses, but once you get to that sort of age a few years here or there can't make all that much difference.

So Prudence thinks, and when she tells Philip about her grandmother who will be arriving tomorrow, and is a simply wonderful person, ready for anything, not at all like an old lady, she is a little surprised when he doesn't seem to be interested in the treat she is planning to offer him. Although he doesn't say anything crude, like he is busy tomorrow, or he plans to visit the classical sites, she senses a certain withdrawal in his manner. They have finished their meal, which was not very interesting, international hotel cooking rather than Greek. Philip dabs his mouth with his napkin and pushes back his chair, smiling at her, controlling a little yawn, and she gets the firm impression that as far as he is concerned this is the end of the evening.

They walk together through the emptying dining room. There is one Greek family left in a corner, and as they reach the door, the red-haired woman from the minibus almost collides with them. Ignoring Prudence, she flutters breathlessly at Philip. She is alone. She has lost or forgotten something, Prudence gathers – her handbag? her handkerchief? Philip touches her elbow reassuringly and turns aside to say something in Greek to the waiter, who responds with a staccato flurry of words, trots to a serving table and returns with a huge pair of very dark sunglasses.

Portia gives a loud squeal of welcome, as if a long-lost child has been miraculously restored to her, and turns to Prudence at last. 'Oh, how marvellous, I simply can't *bear* to lose things, so silly, isn't it?'

Prudence smiles weakly. Such passion over mislaid sunglasses seems more than just silly: unbalanced, disturbed, if not actually certifiable.

But Philip seems amused, almost approving. He has recovered his earlier attentive manner. Perhaps they should have a drink to celebrate? Take the lift and go down to the town. He includes Prudence in this invitation but she shakes her head. It has been a long day, Greek time is two hours ahead of England, and she wants to get up early tomorrow to meet her grandmother when her ship comes in. And she *is* tired, suddenly, like a child who has spent too long with the grown-ups.

All the same, she feels left out when Philip takes her at her word, wishes her a good night, and leaves without a backward look, the middle-aged redhead trotting beside him on ridiculously spiky high-heels. She'll be sorry she wore those after she's marched round the town for an hour! Prudence is startled by how spiteful she feels. She wraps her long arms round herself, hugs herself. Oh, she is *lonely*. Oh, *Daniel*.

They are all asleep by one o'clock Greek time, even Portia and Philip who have spent a comfortable hour in a bar in the main square of the little town, exchanging expurgated histories and old jokes and finding out fairly quickly that although they each enjoyed the other's company, they had no particular urge to end up in bed together.

Portia's feet, swollen by the flight, are hurting like hell by the time she gets back. She sits on her balcony, looking at the black sea and thinking about Bumpy. She is almost asleep in the chair when the *Morning Tide* sails round the headland and anchors offshore.

4

COMING BACK FROM HER MORNING SWIM (in the sea, of
course, not the pool) Amy is surprised to find Tom out of
bed, bathed and shaved, and breakfasting on the balcony.
Miraculously, it seems, a night's sleep and a bath and a
shave have transformed yesterday's whey-faced geriatric;
in the hotel's white bathrobe, a white napkin tucked into
the neckline to catch crumbs and drips, he looks smooth
and powdered and fresh as a newly washed baby.

Pleased with himself, too. As he tells Amy, 'I'd been worrying away at it, who she could be, ever since we got here,
got out of the bus, then, when I woke up this morning,
there it was, clear as anything. Name, rank and number.
Marvellous the way the old brain goes on devilling away
while you're asleep.'

Amy is towelling her heavy hair. She shakes it back, and
sits down, reaching for the coffee-pot. 'What are you talking about? I mean, *who*? One of the old ladies?'

'Not exactly *old*,' Tom says, laughing. 'Our age. More or less.'

Amy reaches for the bread basket, feels one roll and discards it, picks another. 'I thought you must mean the two women sitting behind us. I thought they were somehow familiar. One of them, anyway. But perhaps I'm getting to the age when people start coming round again.'

Tom stares at her blankly. 'I mean,' Amy says, buttering her roll, 'there can only be so many variations on eyes and noses and mouths. There must come a time when you've more or less run through them. Seen the lot.'

Tom says, slowly, smiling, 'It was the redhead at the back of the bus. Talking to that funny couple you seemed keen for us to be best buddies with.'

Amy raises her eyebrows and Tom sighs, reproachfully: surely she understands he was making a *joke*? 'I just thought I'd seen her somewhere before. Seen her *regularly*, if you follow me. As if we caught the same bus occasionally. Or she worked in one of the local shops. You know how it is, there are people who have particular associations, you don't always recognise them out of context?'

Amy thinks, *he's beginning to relax, he looks happier. Really, this place is magic.* She said, 'Go on, then, tell me. I'm not sure I can bear the suspense!'

'Oh, no one important. It never is, is it, when you run up against this sort of thing? She worked at the House, in fact she did a bit of research for me a few years ago, but her real job was P.A. to a man who resigned his seat, which is presumably why I haven't seen her around for a while. I seem to remember someone telling me she'd landed up as secretary to someone or other in the Lords. She was going around with old Bumpy, they were by way of being an item, that was the gossip.'

Amy ignores the gossip, as Tom knew she would, although she frowns at the vulgarity of *item*. She says, 'Bumpy's that nice man who was MP for Cwmgarw before you?'

'That's right. We worked on a couple of bills together since then.'

Amy is looking at him more intently now. She says, 'Funny *she* didn't say hallo, isn't it? If she'd worked for you, you'd think she'd have recognised you. I mean, you can't *both* have been in this uncertain condition.'

Tom thrusts his mouth forward, shaking his chin judicially. 'Oh, I don't know. Not as if she'd been *my* P.A., after all. Maybe she thought much as I did, that I looked familiar, but didn't feel inclined to risk it.'

He frowned. 'What I mean is, no one likes to make a fool of themselves. Hailing strangers as bosom pals.' He gives a short bark of not-quite-amusement. 'Not that we were ever that. And it's a few years since we set eyes on each other, dare say we've both aged a bit. I know I've got fatter.'

Amy tries not to smile. Tom is always hoping she will say that he doesn't need to lose weight, that he looks better now, with rather more flesh on him, than he looked in his scrawny twenties and thirties. Why doesn't she say this, since she knows it will please him? The answer is, like many people whose weight remains constant however much or little she eats, Amy is scornful of what seems to her a petty obsession. But it is not Tom's figure they are talking about, after all.

She says, 'Well, you'd better put it right next time you see her. What *is* her name, anyway?'

'Portia.' Tom produces this name with an air of amused incredulity as if he wishes Amy to know that he finds this a funny sort of moniker; pretentious, perhaps.

'Nice name,' Amy says. 'I've thought so ever since we did *The Merchant of Venice* at school. As a matter of fact I think that was what decided me to go in for the law. Portia what?'

'Donnell, I *think*, I mean it could be O'Donnell. 'Nuff of that, anyway. What d'you want to do after breakfast?'

'Whatever you feel like, darling,' Amy says, a little impatiently. She is prepared to do what Tom wants, this is *his* recuperative holiday, but she doesn't see why she should have to pretend *she* has chosen it. She would like to spend the morning climbing up the hundreds of steps to the castle, but that is not something Tom would have considered even when he was fit and thin and twenty years younger.

Anyway, Amy knows that asking her what she wants to do is only a gambit; a way of changing the conversation to disguise how distressed he is at forgetting this woman's name. Tom is absurdly upset when he cannot remember names, omits to enquire after children, cannot 'place' faces, seeing these minor losses of memory as appalling social gaffes from which no one else suffers and for which he will be despised by everyone around him.

Although she knows it is useless, that his fear is rooted too deeply in what is, to her, an incomprehensible insecurity, she attempts to console him. 'It's obvious, darling, the older you get, the more people you've known, you're bound to forget some of them. Or at least what you know about them is stuffed away somewhere you can't easily find it. I know *I* find myself wondering where I have *put* what I know about someone, like, well, those old ladies in the minibus. It's as if my mind was a dusty attic full of old cardboard boxes where bits of people are stored, not even a whole *person* in some cases, just a smile, or something someone has *said*, or a name . . .'

So Amy goes chuntering on, sweet-naturedly hoping to ease him and, at the same time, nervously defending herself against him, seeing by his lowered head and brooding look that he is finding her tedious. And yet, independently, other areas of her brain (other parts of the attic, or warehouse) continue to function quite smoothly, selecting, arranging, facts, memories, ideas and opinions, throwing up items for consideration, to dwell on or to discard. A conversation she has had with her mother that Tom will have to know about some time is disposed of immediately. It will have to wait until he is stronger. (Or until *she* is stronger?) The Boots surface briefly, Beryl and Daddy; what is the man's first name, wasn't there an estate agent called Boot in that housing scandal? Others, fellow guests, passengers in the minibus, friends and acquaintances flicker past in apparently random order. She wonders what to wear today. What Tom would like her to wear. Should she ask him? Would he be irritated? What would he like to do? Sit and sun by the pool? Walk in the town? There are plenty of cafés where he can sit down. It would be comforting to talk to him about the silly physical thing that is worrying her. Well, not silly exactly, *mortifying* would be a better word. That is, *she* finds it mortifying. She knows this is foolish, but she needs Tom to tell her so. She needs to catch him in a relaxed and affectionate mood. . .

Tom says, 'Look, why don't you go and climb mountains? Or have another swim. Whatever you fancy. I'm going to have a thoroughly idle day. I shall sit here and read. If I get energetic I can toddle down town and see if I can get hold of an English newspaper.'

'Only yesterday's, I'm afraid,' Amy says, feeling guilty. 'And you read those on the plane.'

Although he has been told several times (by Amy) that there would be a day's delay in getting his routine fix, Tom frowns, and sighs, 'How I am I supposed to keep up with what's going on?'

'You've got your radio, you can listen to the World Service. And if you need to have pictures you can watch CNN news on the telly.'

Amy speaks briskly. She has decided to take up Tom's offer of individual activities and has already decided to start up the steps to the castle before the sun gets too high. Much better for Tom to sit here and recuperate, look how much good one night's rest has done him already! If she leaves him in peace until lunchtime, he can have the bathroom to himself for as long as he likes without the fear that she will thump on the door and ask if he is 'all right in there', which she can't seem to stop herself doing even though she knows it infuriates him.

Amy says, 'I think I will trot up to the castle if you really don't mind. And I might get in another swim. Would it be fun to go down to the town for lunch? Mummy and I found a good fish taverna right on the harbour. Very simple, just either fried or grilled, you know, but lovely fresh fish. If they're in season we might have a lobster. They don't always have them, they're so expensive, but there's that cruise boat, rich Americans, probably, so they may have got them in.'

'Whatever you like.' Tom looks suddenly weary. He

smiles with an effort. 'You know, a cruise might not have been such a bad idea. In fact, I didn't tell you, but Vic did suggest it, offered to pay for us if we'd like to go, but I thought you wouldn't really want to be saddled with an old man as well as an invalid.'

'*Rubbish*, Tom.' Amy is genuinely indignant. 'I *love* Vic, you know that! You might have asked me, at least! Besides, poor old man, didn't it occur to you, he might have wanted your *company*? Oh, I know he's wonderful for his age and never complains, but don't you think he must, sometimes, be lonely?'

'Vic is never lonely,' Tom says.

'Vic' is Victor Aloysius Jones, Tom's father, a retired builder and decorator and jack-of-all-trades who, having spent most of his working life hand-to-mouth, just about keeping solvent, robbing Peter to pay Paul, unexpectedly became prosperous in the booming eighties. Vic was an only child, and when his mother and her spinster sister died within a month of each other, he inherited two decayed Georgian terrace houses in a dingy area of inner London that was on the verge of becoming fashionable among the affluent young bankers and brokers and lawyers who worked in the City.

In 1939, at the beginning of the war, Vic had been sent to live with his grandparents in Wales. Before that, for the first ten years of his life, he had been brought up in his mother's house and had no wish to return there, remembering lugging scuttles of coal up the stairs, and the smell of damp plaster. But he was quick to see that this kind of respectable slum property had suddenly become an investment. He knew the houses were structurally sound.

Although his aunt and his mother had refused to let him modernise, preferring to live with peeling paint, ancient bathrooms and kitchens, once he was back again, living in London, Vic had cobbled and patched at regular intervals, replacing missing roof tiles, clearing gutters, examining the timbers for rot. He borrowed from the bank for the first time in his life, employed a skilled carpenter, and a competent plumber.

He had had no formal architectural training. But the inner eye of the boy who had shivered in those chilly, high-ceilinged rooms, played up and down the shapely curves of the staircase, had registered the good proportions; seen that the kind of houses ordinary people lived in could be graceful as well as practical. Jobbing builders had built these houses from a pattern book, and Vic was a jobbing builder. He put in heating, new electric wiring, and did as little damage as he could. He sold the houses at an excellent profit all of which he spent on buying four semi-derelict Victorian cottages in Islington. He was in the middle of negotiating a loan to repair them when his wife had a sudden heart attack and died.

It is Tom's belief that the purchase of those four cottages killed his mother. He has repeated this accusation to Amy on a number of occasions and by now she knows that nothing she can say will change his mind. Indeed, he may be right. Tom's mother had always been terrified of being poor, envisaging not just an inability to pay her bills, but a heroic, cataclysmic poverty: her family evicted in the depth of winter from whatever pitiful hovel they had been reduced to, barefoot and freezing and starving in the gutter. A great-aunt, apparently, had 'ended in the workhouse'.

This would have been somewhere around the turn of the century, ancient history by the time Tom's mother was born, but it gave her the moral authority to live in fear. When Vic got his first loan from the bank, she became physically ill. She couldn't sleep, lost weight, and developed acute stomach pains. That her husband should squander a lucky inheritance on a few abandoned ruins looked to her like the ultimate folly, the bailiff at the gate, the last straw. And it broke her.

Amy is impatient with psychological excuses and explanations. Although she has never said so to Tom, she has always thought of his mother as a tedious bundle of anxieties and malice. It was hard luck on Vic, having to put up with her all those long years. If Amy doesn't think of it as being hard on Tom, that is because Tom has never criticised his mother, not even, she suspects, to himself, seeing her as a martyr to his father's jolly, spendthrift ways, even though he must know (as Amy sometimes remarks when she is having a private conversation with herself) that Vic had supported his wife in adequate comfort all her complaining life. It was Vic who was out in all weathers, on top of rickety ladders, slithering on the greasy slates of old roofs, while Tom's mother 'rested her feet', sitting with a cup of tea in front of the telly so that she could protest later about the rubbish they put on.

Tom says, 'It's a pity she didn't live to see Dad make a bit of solid money, nice if *she* could have had the chance to have some fun.'

Amy longs to point out that had his mother remained alive, she would have ensured that the rest of Vic's life was dedicated to the absence of pleasure, taking-care-of-the-pennies, laying up treasure in Heaven. But she restrains herself. Even if she doesn't always live up to her own high standards, Amy tries to be good. And she is glad for Vic's sake that he has been rescued from his personal Old Woman of the Sea, and is able to enjoy himself in the cheerful and boisterous way that is natural to him. Amy enjoys his company. He is so different from her dreadful father, so different from Tom. Though, of course, it is Tom she loves. She admires him, too, for a number of excellent qualities like rectitude and devotion to duty which he probably inherits from his mother, as well as for the easy sociability and good temper (understandably not much in evidence just at the moment) which he gets from his father. But it crosses her mind, just occasionally, that it might be nice to be married to a straightforward, fairly insensitive, strong, healthy and masculine man.

Vic is all these things. More important, he is a man at peace with himself and his unexpected good fortune. After his wife died, he abandoned work on his derelict cottages for long enough to discover that their value was growing by the month without his doing a hand's turn to assist it. This amused him. He bided his time, sold the cottages just below the peak of the rise in house prices, bought and sold other property, still without stirring off his backside; when he reckoned he had made enough money to buy a decent small pension for his old age, he decided to blow the rest while he was fit enough to have fun with it. He sold his own suburban semi for what seemed even in that crazy time an astronomical sum, went to Greece for the late summer, to southern Spain for the winter, and returned in the spring to find the house market had collapsed. He bought, very cheaply, a short lease on a comfortable flat in the Barbican, twenty minutes' brisk walk from his son and daughter-in-law, chiefly because Amy suggested it. Vic loves Tom, and is proud of him, but he gets on better with Amy. In fact, nowadays, he prefers the company of women to spending time with men; he finds women, 'the ladies', as he calls them, more spirited, readier to throw themselves into new experiences.

He has discovered it is cruises of the better sort (those that have some ostensible cultural objective, not necessarily the most expensive) that attract the kind of feisty females he likes best. He marginally prefers widows to spinsters, but he doesn't mind if they are travelling in pairs. Since the age of the majority of the passengers is high enough to ensure a certain amount of sudden calamity and the resulting last-minute cancellations, Vic has discovered that if he signs on late enough, and isn't too fussy about where the cruise is going, he can often get a double cabin to himself for the price of a single. Sexual encounters are not the main objective of what he thinks of as romantic adventures, but he likes to be prepared.

He had joined the *Morning Tide* the day before she sailed from Venice. Unusually, no one had died or fallen gravely ill; the cabin he was offered was reserved for a professor of archaeology who was giving a lecture at the American School in Athens and joining the cruise in Piraeus. Vic, on a coach tour of northern Italy that was beginning to bore him, had dropped into the shipping office instead of trailing around the Accademia and seized on the chance of a more comfortable method of travel and, with any luck, more amusing company than the uniformly elderly and uncompromisingly paired couples on the bus, as well as the bonus of disembarking in

68

Nauplion and surprising Amy and Tom at the Hotel Parthenon.

That they might not wish to be surprised is not a thought that troubles Vic. He is confident of Amy's welcome and since years of married martyrdom with Tom's mother have left him with an awed respect for illness, he is anxious to see for himself that Tom is recovering. Besides, as he alights from the *Morning Tide*'s tender, the little town looks agreeably fresh and sparkling as it climbs up the mountain from the harbour; the waterfront cafés, expectant and inviting. He deposits his suitcase beside a convenient table and turns back to the tender to assist Mrs Honey with her luggage.

Vic has no designs on this particular widow who is too tall and gaunt for his liking. He helps her, as he would help any woman, old or young, out of natural gallantry. (In spite of rebuffs, he still opens doors for girls in jeans and offers them his seat on the Underground and the buses.) But Mrs Honey's smallish suitcase is not heavy. He says, surprised, 'You travel light.'

Mrs Honey is proud of the way she manages to live for several weeks with just three light dresses, a jacket, a change of underwear and two pairs of shoes, and if Vic had been a woman might have elaborated on her cleverness, explaining that in her view the key to success is a pair of pretty sandals and piece of jewellery handsome enough to impress but not valuable enough to be worrying (she relies on a large pinchbeck brooch set with rhinestones) to liven up a simple shift for the evenings. As it is, 'Women's clothes don't weigh much,' is all she says.

She smiles at Vic but she is looking beyond him, holding out her hands to welcome Prudence who is running towards her, breathless and laughing, her cloud of crimped hair blowing around and behind her.

If he had not been waylaid by Portia, Philip might have accompanied Prudence to the harbour to meet Mrs Honey. He had woken in the early hours in a cold sweat of embarrassment. How shamefully ridiculous of him to have been put out by the girl's entirely natural and innocent assumption that a man of his age would be longing to meet a well-preserved grandmother! Not, of course, that Prudence would have noticed anything wrong. She was much too innocent to realise she had injured his vanity. All the same, once he had stopped smarting, he was anxious to make amends. He would catch her at breakfast; ask if she would like him to go to the town with her. An old lady would need help with her luggage. The hotel must have arrangements for picking up guests who arrived by boat but would not necessarily be eager to offer them: if he were to ask them in Greek, it might make them more willing.

But when he comes down for breakfast Portia is already seated at a table for two on the terrace and beckoning him to join her. 'Rescue me,' she mouths, rolling her eyes and tilting her head to indicate the approach from behind her of Mrs Boot dressed as a matelot, a vision in tight white jeans and gold sandals, carrying a tall glass of orange juice and a good trencherwoman's plateful of hard-boiled eggs, cheese, bread and butter.

Obediently, Philip sits in the vacant chair, raising his buttocks a polite inch or two as his eyes lock with Beryl's.

'Have I taken your seat?' he asks, clearly ready to leap to his feet on the instant, and her soft cheeks turn a charming, pale, marshmallow pink. It strikes Philip that she must once have been quite deliciously pretty. When she was around Prudence's age, for example. Although Beryl is considerably older than Prudence, she is still a sweet-looking woman. Philip thinks, *cuddly* would be the way to describe her. Beryl is about the same age as Portia, he reckons. Several years younger than Matilda, who is fifty-three. *Was* fifty-three. And much younger than he is, so why is he being so disgustingly patronising?

These reckonings (and stern self-reproof) occupy barely a nanosecond of Philip's time. He is on his feet, hands held palms upward, offering to relieve Beryl of her burden of breakfast, put the plate of eggs and cheese and the glass of juice wherever it pleases her. Not perhaps here, at Portia's table, but practically anywhere else, on the terrace overlooking the sea and the mountains on the other side of the bay, or indoors, in the (at present empty) dining room.

Beryl says, 'No, thank you, I'm fine, this isn't all for me, I'd hate you to think I was greedy, I just thought I'd get a bit extra for Daddy in case there's nothing left on the buffet when he comes down. Though they've gone, that big group who were here last night, did you know? I went to look round the town before breakfast and they were getting into the buses already, six o'clock in the morning, I said to myself, what a time, the poor souls.'

'I thought the place felt empty,' Portia says. 'Though not for long, I expect. It's a white elephant, this hotel, subsidised by the government, so it's marvellous value for people like us. But one imagines they have even cheaper corporate rates for groups and for conferences.'

'Anything that gives more trouble than it's worth, a useless gift,' Beryl says and, suddenly, giggles. 'You know, I went to the library the other day and looked up *white*

71

elephant in the dictionary. I thought, it's something people keep saying, and, d'you know, it started off being what the king of Siam gave to one of his courtiers when he wanted to ruin him. A white elephant was terribly expensive to look after, you see, and the courtier could not get rid of it because it was a present from the king. He had to keep it and feed it even if he and his family starved while they did it.'

Philip says, 'How about that?' He likes to hear this sort of anecdote and not only because his publishing firm makes a good profit out of its dictionaries. It comforts him to know there are people beside himself who take an interest in words, their origin and use.

He is surprised, when Beryl has gone, to hear Portia say – spitefully, to his ear, 'Do you think she really doesn't have a dictionary at home? I wouldn't suspect her of being an intellectual, exactly, but she's perfectly bright, if not educated, isn't she? At least the *Concise Oxford*, wouldn't you have thought? Or perhaps they just have no books at all. I wonder if she calls a *magazine* a book?'

Philip realises that Portia is not meaning to be unkind. She is simply indulging in the British habit of species recognition, of 'placing' a stranger. He is well enough acquainted with this curious game to know that it is not necessarily which rung of the ladder Beryl is perched on that interests Portia. As Philip understands it, the social hierarchy in England is not a vertical structure, but a complex pattern in which education, intelligence, money, accent, taste, occupation, birth and background all figure, but in a varying order, and in different relationships to each other, depending upon the observer.

Philip says, 'Maybe they have walls lined with books. All

the children have been to university, which makes her ashamed of her ignorance in front of the family, so she sneaks out to look things up on the sly. Or perhaps she just likes an excuse to go to the library. A nice change from the shopping mall.'

'Don't you ever make judgements about other Americans?' Portia asks with an innocent air. 'Oh, don't tell me, I know what you'll say. Of course you do, but not in that pernickety, niggardly way. I tell you what, though. I bet we have more social mobility in our class-ridden country. I don't mean au pair girls marrying into the royal family, either. I mean people like me. My mother worked as a cleaner while I was growing up, probably for someone like Beryl Boot. Or her mother. Now I could pass – well, I used to work in the House of Lords so it's what springs to mind – I could pass for a peer's daughter. It's a matter of accent and nous.'

She is being serious, not a hint of irony, and Philip is touched. He would like to say – *No one could possibly mistake you for a peer's daughter*. Although Portia may have hauled herself up by her bootstraps, she has a healthy amount of coarse energy that doesn't, to Philip's mind, go along with his idea of aristocracy, or even gentility. He likes this toughness, it makes him feel safe with her, but he is still nervous of teasing her in case she suddenly changes shape, woman into succuba, turning on him like Matilda.

Portia says, 'I *like* her, actually. I mean, she's obviously been up since the crack of dawn, looking around, I like that. It's not what you'd expect from her, is it? It's what I always mean to do, get up and get going. Instead I just laze about, painting my toenails.' She leans across the table and says, in a stagy whisper, 'Do you think her husband is a little bit *sinister*?'

Philip laughs, as he assumes he is meant to, but he is uncomfortable with this kind of gossipy speculation (which he associates with schoolgirls and homosexuals) and changes the subject. 'Tell me about the House of Lords. What's it like working there?' He is not really interested but anything is better than allowing Portia to prattle about a woman who may (although this is not strictly relevant morally) still be within earshot.

By the time the Misses Farrell descend to the lobby, Portia and Philip have finished breakfast and are on their way out of the hotel, Portia to the elevators that descend to the town, Philip to the steps that wind down the other side of the rock, to the beach.

The old ladies follow him slowly. They are wearing canvas shoes, towelling dresses and sun hats, but their regal bearing and consequential air make it hard to imagine them on the beach, let alone in the sea. Philip, idly watching from the flat rock where he has established himself for the morning, expects them to settle on one of the seats in the shade of the trees, the eucalyptus and pines, that surround the little bay. There are more and steeper stairs from the hotel to the beach than he had remembered; the backs of *his* calves are aching and he is a deal younger than the Misses Farrell!

But they do not hesitate. They jump lightly on to the beach, deposit their canvas bags side by side, remove their shoes, their dresses, sun hats and dark glasses, and stand arms akimbo, heads thrown back, worshipping the sun for a still, ecstatic moment before running, barefoot on the sharp shingle, straight into the sea.

Philip raises himself on his elbow. They are both swimming a strong, stately breaststroke, heads high out of the water; the sea is so calm this morning there is no danger they will get their hair wet if they are careful. Keeping her hair dry was one of Matilda's major concerns when swimming on holiday, and Philip assumes that all women feel the same way. Unless they are young, of course. He thinks of Prudence coming out of the pool yesterday evening, wet as a seal and no more self-conscious, and smiles.

His rock is high enough above the beach and the sea so green and clear he can see the women's long white legs and long white arms moving gracefully beneath the surface. He thinks, *like fronds or tendrils*, but those limbs are powerful, too: Philip wonders if the Farrells have been professional swimmers in their time. Though however experienced they *have been*, at their present age they should surely not be venturing so far out to sea! How old are they? As they entered the water they had looked like withered storks. Now, from this distance, under water, their bodies are beautiful.

Philip watches them, frowning. It is nearly mid-June, local children are still in school, and apart from a *kaffee-klatsch* of Greek ladies in black bathing costumes and soft linen hats, bobbing up and down at the edge of the sea in a tight, conversational circle and screeching cheerfully away at each other, the only other people within shouting distance are obviously grandfathers: three stooped, elderly gentlemen, each in charge of a paddling toddler. All the same, there is no reason why Philip should feel he is responsible for the safety of two people he has barely even spoken to, just because they travelled together yesterday, from Athens to the Hotel Parthenon. A couple of hours in the same minibus is not long enough to develop a sense of group obligation. This is what Philip tells himself, anyway.

But he does feel responsible. And, suddenly, finds he is resenting it bitterly. Oh, he has no intention of leaving the beach while those idiot Englishwomen remain in the water. He will stand guard, do his duty. But (so he snarls inwardly) there is no logical reason why he should feel responsible for every damn fool on the planet just because he has failed Matilda.

Why did he come to the beach, anyway? If he wanted exercise he could have swum in the pool and although he is not a hypochondriac, he is sufficiently health conscious to know it is dangerous to lie too long in the sun.

Oh – he knows why. It had been an excuse. He had been afraid Portia might want him to accompany her to the town. She was going to hire a car and thought it would be an advantage to have a Greek speaker with her. Or had *he* thought she might have thought that? He couldn't recall her actually saying so. And his Greek isn't all that good, anyway.

Nor all that bad, either. He had spent school holidays in the Embassy in Athens with the then American Ambassador (his dead Jewish father's useful diplomatic friend in Berlin, and his Quaker father's brother) and then, later on, the year he left Harvard, a long summer walking in the Peloponnese. He has a good ear for language and a good memory. The truth is – and Philip groans aloud as he faces it – he is a solipsistic and prurient bastard. Prissily defending himself against imaginary onslaughts on his celibacy when he could have been of some practical help to a pleasant woman who had shown absolutely no lustful intentions towards him.

Well, serve him right, look where it's landed him. Lifeguarding a couple of crazy old exercise fetishists. Philip sits up, finding himself suddenly in much better humour, and sees that the two women have turned from the horizon and are swimming, steadily, regally, with no sign of exhaustion, back to the shore.

5

PORTIA HAS DRUNK THICK, SWEET, GREEK coffee at two places in the central square, sipped an ouzo on the waterfront, and eaten an agreeably boozy lunch at a tiny table precariously balanced on the edge of a slightly smelly drain outside the back-street taverna recommended to her by her travel editor. She has appraised the good-looking young waiters, fed the thin, pestering cats, visited the small museum, and watched the comings and goings and general behaviour of some of the passengers from the *Morning Tide* who have decided against toiling around Epidaurus and Mycenae in the blazing heat of the day and chosen, instead, to explore the town and compare prices in the tourist shops.

Almost all of these passengers are over fifty and for many of them, Portia has guessed, this cruise is a precious retirement treat, long saved up for, never to be repeated. Knowing this – or believing she knows it – makes her temporarily tender towards people she might otherwise have secretly sneered at: the red-faced, lumpy women in frilly sun dresses and the ravaged old men who trail around after them, weighed down with video cameras and money belts, as well as with their wives' purchases.

However, after lunch, when she is sitting at another café, eating an ice-cream and writing her notes, one of these burdened ancients suddenly halts his shuffling progress and wheels round to point the expensive machine dangling around his lined, tortoise neck, directly at her, only a few feet from her face. He takes Portia's photograph, not only without asking her, but also without even appearing to consider that he perhaps ought to ask her, which she finds a curiously unsettling experience. It is as if, in his view, she is not a human being like himself, whose feelings should be considered and consulted, but merely a subject to be recorded – rather as an old-time colonial adventurer with a camera might have recorded a bare-breasted 'native' woman in a grass skirt as just another feature in an exotic landscape.

Portia, made benign by sun and alcohol, decides to forgive him. He has merely been struck down by an illness peculiar to group travel: he has been so cushioned and cocooned from the first hour of the journey that he has lost touch with reality. Anyone outside the protected circle is only a spectacle to him.

Even those cruise passengers who have broken away from the group and are lunching at the harbour tavernas on lobster and crayfish instead of returning to the safe womb of the ship, seem afflicted in the same way; unable to see the inhabitants of the town as real people. Portia, on her way to the car hire company at the end of the harbour, experiments smiling at a party from the *Morning Tide*, one of whom had appeared to be looking directly at her as she approached them, only to be met by an uncomprehending stare, followed by a turned head and a whispered remark to a neighbour.

'Did you see *that*?' Portia imagines this group traveller saying. 'That *alien creature*, the one with two heads, actually *smiling* at me?'

She is absurdly relieved when Prudence Honey, sitting with an erect and handsome woman who looks like an older relation, an aunt, or a grandmother, looks up from the fish she is dissecting and waves, restoring her, Portia feels, to the visible world of humanity.

And when she sees Amy and Tom outside the shop front of the car hire company, she is reassured further. Even Horsey, Portia feels, has become a member of what the Greeks call a *parea*, the circle of acquaintances a person feels naked without. (Portia learned this useful word from Philip last night and intends to incorporate it in her article on the Peloponnese.) As for Tom, there is nothing so reliable in a crisis as a no-longer lover for whom you still feel some affection.

Portia finds herself wishing she could share this comforting discovery with Tom so they could have a bit of a giggle together, but this is hardly the moment: Tom is climbing, with evident difficulty, into the back seat of a small, blue, two-door car; another man, older and thinner, is preparing to get into the driving seat and Amy, who is anxiously bending forward as if to assist Tom, will presumably take the front seat beside him.

They are, all three, large people; too large for the Nissan Cherry. *How do you get four elephants in a minibus? Two in the front and two in the back.* Returned to childhood by this infantile joke, Portia doubles up with helpless laughter, turning away for concealment into the wide doorway of the nearest shop which has bicycles and scooters in various stages of dilapidation for sale or for hire.

Tom is in pain. *Discomfort* he tells himself, that's what it's called. Discomfort. Pull yourself together, man. For God's sake stop moaning.

Amy, turning round from the front seat, is regarding him with remorse and sorrow. Of course it is not her fault that he has had to crawl into the back of this ridiculous car! 'In the back, lad,' Vic had said, naturally assuming his son would leave the comfort of the front passenger seat to his wife. Amy might have been a bit quicker off the mark in protesting, but she wasn't, that's all there is to it. Too busy smiling at Vic?

Tom tells himself he is delighted that his wife is so fond of his father. He is fond of his father himself. It is just that in his present uncomfortable circumstances, he would have been better pleased if Vic had delayed his surprise appearance for a few days, or if he had at least been less obviously physically fit when he did appear: a real *old man*, of whom one could say he was 'marvellous for his age', instead of a powerful hunk of testosterone apparently able to make sensible middle-aged women like Amy flutter their eyelashes and blush.

Amy is saying, 'Why don't we take a ride around, Vic darling? I don't think Tom's up to a long drive after yesterday's journey, but I'd like you to get the feel of the place. There's a beautiful bay beyond the castle, on the other side of the mountain, you might fancy a swim there, not now, perhaps, we ought to make sure they have a room for you at the hotel, but we might swim later this afternoon, after you've settled in. After siesta.'

'Let the poor man get his breath, Amy,' Tom says, in what is meant to be a jocular tone but which comes across, in delivery, as captious and carping. To Amy's ear, anyway.

Vic says, 'Anything you say, Amy love. You give the orders.' He raises his voice as if his son in the back of the car is deaf as well as sickly. 'OK by you, Tommy lad?'

'Fine,' Tom says. 'Just fine, Dad.'

He sits back, resigned. Amy has shifted her seat forward as far as she can but his knees are still jammed. He twists around to find a more comfortable position, and finally settles with his left leg and left arm stretched along the back seat and his right arm and hand resting on his right knee. As long as he doesn't try to move, this is just about bearable. He will have to put up with it, anyway. Vic has paid for the hire of the car, paid for their lunch, and will almost certainly continue to pay, while they are all three together, for anything that has not already been paid for in advance as part of the package deal. (Tom does not think like this *consciously*, it is his mother's spirit, or memory, thinking inside him: all Tom actually reckons, himself, is that it is only fair to give his father a chance to look around.)

Not that he, Tom, will be able to look around much; the way he is sitting, and with those two big bodies blocking his front view, his only real outlook is through the back window.

The traffic in the centre of the town is undisciplined. Vic whistles (in admiration not fear, Tom judges, knowing his father) as bikes and vans and cars perform unsignalled U turns, hurtle unexpectedly out of side alleys, or scream to a stop in order for the driver to hail an acquaintance on the other side of the street. Though Tom cannot see precisely what is happening in front of the car, he can extrapolate from what goes on behind and sympathises with Amy whose white-knuckled hands are braced on the dashboard. For a minute he contemplates stroking the back of her neck to console her. But it would mean changing position and he is too lazy, too afraid of the pain.

In any case, they are soon out of the town, the little car is labouring up the steep hill to the castle, and the traffic has diminished to rustic proportions; there is even an old man on a donkey trotting in the middle of the road. As they leave him behind, Tom waves at him through the back window.

A Range Rover passes them. There is a red scooter behind it. The rider seems to hesitate, as if uncertain whether to follow the Range Rover, then pulls in behind the Nissan. A pulse jumps in Tom's throat.

Portia is wearing a crash helmet and her enormous dark glasses. She grins at Tom and lifts one hand from the handlebars as if to salute him. The scooter wobbles and she replaces it quickly. Her wide mouth is laughing.

Tom is horrified. This must be the first time Portia has ridden a scooter. If it had been one of her accomplishments she would surely have told him? On the other hand, these little machines are safe and steady enough, nothing like a big motorbike. A child could manage one, probably. As long as she does nothing silly . . .

Portia chooses this moment to show off. She raises her hand again, makes a V for Victory sign, veers towards the other side of the road, then accelerates back towards the Nissan, passing it dangerously close. She gives Tom a triumphant glance and he closes his eyes. A horn blares; an alarming, deep, breathy sound, like a trumpet. Vic swerves, and brakes hard. Amy gasps. Tom is thrown forward, his right foot slips and is caught behind Vic's seat. He opens his eyes.

The bus passes them with a groaning hiss on its way down the hill. Vic says, 'All right in the back, Tom? Sorry, Amy love.'

Amy says, 'You saved her life, Vic.'

'Luck, my love. Looked in the mirror at the right moment, just as she came out from behind us. I suppose she was tucked in too far, couldn't see the blasted bus.'

Vic is pulling out now, passing Portia, who grins and wiggles her fingers.

Vic says, indulgently, 'Silly girl.'

Amy says, 'Isn't she . . .?'

'Who?'

'No, not you, Vic, I was asking Tom.'

Tom is wrestling with his trapped foot. He says, through gritted teeth, 'I can't see much, stuck in the back here. Hang on a minute.' He has managed to free his foot, leaving his shoe behind. Massaging his ankle, he looks out of the back window.

Portia is still there, about ten metres behind them. She is not smiling; her mouth is set grimly. Perhaps she has only just understood how close she has been to her death.

Tom suddenly realises it, too; an aching hollow of fear opens up in his chest, sweat breaks out on his forehead. For a second, wrenched back in time, he cries inwardly, *Oh my darling . . .*

And instantly repudiates this out-of-date sentiment. *Bloody woman.* Though he is still shaken. Mind you, he tells himself, he would feel pretty shaken up if she had been a stranger!

He says, 'Yes, you're right, Amy. I didn't notice before, I mean I saw the bike, but not *her* if you see what I mean.'

'It's the hair.'

Amy sounds breathless.

Vic says, 'Friend of yours? Just as well I didn't run her down then.' He catches Tom's eye in the driving mirror and winks at him.

Amy says nothing. She doesn't turn to look at Tom, which makes him uneasy. Though why should it?

He clears his throat noisily. 'Not a friend, Dad, just an acquaintance, someone who used to work at the House. She's staying at our hotel.' He hesitates. Something more seems to be needed. He adds, awkwardly, 'Quite by chance, naturally.'

Silence. Well, no comment is called for. Amy is looking out of the window. They have reached the top of the mountain and are descending a zigzag road to a wide bay, bare, rocky mountains sweeping down to the sea. Trees fringe the shore; there is a tiny white church halfway up one headland; white crosses painted on the rocks above. Amy says, 'The Germans shot some resistance fighters there. In the war.'

Then, after a pause, 'It's shallow here, you have to walk out quite a distance before you can swim, but it's firm sand all the way. The beach near the hotel, where I usually go, you can dive straight from the rocks into deep water. Better for swimming, I think, but it's nice to have a change sometimes.'

Tom says, 'Ah!' in a sardonic tone that is meant to point up (in an amused way, of course) the slightly absurd juxtaposition of these two pieces of information, but Amy does not appear to hear him. It is at this moment that Portia zooms past them again, driving her scooter more skilfully now but still recklessly, given the state of the road which has become deeply rutted close to the shore, worn away by rivulets of fresh water running off the mountains into the sea. She doesn't acknowledge the occupants of the hired car, perhaps because she is too intent on staying upright on the scooter as she leaves the road and sets off on a path through the trees that is little more than a goat track, too narrow and rough for a car to follow. But it seems to Tom that the bouncing of her tightly blue-jeaned behind, up and down with the ups and downs of the road, is meant to be derisive; Portia cocking a snook in farewell.

It makes him laugh inwardly. He can't see if Amy is smiling or not. Though why should she smile? You would have to know Portia . . .

It is Vic who laughs aloud. He says, 'That is one shapely lady!'

Amy does smile at this. She likes the way Vic relishes women. He has such a wide range of appreciation: pretty girls, mothers and grandmothers; their appearance, their conversation, and (something he believes in profoundly), their superior feminine wisdom. And his delight is so open and innocent that even Amy, who is normally embarrassed by remarks that seem to her to have a sexist, or a sexual, connotation, is able to enjoy his pleasure in the sight of Portia's plump bottom.

Though Amy is not really thinking about Portia. Oh, she is relieved the poor woman is not lying bloody and broken on a Greek mountain road. She is also conscious of a slight urging of social duty: she must remind Tom, who is lazy about people of no particular use to him, to greet this House of Commons acquaintance next time he sees her. But most of her mind is otherwise occupied: with how and when she will tell Tom about the financial arrangements her mother has made for her husband, his stepson, his daughter.

She had decided to put off telling him until the end of the holiday but Vic's arrival has made it more urgent. Up to now Vic has only asked after Bill and Kate, but he will soon embark upon wider enquiries. How is Amy's mother – known to Vic as 'the beautiful Harriet'? How is Amy's step-father, Dick? And (for Vic is punctilious in family matters) how are Dick's two unfortunate children? Once Harriet and her new family are mentioned, brought, as it were, *out into the open*, Amy cannot continue to say nothing to Tom about her mother's intentions. It would feel so dishonest and devious to be discussing her mother with Vic, even if all they are exchanging are polite social bulletins, while Tom remains ignorant of what he will see as much more important. Of course, he will say she has been dishonest and devious, not telling him in the first place.

Amy sighs. They have reached the end of the bay and Vic, turning the car, looks at her enquiringly. He says, 'OK, my lovely? Back to the hotel? Or does something else take your fancy? Your wish is my command.'

Vic's features are finer than Tom's, his bright eyes more narrowly set. Stewart Granger, Amy thinks, remembering one of her mother's film heroes, and long discussions about his appearance and character, after the film, in the cinema café. Amy had always maintained that his eyes made him look foxy and deceitful but her mother had argued for romance, sensitivity.

87

Vic's eyes, Amy considers, twinkle with sense rather than sensibility; the eyes of a robust personality who has survived a pinched and tedious marriage and at last come into his own. She hopes Vic's last years will be happy and glorious. He has just enough money for comfort, and for freedom to travel, and he is cheerfully spending it. There will be nothing for Tom to inherit; that is, nothing worth worrying over.

And Tom hasn't worried, up to now, anyway. Why should he bother about his father's little bit of money when he is expecting to inherit so much more from his wife's mother?

Amy is shocked to find herself thinking so bluntly. Tom isn't *crude*, only anxious. He is in an uncertain profession. If the Party gets in next time, there is a possibility that he might be offered a minor government post, but Amy is afraid that since he didn't get elected to the Shadow Cabinet last year, he has already missed the boat. He has talked about resigning his seat and 'going into the City'. But Conservatives are usually better placed to metamorphose into bankers and company directors than back-bench members of the Labour Party. Before he was selected to stand for the Cwmgarw constituency, Tom had been in the civil service, a principal in what was then called the Department of Education and Science. But he has been in politics so long. If he were to leave, what would he do? He must worry about it.

Turning from Vic, looking out of the passenger window, Amy pretends to be absorbed in watching the sea and the mountains and talks to Tom silently.

I had a chat with Mummy the other day. I should have told you before, but you were feeling so low after the operation . . .

88

No. No excuses. No hinted apologies. A mistake to be on the defensive.

Mummy has decided she must make proper arrangements for Dick in case she should fall off her perch before he does. Not our business really, of course, no need for her to tell us at all, but she wanted everything open and above board between us. Of course, she's left the house to Dick for his lifetime, and enough to pay for its upkeep, well, of course we knew she'd do something like that. What's new is that she's decided she must do something for his children now, to make them both independent, rather than leave them money when she dies. She and Dick are especially anxious about the boy. With good nursing he may go on living for years and with the NHS crumbling, who knows what will happen to paraplegics who are left to rely on the social services? The daughter's situation isn't so desperate, but someone has to look after the children, Dick's grandchildren, and he worries so terribly . . .

No. A mistake to try and get pity for Dick. Amy loves him because he has made her mother so happy, but Tom feels rather differently. After Amy's father died, Tom had suggested they buy a house in the country and share it with Harriet; she would be less lonely now and later on, as she grew older, it would be easier for them to take care of her. One of his friends in the House, an old-fashioned Liberal member for a northern industrial constituency, had sold his London house, bought a flat in Dolphin Square for himself, and converted an old farm in Sussex for his family, adapting an adjacent farm building as a sheltered apartment for his widowed mother, and Tom had been agreeably struck by the freedom it gave him.

'At least mention it to Harriet,' he had pleaded with Amy – to her stunned disbelief. Surely Tom knew that

Harriet was urban by nature; the country was fine to walk in or bicycle through but not a suitable place to *live* unless you were a cow.

'I don't think Mummy would like to live in a cowshed,' Amy had said, faintly but finally, finishing the matter as far as she was concerned. But Tom had apparently continued to cherish a vision of the fine house they would be able to afford if his mother-in-law bought most of it for them, and when she announced she was getting married, he had felt, quite genuinely it seemed, that he had been deceived. He was polite to Dick, even friendly, but (Amy was sure) he still secretly regarded him as a swindler who had deprived him of the country gentleman's existence he had almost begun to believe was his birthright.

On the other hand, Amy reminds herself, Tom has always been fond of Harriet. Certainly, he has always liked her far more than she, for example, ever cared for Tom's mother . . .

Mummy needs to do what seems right to her, I think she'd be miserable if she felt she hadn't provided as well as she could for everyone she feels responsible for. And she does feel responsible for Dick's children; what you and I might think about it can't alter how she feels, and we ought to be grateful she wants us to know – after all, she needn't have said anything, she could have left us to find out once she'd popped off!

They were driving up the winding road to the hotel when Portia passed them on a blind bend. Vic blew his horn at her. He said, 'That reminds me. I should have asked you before. How is the beautiful Harriet?'

She tells him in a rush, in a stumbling hurry, as soon as they reach their room. Then bursts into tears.

Tom is bewildered. Amy so rarely cries. He puts his arms round her and pats her broad shoulders. 'What on earth is the matter? Don't you feel well?'

She shakes her head, sobbing; her hot tears soak his neck.

He makes an unusually imaginative effort. 'Do you think it means she doesn't love you? Is that why you're crying? Don't be a silly girl. Harriet probably thinks we're rolling in money, coals to Newcastle, obviously she has to do something for Dick's kids. Especially for the boy. I mean he's a tragedy. *Bloody* motorbikes – there should be a law restricting licences to men over thirty!' He chuckles at himself, a law-maker, saying this; kisses the side of Amy's wet cheek and nibbles the lobe of her ear, which has been known to make her laugh. He says, 'You must have known this was likely to happen, once she was married to Dick. You know your mother.'

She said, with a doleful sniff, 'You don't *mind*?'

'Fat lot of good it 'ud be, my minding,' Tom says, amused. 'Anyway, what sort of monster do you think I am? I admit, I was fed up to begin with when she took up with Dick, all right, she'd known him since time immemorial, but he still might have been on the make, mightn't he? I was thinking of the kids, really, though I don't suppose she'll altogether forget them. But I haven't been brooding over it ever since. Honest!'

He holds her away from him. Her expression astounds him. 'Is that what you've been thinking? Oh, Amy! For Christ's sake!'

Her colour has risen. Perhaps she caught the sun when she was swimming this morning. But he hopes it means she is ashamed. She bloody well ought to be!

91

She tucks her chin over his shoulder so he can't see her face. She says sadly, defensively, 'It was just, when Mummy told me, I couldn't bear it. I can't bear to think of her dying.'

Beryl Boot has found a dream house at the top of the town. She has inspected a number of half-ruined houses that have people still living in them, in the cellars, or perched like birds on a precarious upper floor. No one could be living in this one. The doors and the window are broken, empty holes in the crumbling walls; inside the house, the internal walls and the floors have collapsed completely. And it is the only house in the quiet upper part of the town with a view of the harbour; there is no building opposite, either on this level or the one below, only the clear air that at this time of the evening is full of swifts wheeling and crying.

Peeping in through the door opening, Beryl sees, through a tumble of rotten wood, lath and plaster, the broken roof and the sky. A total wreck – which is what she is looking for. *Keep you busy*, Daddy had said. *In case I'm away for a while*. Money has been deposited in her name in the National Bank; there is a lawyer and an architect in Athens, both speaking good English, but they – or she – will need to find a local builder. 'No harm in learning a bit of Greek, anyway, Mrs B. If it comes to it,' Daddy has said.

He would prefer to buy land and build. But Beryl's dream is to recover an old house. She likes the idea of a place that has stood empty for a while, long enough to be grateful to someone who is ready to tend and restore it. In a hidden part of her mind Beryl believes that houses have spirits, or souls.

Not that she can really believe she will ever live in this

ruin, or that Daddy will settle happily in such a quaint *foreign* place. But she thinks it would be nice, once the house is fixed up, to sit in one of the upstairs windows, or on a little balcony with twirled and curled iron railings, and look at the sea and the sunset. And they do have television here, with English and American programmes and films, and there is space at the side of the house for a garden. In fact, there *has been* a garden; though it is chock full of rubble, out of it a lemon tree is sturdily growing. Fancy picking your own lemons! Of course it would be hard to be such a long way from the girls and their families . . .

Beryl dusts her hands together and frowns at streaks of dirt on the front of her matelot outfit. She looks at her watch and, as if on cue, the air is suddenly strident with bells.

An enormous coach has delivered its cargo at the entrance to the tunnel that leads to the lifts and the Hotel Parthenon. Cars and smaller buses can drive up the mountain to the hotel entrance, but the road is too narrow for large vehicles to navigate easily and this group of guests will have to finish their journey on foot.

As they alight from the coaches (slowly and carefully, fumbling with walking sticks, scarves and sun hats) the pealing bells greet them, a wild tumble of sound that is cut off abruptly when they enter the tunnel. Here, in the huge shaft driven into the heart of the mountain the silence is absolute; all they can hear is the noise they are making, the patter and shuffle of their feet on the stone floor, little pants and sighs, the creak of their breathing.

Although the tunnel is lit, it seems dark to eyes accustomed to the bright evening and slow to react to a change in the light. When the hotel had been planned, the tunnel had been intended to be a gallery where shops could display their wares, but the display cabinets on either side have remained dark and empty, their glass fronts dusty and broken. And only two of the lifts at the end of the tunnel appear to be working.

It is uninviting and even slightly alarming. There are murmurs of doubt among the group of elderly people who have booked (and paid for) seven nights in a hotel described in the brochure as 'magnificently luxurious', but being old, they are also polite, and the young tour guide does not expect trouble. She says, in her prettily accented voice that has enslaved them already, 'It is like a set for a James Bond film, do you not think it?' and they are reconciled instantly.

By the time Beryl returns from the town they have all settled in comfortably; either sitting in rows in the lounge, grey heads nodding in front of the news on Greek television, or making their way into the dining room where an early evening meal has been ordered, clutching their walking sticks, back cushions, handbags, packets of wheat germ and multi-vitamin tablets.

6

THIS INVASION OF VALETUDINARIANS HAS DRAWN the minibus passengers closer. They have all taken refuge in the bar; ostensibly just a few hotel guests having a drink together, seated in twos and threes, at different tables, but in fact, emotionally, a cohesive force, united against a common enemy.

Philip has had a word with the head waiter. 'Apparently they have arranged to dine early all the time they are here.'

He is speaking to Prudence's grandmother but the bar is small and he has raised his voice for the benefit of others who may need reassuring.

Philip would not have objected to an earlier dinner himself; it would suit his digestion better. Indeed (as he reminds himself now) some of the new arrivals are younger than he is. Their tour is run by an internationally known organisation specialising in travel for older people: the qualifying age is fifty-five. That is younger than Philip, and certainly much younger than Mrs Honey for whom he has just bought a third ouzo. (He ordered this powerful drink for her against his better judgement but did not feel able to tell this poised and statuesque lady that after three ouzos she may find it hard to walk steadily.)

And the two Misses Farrell are older still. Philip reckons they must be in their eighties, perhaps, even, their nineties. They are seated at the far end of the bar and something about them, a dignified remoteness as well as the smallness of the table they have deliberately chosen, discourages anyone from joining them, or even addressing them directly. Amy did wish them a good evening when she first entered the bar, but although they had both smiled politely, dipping their heads at her like two tall, graceful birds, they had not replied. They are not talking to each other either. They are drinking Greek brandy, Metaxa, a large balloon glass apiece, and one of them (Amy is not certain if it is Edie or Jane, they look so alike to her) is smoking a cigarette in a long, jewelled holder.

Amy says, answering Philip, 'It is a bit of a *memento mori*, isn't it? Suddenly finding oneself in an old people's home.' Imagining what it could be like, mind going, body failing, imprisoned in a stiff, uncomfortable chair, incontinent, dribbling, she laughs nervously.

She is sitting on a bench against the wall. Tom and his father are on spindly chairs opposite and Portia (who is the only other person in the bar who is smoking) is sitting beside her. This is not Amy's doing, nor Tom's. Vic had been buying a drink for Portia when they entered the bar. Convivial, gregarious Vic Jones, a glass in each hand, beaming his pleasure at his son, at his daughter-in-law. 'I've been telling this young lady we've a bone to pick with her, scaring the lights out of us back there on the mountain!'

And he had taken Amy's elbow and led her to the bench. 'Portia, my pet. Meet my son's wife. The beautiful Amy. I believe you already know my son. Tom Jones. The MP.'

Behind her dark glasses, Portia has unfocused her eyes, the old childhood trick to conquer embarrassment. 'I think I do. I *thought* I did, earlier, but I couldn't be sure. I haven't been around the House all that much lately.' She holds out her hand. 'I'm delighted to meet you, Tom Jones. Mrs Jones. Amy. You really were the people in that little blue car? I'm so terribly, terribly sorry. If it's any consolation, I was absolutely scared witless. I've never been on one of those horrid contraptions before.'

'Then you need this drink, pet,' Vic says. 'Amy? Tom?'

'I'll get them, Dad.' Tom raises an eyebrow at Amy. 'Orange juice, right?'

'I'll have some wine later,' Amy says, speaking in a humble, placatory voice; apologising, Portia assumes, for refusing alcohol before dinner. Though why should she apologise? For God's sake! *Stand up for yourself, Horsey girl*, Portia urges her, silently.

Portia smiles at Amy. Close to, Horse-Face is prettier than she had expected. She is also, satisfactorily, somewhat older. That fine skin wrinkles early. And why is she wearing that frilly white blouse, that flowered dirndl? As if she were an Alpine peasant woman dressed for folk dancing!

Amy smiles back. She wonders why Portia is wearing sunglasses in this dark bar.

Tom has escaped temporarily. On his way to the counter he has stopped by the table where Beryl and her husband are sitting; she with a gin, he with a whisky. This is the first time Tom has initiated a conversation with the Boots but

97

his immediate circumstances call for desperate measures. He thinks bitterly: it is all right for Amy. She doesn't know. It is all right for Portia. She doesn't care. He is trapped. If it had just been Portia and Amy, he might have worked something out. But Vic, that courting bird, is preening himself like a peacock.

Beryl says, 'It's wonderful what old people can do nowadays. I was saying to Daddy, it's a pity Mother never had a chance to travel with a nice group like that. I don't think she's ever been further than Southend in her life, has she Daddy? Born too soon, I suppose. It makes you think, doesn't it? I mean, how much things can change in such a short time.'

'It would never have done for her, not with her bladder,' Daddy Boot says, hooking out a third chair with his foot and motioning Tom to sit down. He clicks his fingers at the waiter, who ignores him, which is normal behaviour in a waiter employed by the Hotel Parthenon. Tom shakes his head and grimaces ruefully in the direction of Portia and Amy and Vic Jones.

'That's not true, Daddy,' Beryl says. 'I looked at the coach this evening when I came back through the tunnel and it's got all the facilities, two of them, actually, of course I didn't look *in*, but as far as I could tell from the outside they seemed nice and roomy.'

'I doubt if they'd be roomy enough for Mother.' Daddy Boot nods at Tom, managing to convey regret that Tom cannot sit down and have a drink with him and, at the same time, the hope that there will be an opportunity later. Without their womenfolk, preferably. Then his chilly blue eyes twinkle at Beryl indulgently. 'Mother has always been comfortable,' he reminds her.

Reluctantly, Tom moves to the bar, orders an orange juice and a minute cup of muddy Greek coffee. He would prefer ouzo or whisky but he needs to keep his wits about him. Obviously, they will be a foursome at dinner; the best he can hope for is that Vic will want to detach Portia afterwards, take her off to the town for a drink or an ice-cream. Though that kind of tête-à-tête has its dangers, God knows what mischief Portia could get up to with his randy old father, he hasn't the stamina to stand guard all evening. On the other hand he doesn't care to plead illness. Not his illness, anyway; piles, anal leakage. Perhaps he can persuade Amy to say she is tired.

He wishes he were back in the cosy womb of the Commons. Having a drink in the Strangers' Bar, or in the Marquess of Granby. His bloody doctor advised him to take a relaxed holiday, away from the pressures of politics, get some of the stress out of his system! What could be more stressful than this? Perhaps he will drop dead of a heart attack. That would teach Amy! She ought to know better, for God's sake. She's often told him how regular criminals, bold as brass when it is a matter of their own wicked deeds, will break down in court over a domestic disturbance. Accusations of malicious wounding, grievous bodily harm, are received stony-faced. The wife having it off with a neighbour will reduce the same thug to a helpless torrent of tears.

Although this is not his situation, precisely, Tom can relate to it. Formulating this thought makes him chuckle inwardly. It is a light-hearted silliness Portia would appreciate were he to share it with her.

He returns to the table in more confident spirits to hear Portia saying to Vic, 'I would never have thought you were

99

old enough to have a son of Tom's age, you must have been married out of the cradle.'

Portia had not meant Tom to hear that remark. She hadn't seen him approach them; she had been too occupied watching, and listening to, Vic. And it isn't true that Vic *looks* all that young, she thinks now, in fact the skin of his face has the weatherbeaten, well-worn look of a man who has spent years of his life in hard, manual labour. It is not even his obvious physical fitness. There is a calm brightness about him; a sense that he enjoys himself, is content with his life, that is relaxing and energising at the same time, and makes him seem youthful.

Portia likes older men, anyway. She had been happier with Bumpy than at any time in her life. Happier with Bumpy than with Dave, than with Tom, than with a fair number of lovers – Portia doesn't keep score. Is it because her father was away at sea all her young life? That's what a shrink would say, isn't it? Psychobabble in Portia's opinion.

On the other hand, her only legal partner, her only *husband*, was ten years older. But that didn't last, did it? Portia looks at her marriage as a waste of her twenties. Not that she often thinks about it. Nor talks about it to anyone.

She says, 'I didn't mean you look old for *your* age, Tom Jones. Just that your father looks young for his!'

She hopes that calling him Tom Jones, *in full*, will help to establish a suitable distance between them. This is for Tom's sake. Portia is not above enjoying Tom's discomfiture but only up to a point; she doesn't want to see him too miserable. She is not at all miserable, or even uncomfortable, herself.

Tom says, 'Thank you very much, Portia. Nice of you to

100

say it, anyway. And it's true, my father was married young – nineteen, weren't you, Dad?'

Vic Jones looks at his son with a slight tightening around the jaw line. But he says, evenly enough, 'Just off to Kenya on my National Service. Your mother and I thought we'd tie the knot. I don't know why she took the risk. I know I just wanted to make sure no one else nabbed my girl while I was away.'

Portia and Amy interpret this in different ways.

Portia thinks, *what* a nice man! Decent of him to have married the girl! Most boys of nineteen would be glad to be shut of it. Off and away, safe in Africa, who would blame him? And decent, now, to insist that he was the lucky one. Ten out of ten on both counts. Mean of Tom to have brought it up. Upsetting his dad. *Definitely* out of order there. Vanity? Or what?

Amy is incredulous. Tom has never even hinted at this before. Well, at least it explains why Vic married Tom's mother. Who would have thought it of that pursed-up old female! Though she wouldn't have been old then, of course, no older than Vic. And *that* really is hard to credit. Her being young!

Amy says, 'Tom, if you don't mind, I think I will have a proper drink now. Something like Cinzano, with lots of ice and lemon. I'll get it myself, if you like.'

'Your wish is my command, darling,' Tom cries, sounding eerily like his father and leaping up with alacrity. 'Anyone else for a refill? Dad? Portia?'

He could certainly do with something stronger than coffee himself. The evening that stretches before him is a foggy, uncharted minefield and he feels in the need of Dutch courage if he is to plod bravely on.

101

Portia shakes her head, smiling brilliantly at him. Vic says, 'I'll take a raincheck for the moment. I want to pick this young lady's brains about what goes on in the Mother of Parliaments. All the behind-the-scenes gossip you don't tell me, Tom.'

Tom would have been appalled if had known the conclusion Portia and Amy had drawn from one innocent, idle remark. It has never once crossed his mind that his mother might have been pregnant when she married his father. That she had married so young was merely another detail in the holy frieze of her martyrdom. She had been trapped before she had the chance to go to college, do an interesting job, see the world.

These were all things she would definitely have done if she had not married Vic. As she used to tell Tom at least once a week.

'Don't tie yourself down too young. At least wait till you see what's round the next corner.' Or, 'You've only one life, don't do what I did, give it up before you've got started.'

These injunctions, and others like them, were always accompanied by small, groaning sighs, and the continual anxious movement of her fingers, pleating the apron she almost always wore, even when she was no longer cooking, or washing the dishes, or scrubbing the floor: it was a badge of servitude that she wore like a reproach. When he was a little boy, Tom had adored his mother. As he grew older, he loved her less but remained doggedly loyal to her. He could see how her joylessness crushed his father, but it was his mother he felt sorry for when Vic blundered out of the house to go to the pub alone, not for the beer, he rarely drank more than a couple of half-pints, but for friendship and laughter.

'He doesn't think, does he, that I haven't been out of the house all this live-long day,' his mother would sigh. Wry acceptance was the line she took, a little pout of humorous resignation, but if Tom were to suggest, however mildly, that his father would have been glad of her company, she would turn on him savagely.

'So you think I'm a bad wife to your *precious father*? Not a word of thanks for my trying to be a *good mother* to my only son! I happen to think the place of a mother is at home with her child, not roaming the streets like a drunken slut. But, oh no, you think I should go drinking my eyes out night after night because *he* wants me to! In my opinion, decent women don't spend their evenings in pubs. Just because *your father* likes the kind of women who do, is that any reason why I should lower myself to their level?'

And so on. It terrified Tom. And humiliated him. She forced him to choose between her and his father and he wasn't strong enough to stand firm against her. He was forced to appease her because *he* was afraid of her terrible, volcanic anger. It was frightening to him because so irrational. She was not a stupid woman. She had intellectual aspirations. She introduced him to politics by way of political philosophy; she read passages from Hobbes and John Locke aloud to him. To begin with, Tom had shared her belief that she was more intelligent than Vic and grieved with her over the waste of her talents. Later he admitted (only to himself, and unwillingly) that her cleverness was a useless trick, like a dog dancing, and that Vic, uneducated and unpretentious, had the sharper mind.

It made him even more protective of his mother. It seemed to him that all she was left with was her ambition for him. To make up for the saintly endurance of her unfulfilled life, he had to pass examinations, work hard, get into the civil service, get into Parliament. And up to a point he had pleased her, though it was always the *next step* she was rooting for. When he had failed to be elected to the Shadow Cabinet for the second time last year, his first thought was that he was glad she was dead and could not be disappointed. The second, that at least he would not have to defend her to Amy.

Tom wishes that Amy had been able to recognise what was good in his mother. At least she could have understood that for a working-class girl, a miner's daughter, getting married so young had meant giving up her own future; sacrificing herself for her husband and son. She had not just cooked and cleaned, either. She had kept Vic's books, sent out the bills, filled in his tax forms, his quarterly VAT return. Tedious work. She didn't do it uncomplainingly, but she did it, often sitting at the kitchen table until the cold morning hours, frowning, pale with exhaustion, whispering numbers. 'No good leaving it to your father, he has no head for figures.'

When he told this sad tale to Amy she merely said that Vic had always seemed perfectly numerate to her. Tom read this remark as a polite way of saying that his mother enjoyed making rods for her back, which he knew to be true.

Tom cannot really fault Amy. She had always been meticulously pleasant to his mother. She had never once abused her to him, but that is not Amy's way: she shows her disapproval by withdrawal and silence. An annoying habit,

104

Tom thinks now. What is wrong with a bit of hypocrisy? It would not have hurt Amy, since she affected to be too well-bred to speak out against his mother, to say something affectionate about her, or at least to agree with him and admit she'd had a hard life.

Thinking along these lines, Tom grows indignant. This is only partly because of his silent arraignment of Amy. It is also because he is having to wait for her Cinzano and his whisky. Some of the old folk have shuffled in from the dining room and occupied all the vacant tables and the space around the bar, making between them a lot of noise; scraping chairs, shouting merrily into each other's deaf-aids, and thumping on the bar.

Philip, also waiting for attention, raises an eyebrow at Tom.

Tom shakes his head and sighs.

Philip says, 'I think, retreat.'

Tom says, 'In this case, I agree, the better part of valour.'

Although this is the first time they have actually spoken, they have already defined each other's origin and status more or less accurately. Tom has pigeon-holed Philip as an aristocratic, or at least wealthy, east coast American; Philadelphia or Baltimore. And Philip, registering Tom to begin with as a tired-looking man with a nice wife, has heard Vic introduce him to Portia this evening and so knows his occupation and his name.

Philip says, 'Philip Mann,' and holds out his hand.

'Tom Jones,' Tom says, heartily.

Philip says, 'Glad to know you.'

Tom takes Philip's hand in both of his and grips it sincerely.

Connection thus established, they nod, and smile, and

make various other small facial gestures to express friendly intentions towards each other and amused dismay at the suddenly crowded bar; every seat taken and not even much standing room since several of the newcomers have crutches or zimmer frames which they deploy cunningly to give them extra floor space.

Philip is able to escape fairly quickly since Prudence and Mrs Honey, waiting for him by the entrance to the bar, are clearly poised for flight, but Tom has further to go to reach his party, who not only show no sign of moving but are clearly comfortably engrossed in their conversation and each other. Tom can hear Vic's loud and cheerful laugh as he edges through the press; he can see the two women leaning towards his father, smiling. Portia is talking, and waving her hands about, and tossing her head so that her long earrings jangle. *Affected bitch*, Tom thinks sourly.

Whatever she has said has made Vic laugh again, slapping his thigh in his pleasure. Tom arrives in time to hear him say, 'What I want to know is, why's it always the Tories who get caught out that way, never the Labour?'

And Portia says, smiling at Tom, 'Sexual misdemeanours, Tom, that's what your father wants to know about. I don't know the answer. Can you enlighten him?'

7

JUST AFTER ONE O'CLOCK IN THE morning the two Misses
Farrell return through the tunnel to the Hotel Parthenon. A
group of the newly arrived senior citizens, also on their
way back to the hotel but lingering in the warm night air at
the tunnel entrance like reluctant children at the end of a
party, stand aside to let them pass. This courtesy is only
barely acknowledged; no smiles, no meeting of eyes,
merely a slight inclination of two regal heads. They stride
on into the chill of the tunnel, tall as baseball players,
upright as grenadiers, a different *breed* of old person. The
group watching them falls briefly silent, seized by an un-
defined sense of unease.

The old ladies have been observed elsewhere in the town in
the course of the evening. Portia saw them as she strolled
with Vic Jones through the *plateia*, sitting at a round
marble-topped table with small cups of Greek coffee and

large glasses of brandy in front of them. She thought, affectionately, *funny old things*. And dismissed them.

Portia is feeling affectionate towards the whole world at the moment. A fortunate conjunction of people and events is conspiring to entertain and amuse her. She enjoyed her dinner, sitting next to Tom and opposite Vic and Amy, happily conscious that a few words from her would blow this civilised social occasion apart, scattering, spattering, blood, bones and sinew to the wind's four quarters. After they had finished the main course, boredom with her own good behaviour stirred her to devilment. She slipped off her right shoe, placed the ball of her foot gently against Tom's left leg, and wriggled her toes against his ankle bone.

Tom removed his foot, at once, but cautiously. He had continued with a supposedly funny story he was telling them about the Shadow Home Secretary, but ran into the sand before he got to the punch line. And Portia saw him redden.

After that, he didn't once look at her. He told no more stories. He refilled his own wine glass but nobody else's. When Vic suggested they all went for coffee and drinks in the town and Amy made fulsome excuses (she was tired, had got up early this morning, swum rather too long, would they all *please* go out and enjoy themselves and not worry about her, not for an *instant*), Portia knew Tom was bound to insist he must stay with poor, fragile Horsey. What a convenient cop-out for Tomkins! Catching his eye at last, Portia had allowed herself a sly grin, and was surprised that he didn't look sheepish.

Instead, he said, with an indignant and defiant air, 'Actually, I'm more than ready to lie down myself. If you want to know, Portia, I've just had my piles seen to, and that makes bed a more enticing prospect than going out on the razzle.'

He laughed, but his father had blushed. If Vic could have brought himself to speak about Tom's operation in front of a woman who was not a nurse or a doctor, he would have been much more delicate; mystifyingly so, Portia suspects. Although this thought amuses her, she finds Vic's old-fashioned gentlemanly approach to 'the ladies' original and sweet. She guesses he is rather in awe of her, which also pleases her; he is impressed by the fact that she writes for 'the papers', and that she is here to do a job, not just on holiday.

He says, 'I haven't really got used to it, myself. Travelling around and nothing to do. I tell myself it's education, catching up on what I might have done if I'd stayed on at school, gone to college. But it won't get me anywhere, too late for that. And there's so much. It's hard to know where to start.'

'Education doesn't have to get you anywhere,' Portia says. 'If you think about it, most of us only need a very little bit to get by.'

They are standing at the end of a long jetty with their backs to the lights of the harbour front and the town. The moon has not yet risen and the sky, though pricked out with stars, is black and unfathomable. There are occasional flashes of white light in the sea, but the mountains beyond it are dark. Portia can only just make out Vic's face; a gleam in his eyes, on his mouth.

She thinks, why not? He is funny, and cheerful, and nice. He makes her feel successful, desirable, witty and young. It is only for a week. And he is an excellent driver, as she has reason to know! She has already sent a fax to Dave. It would be one in the eye for Tom.

She says, 'No time like the present. Here you are in Greece, which is where it all started. Western civilisation, I mean. Not a bad place to begin.'

A little after midnight, Philip and Prudence and Mrs Honey (who had remained, to Philip's amazement, not only steadily upright but apparently perfectly sober after three large ouzos and the best part of a bottle of wine at dinner) found themselves at the same *zaharoplasteio* as the Misses Farrell.

Edie and Jane had appeared not to recognise their fellow hotel guests. They paid no attention to anyone. They sat, eating from tall glasses of ice-cream decorated with scarlet paper umbrellas, occasionally touching their lips with a wisp of a handkerchief. From time to time one bent towards the other, whispering behind a raised hand as if it were a fan. They were wearing light, floating garments that Mrs Honey has enviously identified as expensive, and packable.

If Mrs Honey had been on her own with Prudence she would have attempted to introduce herself to the Farrells if only to find out where they bought their clothes. Ridiculous, anyway, to sit at a café so near to people who are staying in the same hotel and not speak to them! But Philip has had some practice in controlling inquisitive elderly ladies, of whom there are a good many in his adoptive family. 'I think they like to be alone,' he said firmly.

A remark (or rebuke?) that is still echoing in Mrs Honey's head after the ladies have left the café, trailing past on the marble flags of the harbour front, their gossamer skirts flowing around them like water, looking neither to right, nor to left.

'It's all very well wanting to be alone,' Mrs Honey says. 'Though if that's really what they wanted, you'd think they wouldn't just come and sit plumb in the middle of a whole crowd of tourists. But they weren't so much ignoring us, as just not *seeing* us. As if they were used to paying no attention to underlings. D'you know what it put me in mind of?' She leans towards Philip and Prudence and says, in a low voice, charged with significance, '*Royalty*. That's what I think.'

'Oh, Granny!' Prudence says lovingly.

Philip says, 'Waiters. How about waiters? That's another group who are skilled at not noticing people. Years of practice in avoiding one's eye! There must be others, but it's waiters who spring to my mind at this minute.'

'It would have worn off, the age those girls are by now.'

Mrs Honey (who is wearing her evening shift, the pinchbeck and rhinestone brooch glittering splendidly on her right shoulder) is disposed to tease Philip, flirtatiously, but not to concede an argument. 'If they had ever been waitresses, it would have been – how long ago? – half a *century* surely! Do you remember those girls in Lyons Corner Houses? What were they called? Nippies? Oh, you won't know, you're too young, besides being American. But even if that had been their job, they would have lost the trick long ago. Royalty now, never lose it I'd stake my life, one of those women is at least a duchess.'

'Oh, Granny!' Prudence protests again, still loving, but with a helpless, shy glance at Philip.

But he is smiling. 'Polish princesses? Or Russian? Last seen at the Winter Palace? How about that?'

'Now you are laughing at me!'

Mrs Honey speaks with mock-severity. She is enjoying herself. She would have enjoyed herself if she had been alone with Prudence but she has always found that a handsome man adds spice to an evening; supplying the sexual fillip lacking when two women, however devoted, are dining alone. (Prudence's grandmother has nothing against lesbians, or, indeed, gay men; it is just that their activities and emotions are incomprehensible to her.) And because Prudence is here, as a chaperone, she can flutter her eyelids and generally behave like a cheerful old tart (which is how Mrs Honey likes to think of herself) without giving the impression that she is doing anything other than entering into the spirit of things. Certainly not chasing after someone younger than she is. Not that she considers herself all that much *older* than Philip.

Philip is also comfortable with the way things have turned out. Prudence is here with her grandmother. This is a relationship that puts her in another sphere, out of his reach, so he can enjoy looking at her without betraying Matilda. He knows this is not exactly logical, but it makes sense to him. In a convoluted way that has to do with Mrs Honey's greater age, her presence reminds him that although he is not yet old enough to be Prudence's grandfather, Prudence is young enough to be his daughter.

As for Prudence herself, she is wondering why people say two is company, three is a crowd. It is just the right number this evening. The two old people can talk to each other, leaving her free to think about Daniel. And it puts off

112

the moment when she will find herself telling her grand-mother what has happened between them. She doesn't know why this prospect dismays her, when confiding in Philip last night seemed so easy and natural. Unless she is afraid of the *relish* with which Mrs Honey always approaches affairs of the heart.

She allows herself to drift into an erotic dream. Daniel has decided to join her in Greece. A long-vanished uncle has died and left him some money. He has just appeared, oh, yes, *there*, at the harbour end of the jetty. Landed from a boat? He is still wearing his white hospital coat. He is walking towards her and smiling. Oh, Granny, look, there's my friend, Daniel . . .

Her body is suddenly soft and pounding with pleasure. Her cheeks flush, her lips glisten, her hand flutters to the pulse in her throat. Mrs Honey, observing her grand-daughter, diagnoses her condition correctly, but assumes that the cause is nearer at hand than a London hospital. Sex does wonders for the complexion, but she hopes history is not about to repeat itself. Oh, of course not! Prudence has only been here twenty-four hours. Even if love develops fast in this climate, she is not a silly, pliable fool like her mother.

Philip, watching Prudence, thinks how exceptionally lovely she is looking this evening. Although he had thought her pretty last night, a day in the sun has given her an additional glow. He has heard from his English friends how hard young hospital doctors are forced to work in the National Health Service, but it is wonderful how quickly the young recover. Twenty-four hours has turned Prudence from a pretty child into a beauty. Almost voluptuous. A voluptuary. Though perhaps that is not a word a man should use of a girl he is training himself to regard as his daughter.

This pedantry makes Philip laugh at himself. Prudence looks at him sleepily. 'My grandmother's hobby is the royal family,' she tells him. 'Her hobby-horse. Any royal family.' She yawns and stretches herself as if she has just got out of bed. She says, 'Maybe it's height with those women. You're a girl, and you grow up like that, you either crouch down and hunch up or you make a big thing of it, lift your head, stand up straight, and that makes you haughty. I think they are probably nobody important. Just born to be tall.'

Tom has spent the evening in the foyer bar. He left Amy sleeping. She had gone to bed as soon as they went to their room after dinner and fallen into a heavy sleep almost at once as if drunk, or drugged. She had looked suddenly and uncharacteristically pale, puffy under the eyes, and Tom felt guilty and threatened. Amy was never ill; was she punishing him for landing her in this stupid mess? Though why should she punish him if she wasn't aware there was anything wrong? Was she *unaware*? Consciously, yes, he would swear it. But knowledge can flicker elusively on the edge of the mind without being admitted. Did he *want* her to know?

Well, he did and he didn't. If his father had not turned up it would have been a damn sight more simple. Either he would have made a clean breast of it and prayed that Amy would see the funny side, or he would have kept his mouth shut and relied on Portia behaving herself. Since it was rapidly becoming clear that was a faint hope, the first course would have been the sensible option.

But one that was blocked off now Vic was here, requiring

constant attendance, meals, entertainment, leaving them without a splinter of time to themselves. There would have been time this evening, of course, if Amy hadn't suddenly decided to take to her bed! That was perverse of her, surely! Maybe she was tired, but it was of her own making: no realistically well-adjusted person gets up at the crack of dawn on the first day of a holiday just to go swimming!

Vic hadn't said how long he was staying. In the ordinary way, Tom would have expected no more than a day or so; Vic liked to come and go, was enjoying his freedom. A pity he had snapped up Portia before she'd had a chance to pair off with someone more suitable. That pleasant-seeming American, for example. More sophisticated than Vic, more literate. Though those characteristics were not, perhaps, what Portia was after. And Tom cannot deny (though he would like to deny it) that his father is attractive to women.

The foyer bar is dark and unfrequented. There is no barman on duty; when Tom wants a drink he summons the receptionist. He has had quite a few drinks by the time Vic and Portia appear in the marble wastes of the entrance hall and calls out to them with a belligerent bonhomie that seems to alarm them; they peer with a look of guilty surprise into the dark of the bar. 'Startled rabbits!' Tom booms. 'Caught in the act of nibbling the lettuces by the man with the gun.'

'Oh, it's you, Tommy lad,' Vic says. 'Couldn't see to begin with. You sitting in the dark.'

'Thought you were going to bed,' Portia says. 'Nice early night, you said.'

She sounds carefully distant; a friendly new acquaintance, not an old lover.

115

'Couldn't sleep. Amy went right off straight away but I wasn't tired suddenly. Felt like a bit of company but everyone's flown the coop, seemingly. Not a soul anywhere bar a few oldies snoozing in front of the telly and they hardly count. What'll you have? Portia? Dad?'

Tom makes to get off the stool but it rocks precariously. He steadies himself, clinging to the edge of the bar. He says, 'Not much service in this place, dire shortage of uniformed minions. A man could die of thirst.'

'I'll have a lemon Fanta,' Portia says.

Vic is frowning. Tom takes the frown to mean that his father is not exactly delighted to find his plans for the rest of the evening frustrated by his tipsy son. But it seems Vic is merely searching for a polite way to explain a necessary disappearance. He spreads his hands out palm upwards, as if inviting inspection. 'I think I could do with a wash and brush-up. Won't be a tick.'

Portia watches him go. She says, 'I like your father.'

'Most people do.'

Portia smiles at Tom sweetly. 'You mean I am just like everyone else? How disappointing.'

'Oh, shut up.'

'Drunken pig,' Portia says calmly. She perches on the stool next to Tom. 'Your father has kindly agreed to drive me round the Peloponnese. I hope you have no objection. The paper will pay for the car hire, the petrol and the expenses. So your father won't be out of pocket. Okay?'

'No. Not at all OK.' Tom's voice breaks with horror. 'You can't do that, Portia. You can't *kidnap* him. What the hell! He doesn't know anything!'

'Tell him, then. *I* don't mind, why should I? Only I

116

thought you might prefer discreet silence. A little secret between you and me. Or have you told wifey?'

Tom says nothing. His face appears to swell and ripen.

Portia says, steadily, 'To be truthful, I would prefer not to tell your father that you and I were once rather more closely connected than we are now. I don't see why he should be made uncomfortable. And he might feel it improper to go travelling around Greece with his son's relict. But I can drive myself if I have to. So if you want a public announcement, say when. Tonight, or tomorrow?'

Tom hisses, 'If you should *dare*!'

'Don't you threaten me.' Portia fixes Tom with a bright, taunting gaze, then relents. 'Look. You can't harm me. I don't especially want to harm you, but I don't care all that much if I do. OK, sweetie?'

Portia laughs. She says, in a different tone, suddenly and chattily sociable, as if Tom were a distant acquaintance she had met by chance at a professional party and felt it her duty to talk to, 'Did I tell you I'd been asked to write Bumpy's biography? I haven't made up my mind yet, yes or no. It's a tremendous *sweat* in prospect, though it could be fun, too. Don't you think? Bumpy left diaries behind which could help with a bit of the leg work. You are mentioned, as a matter of fact.'

She looks at Tom, her slanting, topaz eyes glinting, her mouth curving in what he used to call her Mona Lisa smile; little cat, been at the cream. He can feel his pulse thudding. He says, watching her warily, 'I hadn't seen all that much of him recently. We did work together on the Disability Bill, but that was some years ago.'

She nods with a purposeful air. Then glancing beyond Tom's right shoulder, twisting round on her stool, beaming

117

at Vic, 'I've been telling your son that you're going to give me a new *angle* on all those old ruins. A modern builder's view.'

And, to Tom's disgust, Vic smooths back his hair that he has just slicked down with water, and gazes at Portia with fatuous devotion.

Portia says, 'I think I'll give the Fanta a miss, Tom. If you don't mind. Thank you for a lovely evening, Vic. We'll settle down to look at the maps tomorrow and make proper plans.' And, with a winsome smile, and in a tone that Tom finds insufferably arch, 'If you don't change your mind, that is. I would hate to think I had hijacked you.'

'I wouldn't mind if you did,' Vic says. 'You can take me hostage any time you fancy.'

'Do you want a drink, Dad?' Tom says, hoping to restore his father to sanity.

But Vic shakes his head without even looking in his son's direction. 'I'll see this young lady safely to her couch, and then I think I'll follow her example.'

*

Tom glowers after them: Portia trotting like a smart little pony, Vic limiting his long stride to hers, bending his head towards her in a courtly fashion. Tom observes, resentfully, that his father's hair is still thick and dark, his waist slender. He regards his own image, reflected in the amber-coloured glass at the back of the bar, with grim dissatisfaction. A sedentary life, too many whiskies, too much cheese, a passion for chocolate. Well, from tomorrow, all this will change. Up early, a swim before breakfast, no lunch or, if forced into it, only a salad.

He feels better already. Getting off the stool, he sucks in his stomach and pats it appreciatively. He is in high good humour as he approaches the lifts. The two tall old ladies are already waiting, and as the lift door opens he makes an exaggerated theatrical bow, one leg forward, one arm across his chest, the other at full stretch. He staggers, laughing at himself, and Edie (or Jane) sweeps past him into the lift with a contemptuous glare. But Jane (or Edie) giggles; a light, girlish sound, fresh as spring.

8

I<small>T IS A CALM AND BEAUTIFUL</small> morning. The sea barely moves on the pebbles; Beryl, flat on her back on a rock, body lavishly creamed to receive the sun, listens to the whisper of the little waves, and sighs with contentment. She has decided she prefers basking by the sea to lying beside the hotel pool, even though her expensive bathing gear (purchased from a shop in Knightsbridge famous for supplying brassières to the Queen) is unlikely to attract informed tribute from the group of plump Greek matrons, all robed in shapeless black and chattering like starlings in the shallows.

There is no one else on the beach to admire Beryl's outfit. The Farrells were here when she first arrived but now, sitting up before she turns to lie on her stomach, she fails to see them and assumes they have gone back to breakfast in the hotel. That they might still be in the sea does not occur to Beryl, who is not a swimmer and does not intend to risk ruining her hair or damaging her designer swimming suit with salt water.

And she is preoccupied, anyway. She doesn't usually listen when Daddy is talking to the boys. She wasn't consciously listening last night, just lying in the bath, in her warm, scented bathroom, splashing the water over her plump, silky tummy and savouring the day she had spent looking at houses and exploring the town, *thinking herself* into living here. Around midday, she had descended a flight of pink and white marble stairs to a small square with a little white church and rested on a bench by an old Turkish fountain while an unseen pianist in one of the shuttered houses played such sweet rippling music that she had felt her heart swell with pleasure. Lying in the bath at the end of the day she had thought, *that was perfect!* The tumbledown dream house she had found last night was higher up the hill, the shops lower down, clustered around the main square and the harbour. This square, the pianist's square, another enchanted discovery, would be the perfect place to stop and rest her feet before the last lap, up the pink and white steps with her shopping.

It was only a dream, she had thought. She had been brought up in Essex, on the edge of Epping Forest, and had hoped to go back there one day. She hated the city, the broken pavements, the dog mess, the traffic, and Daddy had promised her that one day they would leave London and settle in a small country town with a market-place. Now it seemed he had changed his mind, although, as they drove to the airport, he had denied it. 'I said a small town, Mrs B. I didn't say *where*. I didn't say a small town in *England*.'

Still she hadn't believed him. She had gone along with

what she saw as a game: sending her to look for a suitable property was Daddy's way of keeping her busy and out of his thinning hair, while he read the newspapers, did the crosswords, shouted at the boys on the telephone. Beryl has never interfered in the business, nor asked questions about it, and she has never paid much attention to the way he shouted at his sons. When she married Daddy, she had taken on his daughters, his three motherless little girls, but the teenage boys, Alan and Eric, were already what Daddy called 'away' (at a school for young tearaways paid for by the social services) and once what Daddy called their 'education' was over, he threw out the tenants in the flat above his estate agency, and put his sons to live there.

To begin with, Beryl had gently protested. After she left secretarial school, she had gone to work for Daddy Boot in his office, drifting into the job rather as some twelve years later she drifted into marriage with her employer when his wife died. Beryl was intelligent and good-natured, but too idle and amiable to be resolute about anything. When she murmured to Daddy that the best place for boys of seventeen and eighteen might be at home with their father, she was easily persuaded when he explained that if they didn't live in the flat, he would have to spend a lot of money to make it legally habitable. The previous tenants had been kicking up trouble with the local housing department. Claiming that he needed the place for his family had been the easiest way to get rid of them. Otherwise he might have had to get rough. 'Put the boot boys in,' he had said, with only the ghost of a grin, so that Beryl was doubtful if a joke was intended.

She sometimes cooked for Alan and Eric, Saturday or Sunday, at lunchtime. She found them agreeably cheerful but uncouth, unlike the girls, who had been nicely behaved from the moment she met them. But their mother, who had died so sadly and suddenly, had been Daddy's second wife. His first wife, the boys' mother, had 'never been much good', according to Daddy; offering Beryl the bare bones of the story so reluctantly that she had the impression he would have told her nothing at all if he had not felt the need to explain why Alan and Eric were less well integrated into society than he might like them to be. When they were ten and eleven, their mother had disappeared after an evening's drinking at the local pub and been fished out of the river some weeks later with her throat cut. Three men had been taken in for questioning, one after the other, but they had all been released and no one had ever been charged with her murder.

Beryl finds the idea that she is even distantly involved with such a ferociously dramatic happening incredible as well as disturbing. She shrinks from violent events, strong emotions, all untidiness. She has been sorry for Alan and Eric, but they have had Daddy to help them, employ them, and find them a place to live. It is Beryl's opinion that he has been a wonderful father. If she has sometimes thought that now the boys are nearly forty it is time they stood a little more sturdily on their own feet, she has kept it to herself. And as it turns out (so Daddy has casually mentioned, perhaps sensing criticism in her silences) they have recently been more than earning their keep. One of the reasons the business has become so lucrative has been their initiative in what Daddy calls 'welfare housing'.

Beryl rarely reads newspapers. But she does watch television and sometimes she turns it on while the news is still running. This was how she caught a piece on the

South-East news about terrible conditions in a run-down London hotel, full of immigrants and other poor people. The owners of the hotel, clearly culpable, had not only been refusing to do the most basic repairs, get rid of the lice and the cockroaches, but had been meeting immigrants at Heathrow with claim forms for housing benefit which was then paid directly to them.

Beryl had said, 'Isn't that *illegal*, Daddy?' and Mr Boot had switched channels immediately. He had not answered Beryl (he often didn't answer her) but she had noticed a dark flush on his cheekbones, and wondered.

Now she was certain. What he had said (to Alan or Eric) last night on the telephone was, 'I am not coming back to carry the can, get that straight, will you?'

She doesn't know what this meant, not precisely. But it is clear to her that Daddy's apparently sudden decision to fly to Greece (he had given her just three days to get her wardrobe together) was more in the nature of a strategic retreat than a husbandly impulse to 'give Beryl a break'.

How long for? What about Mother?

She feels chilly suddenly. A unexpected cloud has invaded the sky and covered the sun. Looking out to sea, Beryl sees that more clouds are puffing up from the far side of the bay and reaches out for her beach wrap. A pity to lose the sun at this time of the morning. If you sunbathe later on in the day, you can die of skin cancer. Especially if you have Beryl's fair skin.

The Greek ladies have finished their morning swim. Well, not swim, exactly, Beryl thinks, more of a Women's Institute meeting. They are making much more noise now they have come out of the water; one or two are actually screaming . . .

Screaming and clutching each other. Pointing to the horizon. Beryl thinks, *dolphins*, and seizes her beach bag which holds her (newly acquired) distance glasses.

Descending the steps, towel over his arm, Tom hears the cries echoing round the steep red cliffs that surround the little bay. In a gloomy mood, he assumes this hideous cacophony is only what he has to expect if he really intends to pursue his resolve of the night before and join the growing band of sporting fanatics. At least the House gym is not as noisy as this. No keening foreigners, anyway!

A couple of old Greek women are running towards him and shouting, shrouded in what look like black sails, billowing around and behind them. And Beryl is almost upon him – that odd little Boot woman, is how Tom thinks of her. She is wearing a vivid, fluttery garment over a matching bathing suit. Extraordinary colours. Purple, orange and silver. At least he can understand what she is saying.

'Oh, please, I can't swim . . .'

One of the Greeks is thumping her breastbone, throwing her head back and wailing.

Tom says, 'What on earth . . .? Oh, my God . . .'

He can only just see them, they are so far from the shore. Two pale heads bobbing in the bright sea, out beyond the line of buoys that marks the limit of safety. One seems to be supporting the other. One white arm is waving, but wearily.

Tom says, 'Is there a boat? God, there must be.'

But there is no boat, no pedalo, only the empty sea and the drowning women. And, apparently, no one else physically capable.

Beryl says, 'Oh, I'm so sorry, I've never been out of my depth in my life.'

125

'*Christ.*' Tom flings down his towel. He is in a raging temper suddenly. He hops, kicking off his canvas shoes, tugging off his jeans. He yells at Beryl. 'Why the fucking hell can't you swim?'

And stumbles down the stony beach and into the sea.

For the first couple of minutes, the shock of the cold water numbs him. And the rage that fills him is an additional anaesthetic. Education is one of Tom's subjects. It appals him that a woman who must have been at school since the Butler Education Act has not been taught to swim. It's not as if Britain is a landlocked country in the middle of a bloody great continent! It is a bloody *island*, just like Greece, for God's sake, a country of mariners, merchant-men, surrounded by sea. Learning to swim is as much part of education as mathematics. You could say it was more necessary for survival than Pythagoras, or even the alpha-bet! And there are bloody swimming baths in every reasonably sized town in the length and breadth of the country. No excuse for any school, anywhere.

The sea is choppier than it seemed when he first hurled himself into it. And the pain has begun. Like a red-hot poker stabbing him through the anus. Who was that poor, bloody king who was murdered that way? Oh, for God's sake, please God, don't let the stitches burst, if there are stitches, why the hell didn't he pay more attention to what they said before he went home from the hospital! Amy probably knows, but Amy isn't here, is she?

He rears himself up in the sea, hoping against hope for a sign of help coming: a boat, a wind-surfer, another younger and fitter swimmer. The line of buoys is now within a possible distance, and the women are not so far beyond them.

126

If he can get them back to a buoy they can hang on till help comes. Surely the Boot will have the sense to get help? Some strong young man. Not a poor bloody middle-aged one, past his best, with a burning rod rammed inside him.

His eyes are smarting and his heart hammering. A heart attack any minute. Well, at least that would put an end to it all, not that he really wants to die but it seems a less disagreeable option than usual at this precise minute. He lifts himself as high as he can out of the water, waves his fist, and shouts. Or endeavours to shout. And she has heard him. Her blind white head, a maggot, a sea monster, is weaving about, searching the sea for him. Only one head? No, the second is resting against her friend's shoulder.

Tom feels sure he is finished. Thank God for this buoy. He is holding on now, taking a rest, pressing his legs together like a tail and letting it drift with the sea. Only a little way further, to reach them. He waves and one of the women waves back to him. And calls weakly and faintly, 'Oh, thank you, oh, I'm so sorry . . .'

He guesses she has been trying to swim to the buoy with her burden; her friend must have given up further out, cramp or exhaustion, round the headland, out of sight of the beach. Bloody idiots, *half-wits*, to have swum out so far in the first place. Old enough to know better! This nanny-ish phrase makes him snort laughter. He is almost there. But now he can't see her.

Panic. Pain and panic. She has slipped under the water; her ghost-pale face floating dreamily just under the surface. Her head bumps his shoulder and he clutches at her, one hand under her armpit, drawing her close to him. He took his Life Saving certificate when he was twelve years old in the public baths; it should be like bicycling, something

127

you never forget, but he cannot remember. He is swimming with his left arm, his right clasping her like a lover, fighting to get back to the buoy. She is trying to push him away, eyes and mouth full of sea and slime, spluttering. She gasps, '*Jane* . . .'

'OK, OK.' He wants to tell her he hadn't really forgotten the other one, or only for the tiniest fraction of time, and that once they have got to the buoy, he will go back and find her, but he hasn't the breath. And, luckily, she hasn't the strength to fight him. Her body trails, limp in the water, but she is only exhausted, not unconscious or helpless. When he fastens her hands on the fat and slippery buoy, she has enough sense, enough grit to hold on, twining her legs round the weedy rope, rising and falling with the buoy, with the rise and fall of the sea.

Tom hears himself saying, 'Hang on, old girl.' In a high, histrionic voice. Like an actor.

He dives. The agony is not as acute as he had been expecting. He opens his eyes under the water and sees small black fish darting in and out of what looks like a broken, half-buried amphora. He remembers. Amy has told him. There is an ancient, drowned city under this sea. Thousands of years ago it was land, streets and houses, people lived here. Is this what those silly women were looking for? A tourist attraction? He swims along the ruin of an old stone wall covered in barnacles and black, spiky sea urchins, twisting his head, searching, until he feels his lungs about to burst. He rises to the surface and bursts into sunlight.

He has swum, or been carried by the current, much further out than he had expected. The buoy, disappearing and reappearing in the heaving sea, now looks almost halfway

to land. The woman is clinging with one hand and waving – though it seems not to him. He thinks he can hear an
engine but when he turns, he sees nothing.

He takes a deep breath and dives again, swimming, as
well as he can judge, back towards the buoy, looking for
the other woman, for *her body*, he tells himself: it would be
a miracle, surely, to find her alive. Although he doesn't
know how much time has passed. Nor how long it takes a
person to drown. But he can't give up, anyway. Or be seen
to give up.

He comes to the surface, draws breath, dives again. His
eyes are stinging with the salt water. He can't *see* any more,
or not properly. There is something ahead, flexible limbs
waving gracefully, like the arms of an octopus. As he
reaches out they are drawn upwards and away from him;
long, white feet kick his hands away. He comes up under
the buoy, cracking his head against metal and opens his
mouth. As the fishermen pull him over the side of the boat,
he is choking on sea water and vomit.

Philip has breakfasted alone, in the town square. He had
fled from the hotel, from the old folk creeping into the
dining room with their paraphernalia of handbags, zimmer
frames, crutches; each clutching a jumbly collection of
cherished and particular remedies: ginseng, garlic, vita-
mins and fibrous concoctions to relieve constipation. Philip
has nothing against these good people; it is just that in his
present low mood he finds them a depressing reminder of
the future that is rushing towards him like an express train.
Besides, although Portia as well as Prudence had waved to
him from a table they were sharing, he wants to avoid
being drawn into what he fears is becoming almost a family

129

circle; relationships developing beyond the ordinary calls of propinquity and politeness. Last night, for example, although he had enjoyed himself, he had begun to feel uncomfortably *obliged* – as if Mrs Honey were his older sister and Prudence his niece, or his daughter. Prudence who is mourning her inconstant lover. Inconsolable Prudence, whom he would, perhaps, like to console . . .

He is sitting in the square over the remains of his breakfast, wishing he still smoked, feeling lonely.

Seeing Amy (to Philip, 'that British politician's nice wife') crossing the *plateia*, wearing a dazzlingly flowered cotton frock, sandals and sunglasses, he has an impulse to call out, offer her a cup of murky Greek coffee. But he restrains himself. She has such a purposeful air, as if engaged on a specific and urgent task. She would probably be annoyed if he accosted her. Why should he imagine otherwise? Though she wouldn't show it. She is a gracious and amiable woman.

There are three restaurants in the *plateia*, separated from each other by rows of plants in tubs. Amy has disappeared from view; to find out where she has gone he would have to stand and peer over the sprawling, green hedge. Which is out of the question, of course.

Philip sighs. He is not missing Matilda. He has given up trying to miss her, given up hoping to find her young, eager, long-ago self. She has left him for ever and all he feels now is a dull, aching emptiness. It was a mistake to come here. He is bored as well as lonely. The sensible course is to cut his losses. Clear off tomorrow, get the bus to Nemea, visit the tiresome old novelist in her mountainous eyrie, then straight back to Athens.

He feels better already. He manages to decipher the

almost indecipherable bill, puts the money under his coffee cup, tucks his wallet into the inside pocket of his linen jacket, and pats all his other pockets, generally assessing that he has everything with him, dark glasses, pens, diary, address book, a few jingling coins. No handkerchief.

There is a pharmacy in the *plateia*. He can buy a packet of tissues and, in case he decides to go swimming this afternoon, a tube of some kind of sun stuff. Not that he intends to lie in the sun.

Amy is already there, standing with her back to him, inspecting a wall of glass-fronted shelves. If he had not already greeted the pharmacist in the elaborate Greek fashion (good-mornings followed by an exchange of health bulletins) Philip might have slipped out of the shop before she caught sight of him. There is a certain delicacy to his mind about hailing women in drug stores, and when Amy blushes helplessly the moment she sees him, this gentlemanly instinct is vindicated.

She says, 'Oh. Hallo.' And, like a large, embarrassed child, puts her hand up to her cheek.

'Hi, there!' he answers. 'Pretty day!'

Nodding abstractedly, hoping to release her by suggesting that he is too busy at the moment for further pleasantries, he moves to the counter. But when he has bought the tissues, and (after some discussion) a tube of Clinique cream, and turns to leave the shop, she is still standing where he left her. Although no longer crimson, she has a square-jawed, nobly determined look. Philip thinks, like a martyr.

He says, 'Ah!' Uncertainly. Then, 'Can I help? He doesn't speak much English. The pharmacist.'

She draws a wavering breath and juts her chin. She says,

'I'm sorry. I mean, sorry to be so silly, make such a miss-ish fuss, when obviously you *can* help me. Speaking Greek, I mean. I want a pregnancy testing kit. I thought I might see one on the shelves but there doesn't seem to be . . . I don't know if . . . Of course, they may not have . . .'

A fresh wave of colour surges high in her face but her eyes remain steady.

Philip says, 'I'll ask.'

He doesn't know the exact term, but the gist is easy enough to convey. The purchase is completed and he is able to hand Amy a discreet package, neatly wrapped in grey paper and sealed with Sellotape.

She says, 'Thank you. How much do I . . .?'

Philip shakes his head, smiling.

Amy laughs, a little ruefully. 'Well. Thank you.' And, as they walk out of the pharmacy, 'There is just one thing. I haven't said anything to Tom. To my husband. That is, I mean, not yet.'

Philip wonders about that. Why ever not? But he is not really interested. What occupies him suddenly, bringing him in a fraction of a second to the verge of tears, is the memory of Matilda running down the steps from the doctor's office, looking for him, for the car, up and down the street, and then, seeing him, jumping up and down and waving like an excited little girl. Which baby had that been? Phyllis? Matthew? But as he puts this question to himself, as he reaches out for her, Matilda vanishes – *that* Matilda, anyway; his young Matilda, untroubled, unafraid. The loss clutches at him, claws him, twisting his guts.

'You OK?'

Amy is looking at him anxiously.

'Sorry?'

'No, it's all right. I just thought . . .'

Philip blinks at her, waiting for her to continue, wondering how to explain his sudden distraction, afraid it must have appeared as illness, or rudeness.

But she is looking beyond him. There seems to be some excitement going on in the pharmacy; men shouting in the dark of the shop. The pharmacist appears, looking wildly around the *plateia*. His eyes fall on Philip and he runs towards him, flapping his arms like a goose taking off, gabbling in loud, rapid Greek.

An angry language, it sounds to Amy. Like spattering gunfire. Philip translates as he hurries towards the harbour while she runs beside him; although Amy is tall she cannot keep up with his lanky, American stride. A couple of foreigners, English or American, have been fished out of the sea in the bay below the Parthenon, brought round the headland and landed here, on the quayside. The pharmacist will be coming to see if a doctor is needed; in the meantime perhaps Philip's Greek might be useful.

Amy is ashamed to find herself welcoming this timely diversion. Although no one could have been more tactful than Philip, she feels such a fool! She is also ashamed of the terrible embarrassment that still rages inside her. Should she have told him or shouldn't she? It is the sort of quandary that made childhood a misery. But she is *grown up*. In her *forties*! It would have been childish to pretend she merely wanted a toothbrush. Fussy and mimsy. And, in some way that she cannot identify, self-regarding.

She doesn't want Tom to know. Not until she is certain. If it is an early menopause she would prefer to keep it to herself until she is used to the humiliation. It is ridiculous to feel humiliated; she knows that. But she does, she does: it turns her into a middle-aged woman, even more spectacularly dried-up and gawky beside the young, luscious girl Tom had that affair with and probably still hankers after. Amy tries not to think about her, about *that woman*, and has largely succeeded, *put her away, out of mind*, as Tom had begged her to do. But there are times when she surfaces without warning from some dark, subterranean region, a menacing goddess, all the more threatening for being unknown, disembodied, a woman without a face or a name.

Philip is saying something, head turned towards her, waiting for her to answer him.

Amy says, 'Sorry?'

He shakes his head. Oh, it doesn't *matter*, don't bother to listen to *me*, is that what he's saying? Is he reproving her? Appalled, Amy lies. 'Sorry, I was thinking. Wondering, if they were picked up in the bay, could it be someone from the hotel?'

A pulse begins to thud in her throat. *Tom.* They had had an early breakfast on their balcony. She had said she was going shopping. He had said he was going down to the beach. She hadn't paid much attention.

'That is what I am afraid of,' Philip says grimly. 'As I was just trying to tell you . . .'

They have come to the harbour. The sun dances sharp points of light on the sea, the little, painted boats rock, the awnings crack above the café tables. A crowd has gathered round the landing stage at the jetty. Philip starts running. Amy tries to keep up with him, but her legs have gone rubbery; weakened beneath her. And she feels sick.

Everyone seems to be shouting. Amy remembers her

134

mother saying when they were here together, 'It seems to be the natural Greek response to any emergency, however minor.' She cannot remember when her mother said this, or why, but thinking of her mother steadies and comforts her. She catches Philip up as the crowd opens to admit him. She hears him say, 'How is she, Prudence?'

One of the Misses Farrell is half sitting, half lying on a couple of blue canvas chairs, covered from chin to foot with a rough-looking brown blanket. Except for her pallor, ivory-yellow, like a stick of forced celery, she looks well enough; alive, anyway. But she has a lost, bemused look. Amy assumes that Prudence, who is holding the old woman's wrist, must be a nurse or a doctor. She has that kind of competent and professional air. She says, turning to Philip, 'Exhaustion. And shock . . .'

'Frustration, too. And no bloody wonder.'

Hearing her husband's voice, snarling with fury, Amy pushes past Philip to find Tom seated at a table with a denim jacket round his shoulders and a large brandy in front of him. She rushes at him, whimpering, and he fields her neatly, restraining her with a kindly arm from hurling herself on his lap, while he continues to bellow at Philip. 'Thank God you're here. Do you have enough Greek to tell these bloody idiots there's another woman still in the sea? I knocked myself out when they hauled me into the boat, took a while to come round, when I did this poor soul was screaming herself hoarse to no purpose. *Christ*! I suppose they thought she was batty and past it.'

Voices begin rising; everyone starts yelling again. Tom grins at Amy. 'It's all right, darling, I'm all right, better than you by the looks of it . . .'

His voice seems to be vanishing down a tunnel. Amy's

head is booming like a gong, the ground is tilting. Tom is roaring again. Someone takes her by the elbows and helps her into a chair.

Prudence says, 'Put your head down, you'll be OK in a minute.'

Amy feels the girl's hand cool on the back of her neck, her voice saying, 'Someone should tell you, your husband is a hero.'

And Tom's embarrassed laughter. Slowly, the dizziness fades and passes. Amy sits upright. Prudence puts a glass of water in her hand.

Philip is saying, '. . . did understand. They are looking for her now. The coastguards have been called out. They have sent for a helicopter from Athens.'

He is bending over Tom, lowering his voice. 'They say the current is strong. They won't find her easily and they are unlikely to find her alive. The boat that picked you up thought it best to bring you straight here, to the town, in case you needed to be taken to hospital.'

'No thank you,' Tom says. He looks *well*, Amy thinks, surprised.

He takes a gulp of brandy. 'She called out for her sister. They both look alike to me but she called out for Jane. So she must be Edith. You've talked to them, Amy.'

He had spoken softly, for Amy's ear only, but the old lady has heard him. She turns her head, her eyes cold and bright.

'No, no, no,' she says. 'I am Jane Farrell. Edie is dead.'

9

'MY HUSBAND'S NAME WAS FARRELL,' THE old lady says. '*She* never married.'

Prudence is endeavouring to settle her comfortably on the Hotel Parthenon's rock-solid pillows. There is a delicate chiffony nightgown fanned out on the other bed. Prudence hesitates, but only briefly, before folding it into a soft pad to slip beneath the bony head. Although old women can be fussy about the proprieties, this one is too exhausted to be finicky about the use of a dead person's clothes. And it is her sister's nightgown, after all.

Though Edie may not be dead. She may have been picked up by another boat. The current may have carried her to shore further along the coast. So Prudence has been hoping to reassure her patient, anxious to calm her, persuade her to sleep. She is a strong old woman, strong lungs, strong heart; but she will recover faster if her mind is rested. Not that she appears in the least concerned about

137

Edie. She seems to have quite forgotten that she pronounced her dead earlier. Unless, with the eerie calm that sometimes descends on the very old, she has simply accepted the death, and moved on.

Her preoccupation at the moment is not her sister but her own identity. She reaches up a long, narrow hand to scrabble at the front of Prudence's shirt and jerk her closer. 'I am Jane. D'you hear me? *Jane*! Mrs Jane Farrell. I was the one who married and had the boy. All she ever had was her famous career, all that fuss. She was always jealous.'

Prudence removes the hard, clutching fingers and tries to still the agitated hands between her own. She says, in a soothing monotone, 'Mrs Farrell. Jane. Please don't upset yourself, it's bad for you. I know who you are, and I think you know who I am. I'm Prudence. I'm a doctor and I want you to rest, go to sleep if you can. Only, first, if you could tell me, is there someone at home I can get in touch with? Your son, perhaps?'

She wonders how old she is. Well into her eighties, certainly. Perhaps she should get a local doctor to look at her? Though the little town is unlikely to yield a skilled geriatrician.

'I don't know. Why don't you ask *her*. She looks after that sort of thing.' The old woman is twisting and turning her head on the pillow. She says, in a fretful, surprised voice, 'Where *has* she gone?'

Prudence wishes she were older. She says, 'They haven't found her yet, dear. But they haven't given up.' She hesitates. How confused is she? She says, nervously, gently, 'You were both in the sea. Do you remember?'

Jane smiles. She has a wide and beautiful smile. It

tightens the loose skin round her jaw and shows her high cheekbones.

She says, 'Full fathom five.'

And closes her eyes.

Vic and Portia are high above the town, leaning over the castle ramparts. They can see the *plateia*, the Byzantine tiles on the roof of the museum, the dome of the cinema that had once been a mosque. A fishing boat putters into the shelter of the jetty but it is only one of many small boats, so far below that they are just specks of colour on the shining sea. And, anyway, they are absorbed in each other.

Portia is saying, 'I got married when I was twenty. It seems so long ago now, as if it wasn't me, you know, but another person altogether. I suppose it would have been different if I had stayed married. I can't imagine what that would be like. And I'm not sure it would have suited me either. But then I am who I am, that is, someone it wouldn't suit to live with the same man for ever, just because the first man walked out on me.'

She laughs. 'You're the first person I've told that to for, oh, I don't know, must be *years*. I suppose it humiliated me. *He* hadn't wanted me, so other people would think I was worthless. I used to skirt round it. Just say, my marriage broke up, fixing whoever I was telling with a cold eye so they wouldn't dare ask any more. Then when I was about thirty, people stopped putting that sort of question. I suppose by that time you might be thought to be single by your own choice. A free woman.'

Vic says, 'He must have been a fool.' And then, 'I'm honoured you've told me.'

This is not a flirtatious response. He speaks confidently and gravely and puts his hand over hers and holds it; their clasped hands rest on the warm, crumbling stone. Portia's eyes dampen. She looks away and says, 'My husband wanted children. I didn't, particularly, though I was quite *willing*. But it seemed I was barren. He used to call me, *my barren wife*.' She blinks fiercely. 'I think he thought it was a joke. Then he went off with a more fecund lady. She had a baby. A little boy with cerebral palsy. I was sorry. I mean, I really *was* sorry. That was the last I heard of him. They went away. I wrote, but the letter came back. Address unknown.'

She turns into Vic's embrace and he rocks her gently, stroking her hair, saying nothing.

Towards midday, they return to the hotel. Amy and Philip are standing at the reception counter when they enter the foyer. As Amy advances towards them, Vic releases Portia's hand. He doesn't want to embarrass her by seeming proprietary.

He says, in his heartiest manner, 'Good morning, Amy my lovely. This young lady and I have spent the morning up at the castle. Marvellous place, built to last, and that's a professional opinion. Hope it didn't inconvenience you, but when I didn't see either of you at breakfast, I assumed you were both having a lie in.'

'It was my fault, really,' Portia says sweetly. 'I requisitioned the poor man, *captured* him, gave him no chance to say no.'

Amy reads their happy, unguarded faces, and sighs. She is conscious of a faint and undiagnosed surge of irritation. She says, abruptly, 'There's been an awful accident.'

140

For a second, Vic stares at her in disbelief. Then cries, 'Tom!' – in such agony, it stabs Amy's heart. Oh, why is she such a fool, so stupid, so clumsy? Why does she never *think* before she speaks!

'No, no,' she stumbles. 'Oh, Vic, I'm so sorry, Tom's absolutely OK. Quite, quite safe. Not only that, he's been tremendously brave, you'll be so proud. But he couldn't save them both, that's what I meant, one of them drowned . . .'

She feels she is drowning herself, bitter bile rising in her throat. She glances over her shoulder at Philip. But he cannot rescue her; he is busy talking to the hotel manager. She grimaces helplessly.

Portia looks from her white, distracted face, to Vic's shocked expression. 'I think what we all need, my dears, is a simply enormous *drink*. Then you can tell us from the beginning.'

Prudence and Beryl Boot are already on the terrace. Beryl has changed out of her beach clothes into a pink and orange skirt and matching blouse. She had meant to wear the halter top that also matched the skirt, but when Philip rang her room to say the police would like to speak to her, she decided a blouse would be more suitable. She had been a teeny bit disappointed that the nice young policeman (speaking only a little, halting English) had asked her so few questions, but at least he didn't shout at her for not being able to swim, as Mr Jones had done.

That had really upset her! Watching those poor women fighting for their lives in the sea had been bad enough without being shouted at! Indeed, as she has told Prudence, she is afraid she may be suffering from shock, just from being there on the beach and seeing this whole, traumatic thing happen. Luckily Prudence (who is a proper doctor, it seems, Dr Prudence Honey) has been a real help to her. As soon as she finished taking care of Mr Jones and Mrs Farrell, left the gentleman sleeping and her grandmother sitting with the old lady, she came looking for Beryl to see how she was feeling. They have had coffee and a nice chat together.

Prudence seems a kind girl, a kind and sympathetic doctor. In fact, Beryl has almost decided to ask her advice about one or two tiny health worries that have never seemed important enough to warrant bothering her real doctor, at home. She might even be doing Prudence a good turn! Young doctors have to earn their trade somehow and she would probably be grateful for some extra practice.

Not that Beryl expects something for nothing. Nor is there any harm in chalking up a bit of credit when you think you may want something later. She says, to Prudence, 'It's lucky for that poor soul you were here. They'd have had to get a foreign doctor otherwise. But if there's anything I can do, you only have to ask. At least, I can take my turn sitting with her if you think she can't be left alone. No need for you and your granny to do it all, you know! And Daddy won't mind. He's got his crosswords.'

Prudence smiles her thanks. 'I hope she'll be all right to take care of herself, but it's hard to tell yet. We'll have to wait until the shock wears off. Then we'll see.'

Beryl is alarmed suddenly. Daddy won't like the sound of that 'we'! He'll blow his top if she gets involved, allows herself to be made use of. She knows what he will say, and she says it. 'It's none of our business.'

Prudence looks at her doubtfully. Beryl gives one of her

142

nervous shrieks, and says, 'What I mean is, it's all very well to do what you can, and I'm always willing myself, even though my husband always says people don't like to be interfered with. But if you don't mind my saying so, those ladies never looked as if they'd exactly say thank you for anything.'

'There's only one of them now. She may feel differently.'

Prudence is barely listening to Beryl. She is watching the door to the terrace, watching for Philip. He has been such a rock: taking control from the moment he arrived at the harbour, seeing what needed to be done and doing it. How could she have managed without him? One moment she had been strolling along the quayside with her grandmother, dreamily idle, on holiday: the next she had been thrust into a leading role in what felt like a parodic edition of *Casualty*. Tom Jones and Jane Farrell both looking like death (though, mercifully, neither of them anywhere near it) and the Greeks, the waiters, the fishermen, shouting and carrying on and her grandmother prodding them in the ribs to get them to make room for Prudence. 'Let her through. Don't you understand? She is a doctor. A *doctor*.'

Then Philip had come and turned all this ludicrous chaos to order. No fuss, no bluster, just the entirely natural authority of a person born to take command in a crisis. The image of a mature, handsome officer, wearing an old-style military uniform, Napoleonic, perhaps, a tight scarlet jacket with gleaming buttons, flits briefly through her mind. How had she ever thought of him as an *old man* in that stupidly dismissive way? As if once a person had reached a proper maturity he was rightly doomed to the scrap heap! What was so wonderful about being young?

She says, 'I hope Philip can find out how we get hold of

her family. There may be something in their passports. A name and address in case of accidents. Though not everyone fills those bits in. And the hotel may not have them still. The police may have taken them. I don't know.'

She looks at Beryl helplessly. 'I mean, I don't know what happens when people die like this. Away from home. In a foreign country.'

Beryl realises for the first time how young Prudence is. It is only her being a doctor that makes her seem grown up. Beryl stretches out her little freckled hand to pat the girl's smooth, rounded arm. 'Now, dear, it isn't your worry. Just you tell yourself that. I'm sure that nice Mr Mann will look after everything. He seems to know what's what, even though he is an American, which may make a difference. If the poor soul is found, that is. I don't suppose the Americans have the same rules about sending bodies home as we do in England. They are such a hygienic nation, there are bound to be a lot of health regulations. I suppose, really, it would be more convenient if she's just lost at sea.'

'Same date of birth,' Amy tells Tom. 'June 1909. So they must be twin sisters. And *ancient*. But not the same names. One is Jane Farrell. The other is, that is, *was*, I suppose I should say, though it seems a bit unfair, a bit *final*, is Laetitia Palmer. I wonder why she called herself Edith Farrell? Laetitia Palmer? Doesn't that sound somehow familiar? Or is it just one of those good *sounding* names, the sort you feel you must have heard somewhere before. Like, oh, I don't know, Mary Witheroe. Artemis Follett.'

No answer. Amy does not really expect one, Tom rarely pays attention when she does what she thinks of as *drivelling on*. But he is not deliberately ignoring her this time.

Although he had wakened briefly when she first sat beside him, he had slipped back below the surface of sleep almost immediately. Now he turns his head, rasping his tongue over his lips and mutters something that sounds like 'Clack Teeth . . .'

'What is it, darling?' Amy leans over him, wondering if she dare dampen her handkerchief and moisten his dry mouth. He hates being fussed over physically, she knows it, but he looks particularly dear and defenceless to her at this moment, an exhausted hero, and she is feeling soft and maternal. The thought that she might be pregnant again is sweetly disturbing. Not that it is really *likely*, of course, not at her age, and it would in fact be most incon-venient: the two senior partners in her legal aid firm are single women in their fifties who might feel – whatever they *said* – that shelling out for maternity leave was not something they had bargained for when they asked her to join them. And she couldn't afford to dispense with it. Tom's salary as a back-bencher is inadequate to support them in the comfortable way they are used to, daily help in the house, Bill and Kate both at university, let alone a new baby . . .

On the other hand, just to think about a small living creature unfolding inside her, tiny hands, heavy tadpole head, produces a delicious rush of sexual warmth that is almost orgasmic. She gives a soft, involuntary moan that brings Tom fully awake.

He says, 'Hey, *hey* there! Oh, love, you're not crying? It's all right, I'm OK!'

He heaves himself up to a sitting position, red-faced, apologetically smiling, grabs her hands and kneads them affectionately against his sweaty chest. 'Sorry! Didn't mean to scare you. *Did* I scare you? God, I've been having a series of hideous dreams. On the carpet at school. Having my mouth washed out by my mother.'

Amy stares at him, speechless. He says, 'I know why, of course, I swore at that poor bloody woman, Bott, whatever her name is, I don't often, you know that, but I was feeling quite desperate. How is she? Not Violet Elizabeth, William Brown's bane. Jane, what's-her-name, Farrell?'

Mrs Honey, sitting beside Jane Farrell's bed, is occupying her mind arranging her own funeral. Her patient appears asleep, breathing lightly but steadily, and she has always found choosing the hymns and preparing the eulogy an excellent pastime for such idle moments. (Although she has no need to earn money, the late Mr Honey having been a thoughtful husband and a careful accountant, she had enjoyed her nursing career and still likes to keep her hand in occasionally, a week or two now and then, helping out families caring for an old or convalescent person at home, sitting with the chronic sick, watching over the dying. There are bound to be patches of boredom in this kind of work but Mrs Honey has never felt it proper to take a book along with her, or knitting, relying on plotting and planning of one kind or another to keep herself wakeful.)

She reaches the conclusion that a church service would be the most agreeably theatrical way to go: a choir, candles, robed priests, perhaps a whiff of incense, but as she has not been inside a church since her daughter's christening (a ritual insisted upon by her husband's Anglican family) Mrs Honey reluctantly abandons the idea of a properly religious venue.

It will have to be a crematorium. But that does not

preclude a few rollicking hymns of a kind she remembers from Morning Assembly at school. Carols were always her favourites, 'O come, all ye faithful,' 'Hark! the herald angels sing', 'The holly and the ivy', but they would hardly be suitable. 'Immortal, invisible, God only wise', is one hymn she must have. She feels that the lines 'All laud we would render; O help us to see. 'Tis only the splendour of light hideth Thee', are particularly appropriate for an agnostic, suggesting she would if she could, so to speak, showing willing. Then there is the lovely Bunyan song, 'Hobgoblin nor foul fiend, shall daunt his spirit. He knows he at the end, shall life inherit,' which she feels reflects and flatters her own dauntless spirit. And something from Shakespeare. If Prudence manages to produce a child before she is ready for her box (say in twelve years or so, which would give her a decent life span but still catch a great-grandson before his voice breaks) he might sing a solo. 'Fear no more the heat o' th' sun, Nor the furious winter's rages; Thou thy worldly task hast done, Home art gone and ta'en thy wages.'

In her head, Mrs Honey hears the pure voice rising to the carved wooden angels flying from the roof of the Norfolk church where her grandparents used to take her when she visited them in the summer – always warning her, before they put her back on the train, not to tell her parents she had attended a church service. Although they had taught her father in his boyhood to despise religion as the opium of the masses, a fairy tale to keep the poor docile, they didn't want him to know that as age wore them down they had yielded to the sentiment and the story.

Thinking of her good grandparents, those innocent erstwhile Marxists, Mrs Honey dabs the corners of her eyes with her finger and reminds herself that she has ruled out a church for her last rite of passage. Would the dirge sound as fine in a low-ceilinged crematorium chapel? She begins to sing it softly to herself, conducting with her right hand, seeing the sweet, bony face of her unborn descendant rising before her. (He looks like Prudence only a touch more ethereal.) '"Golden lads and girls all must, As chimney-sweepers, come to dust . . ."

"Fear no more the lightning flash; Nor th' all-dreaded thunder stone; Fear not slander, censure rash . . ."'

Unexpectedly, the old woman, lying flat on her back, beaky nose pointing at the ceiling, is singing too, and with a strength and volume that Mrs Honey cannot match. All the same she does her best with Arviragus's line, '"Thou hast finish'd joy and moan,"' and then continues to sing, along with Jane's fuller voice, the next couplet. '"All lovers young, all lovers must. Consign to thee and come to dust."'

The two women look at each other with satisfaction. 'What about the last verse?' Mrs Honey says, but Jane shakes her head and murmurs, so softly that Mrs Honey has to bend close to hear her, '"We have done . . . Come, lay him down."'

Then she lies still, her chest heaving, and Mrs Honey feels for her pulse.

'Steady,' she reassures herself. 'Steady as they come.'

And to comfort her patient, 'We mustn't overdo it now. Though I must admit, that was nice, you've still got a pretty voice. Did you train as a singer?'

Jane's pale eyelids flutter; she shakes her head. 'That was my sister. Gone now.'

Mrs Honey takes her hands, expecting tears; instead, to

her surprise, Jane gives a sudden, sharp, sly giggle. 'Oh,' she says, 'Poor Tish.'

Walking into the sunlight of the terrace Philip is surprised to see Prudence convulsed in some kind of seizure; laughing, coughing, scarlet-faced. Beryl Boot, beside her, is looking indulgent.

'She's upset about the poor old lady,' she confides in a loud whisper. 'Of course, it takes people differently.'

Prudence's voice is strangled. 'Beryl thinks, I mean, Beryl is worried, about what happens if . . .'

Beryl translates crisply, 'All I said was, it would be easier all round if the body didn't turn up. Flying a body back home is expensive and there would be a lot of paperwork.'

'True,' Philip says. 'You're right about that. Though I fear it's not something we can have any influence over.'

Prudence makes a small, desperate sound; a kind of choking howl. Philip takes a white handkerchief from his breast pocket and hands it to her. 'Sneeze,' he says. 'It frequently helps.' And while Prudence covers her scarlet, blushing face, he beams at Beryl. 'Hay fever,' he tells her. 'I get these attacks myself sometimes, and you are quite right, Mrs Boot, emotion does play a part in bringing them on.'

He longs to laugh himself. He is feeling oddly lighthearted, which is ridiculous – *no, appallingly crude*, in the circumstances. All the same he is not inclined to rebuke himself. He does not even feel mildly guilty. He says, 'I have some medication in my room that might help. Shall I fetch it, Prue? Or I can give you my key. The stuff's on the shelf in the bathroom and clearly marked.'

She shakes her head. Though her colour remains high, she is doing her best to breathe deeply and steadily. She says, 'No, it's all right, thanks all the same, I'm all right, I was upset suddenly, nothing Beryl said, just thinking of poor Mrs Farrell. And her sister. I wasn't sure if Jane realised that she must be dead.'

Philip smiles at Prudence. He is proud of her. He smiles at Beryl, too. He feels protective towards them both as, indeed, so he realises suddenly, he feels protective towards the whole of his group of chance travel acquaintances. His *parea*. There is really no equivalent word in English. And not only because he speaks Greek and so can interpret for them and to them, though that is part of it, gives him an obvious, serendipitous role. What seems to have lifted a cloud from his spirit is that he feels capable again. *Capable*. That is exactly the word to express the sense of power and renewal that fills him.

He says, 'I guess they'll find her. The manager tells me there have been drownings along this coast before, and the bodies have always been recovered. There will have to be a post-mortem and an inquest, of course, but I don't see any complication there. The hotel has her registered as a Miss Farrell, and the name in her passport is Palmer, but that shouldn't present any difficulty as long as her sister can identify her.'

'Why should she have done that?' Beryl says. 'Put the wrong name in her passport?'

'You can call yourself what you like,' Prudence answers her – rather sharply, it seems to Philip. 'As long as you are not trying to defraud someone. Miss, Mrs, Lady Muck, if you fancy a title . . .'

She catches Philip's surprised expression and adds, hastily, 'I suppose, two sisters travelling together, one married, one not, it would be a convenience to use the same name. Or maybe Jane made the bookings. Though she said, I remember now, it was Edie who did what she called *that sort of thing*. Martha to her Mary, was the implication, I thought . . .'

She frowns at whatever it is she is thinking, placing a forefinger on the cleft in her chin, just touching her sweetly curved lower lip, and Philip is enchanted. He thinks, *Greuze could have painted her*.

Her eyes widen. Philip sees them as if for the first time; grey, flecked with gold, like pebbles in a stream. She says, looking in his direction but not seeing him, she is so caught up with remembering, 'But then she said, that is *Jane* said, something about Edie having what she called "the famous career", *all that fuss*, she said, so I wonder . . . I mean, I wonder now if perhaps Edie was a writer, a poet or a well-known novelist, so that Palmer was her pen name. Her *nom de plume* . . .' She looks at Philip now, mischievously mocking herself for using this comic French term. 'Edith Palmer.'

'Laetitia,' Philip says. 'The name in the passport is Laetitia Palmer.'

'Tish,' Mrs Honey says behind him. 'That's what Jane called her . . . It's all right, Prue, no need to worry, she's sleeping beautifully or I wouldn't have left her . . . And she seems to be fine now, in her right mind, that is, not confused any longer . . . Oh, thank you Philip . . .'

She takes the chair Philip has placed for her next to her granddaughter and sits very upright, both hands fastened tightly on the polished brass clasp of the crocodile handbag she holds on her bony knees. She is tense and quivering and there is an excited flush on her cheekbones.

'And I *was* right, darling Prue! Or, at least, not so far

151

wrong! Do you remember, last night when I said she and her sister were behaving as if they were royalty? Well. Do you know who she is? The one that drowned? That was *Tish Palmer*.'

And looks from one uncomprehending face to another.

🌸 10 🌸

'I THOUGHT SHE WAS DEAD,' PORTIA says. Then, hastily, with a wry glance at Vic, 'I mean, dead long since.'

'At least you knew who she was!'

Mrs Honey's disappointment at the lack of a satisfying response is palpable. Only Amy, arriving on the terrace at the same time as Portia and Vic, has been properly impressed: disbelieving at first, and then awestruck.

'I think I did know her, Granny,' Prudence protests, automatically placating her grandmother. (This is a habit both she and her mother have recently fallen into without either of them complaining to each other, or even privately thinking, that as she grows older, Mrs Honey is becoming a spoilt, self-regarding old woman. They love her too much, perhaps.) 'I just didn't remember to start with. Though I don't think I've ever actually seen her.'

Mrs Honey raises her eyebrows at Amy. 'Can you credit it? Oh, I suppose Prue might not have heard of her at a pinch. At her age, and with all her studies. But Philip is old enough, I'd have thought, surely . . .'

Philip says, apologetically, picking up Prudence's tone, 'I hardly ever went to the movies when I was young. My foster parents are Quakers. They didn't forbid me to go to the cinema, I suppose I just fell into line. But I should have remembered her name. I believe we did a biography. But that was some years ago.'

'I'm astonished,' Amy says. 'Absolutely and totally amazed! I read that biography. It came out about four years ago and I gave it to my mother for Christmas. But I would have thought everyone knew her! That if you were a Tibetan monk you could hardly escape her! She was as famous as Garbo.'

'I wouldn't be too certain that my mother and father knew who Garbo was either.'

Amy sighs her disbelief and shakes her head at Philip playfully.

Prudence smiles at him, feeling tender. She loves the way his face remains still and grave when he says something like that, something just a little bit funny, meant for her ears alone. Only his eyes move, dancing and shining as they meet hers. He twitches a lower lid in the ghost of a wink and she feels a delicious commotion in her chest. Her heart turning over.

Beryl gives a sudden, startled shriek. 'Oh, I *am* silly. Mother doesn't sleep all that well, so she often watches old films on late-night television, even if they're in black and white. And usually tells me the story, beginning to end, the next day. *Of course*! Tish Palmer was English, that's what Mother liked most, she always said she was more of a lady, better class than someone like Joan Crawford. And there was something else, wasn't there? Some old story? I'm afraid I don't always listen to Mother quite as closely as I should, but there's always so much to look out for with an old person and she's naughty about taking her tablets sometimes. That's often taking up my mind when I ought to be listening.'

Mrs Honey can bear it no longer. She raises her voice. 'That *old story* was that she had a child, a boy, early on in the thirties, and the father was supposed to be the Prince of Wales.'

Amy groans. She is speechless. At the opposite end of the terrace, a splinter group from the old people's tour (the concentration of crutches and zimmer frames suggests the less mobile, left out of today's trip to Mycenae) turn as one, falling silent.

Mrs Honey places herself with her back to them and sinks her voice to an almost sepulchral level. 'They met at a dinner in Belgravia. Then later on, at a house party in Kent. Naturally, the whole thing was denied, hushed up in the usual way, first of all by the royal family who didn't want a commoner on the throne, let alone an actress. Though of course Elizabeth Bowes-Lyon was a commoner, strictly speaking. I wonder sometimes if they were sorry afterwards, seeing what happened with Mrs Simpson. At least Tish Palmer was English and a vicar's daughter. Then Metro Goldwyn Mayer stepped in. She was under contract to them and they liked their stars to be pure as the driven snow. So they called her back to Hollywood, threatened to sue any newspapers that repeated the libel and fed them the story that there was indeed a baby, but he had been born to Tish's sister who was decently married. Of course, no one believed it . . .'

155

Amy finds her voice. 'Oh,' she says. '*Really*. I'm sorry, Mrs Honey, but that is absolute rubbish. The baby was Jane's, and her husband was its father. The two girls were close. Of course they were, they were identical twins. And they had both met the Prince of Wales. Not because Tish was a film star but because they came from the kind of family who lived in country houses and gave weekend parties. Their father was a vicar in Bow, in the East End of London, because he believed that was where God wanted him to work, among the poor. But he was what used to be called well connected.'

Mrs Honey is breathing hard, snorting through her nose. 'Excuse *me*, I don't see what Tish Palmer's social standing has to do with it. You're not suggesting, are you, that because she was a *lady* she was unlikely to fall for an illegitimate baby?'

'Of course not.' Amy is as angry as Mrs Honey. 'It's just that to talk as if the only important thing about her was that stupid old scandal seems, oh, so vulgar, so shameful . . . Tish Palmer was a wonderful, wonderful actress, she gave pleasure to *millions*. And she's dead. She drowned here, this morning, in that calm and beautiful sea! Her death was the death of a *legend*. We should be mourning it, not raking up grubby bits of her past.'

'I am sure I am as sorry as you are that the lady is dead,' Mrs Honey says, with some dignity. 'I am sure she made some very nice pictures but of course I was too young to have seen them when they first appeared and after that they were only shown in what we used to call *flea pits*. I'm sorry if you think it was vulgar of me to bring up the fact that if things had gone differently, she might have been Queen of England but it doesn't seem to me to be quite without interest. I am as upset by her death as you are. I must remind you that I have been sitting with her poor sister.'

'Clash of Titans,' Vic whispers unexpectedly, mouth close to Portia's ear. Then speaking, as it were, for general release, 'In Wales, in the war, I used to go to the cinema with my grandad. He was one of her greatest fans. He'd go any distance to catch one of her early films and of course he pushed the boat out if there was a new one. The best seats, and we'd see it round twice. No one else in the family would go with him because he would jump up at the end and clap his hands and wave his arms about and shout Bravo.'

Amy smiles at him gratefully. 'My mother would have agreed with him. She belonged to a film club, this was before there was a video shop around every corner, and the club showed the films in the church hall and she used to take me for a treat. I think Mummy admired her particularly because she wasn't a threatening kind of woman. I mean, she was beautiful and a marvellous actress, but she was like someone quite ordinary, too. Someone we might have known. The girl round the corner. And she had that husky, cracked little voice, and that sweet, sudden giggle . . .'

Vic had done his best to comfort Horse-Face, Portia realises. Like the natural gent he was, he had responded to the tears welling up in her eyes. For herself, she wasn't sorry to have seen old Amy given her come-uppance. Not that she cares much for Mrs Honey whom she has typecast as an arrogant old bitch, used to having her way, and speaking her mind, and riding rough-shod over anyone who disagrees with her. Indeed, if Amy hadn't stood up to Mrs

Honey so surprisingly bravely, Portia might have felt obliged to do so herself.

Amy says, 'It was a kind of cockney, only not quite. It was imitation cockney, the sort of accent that a flapper from Mayfair in the twenties and thirties might have tried to put on. It was fashionable then, wasn't it?'

'Well, I can't say yes or no to that, Amy love,' Vic says. 'It was a bit before my time and I've never taken much notice of fashion. All I'd say is, that woman's voice was the kind to break a man's heart. Heartbreaking. Such a tall girl, and that little voice, with a catch in it, like she might cry any minute if you didn't look out for her. Powerful stuff.'

Mrs Honey says coldly, 'I can't see, *myself*, how putting on a common accent can make a person a good actress or even an attractive one, but I suppose since you're all agreed, I'll have to take your word for it. Now, if you don't mind, I think I'll go and have some lunch. It's been a long morning. Are you coming, Prudence?'

She sweeps out without waiting for an answer, an unbecoming flush staining her cheeks, but with her head held high.

Amy says, mortified, 'I'm sorry, Prue. I didn't mean to upset your grandmother. Only it did seem . . .'

'It's her recreational drug,' Prudence says. 'Some people read romances. Others watch television or go to football matches. With Granny, it's royalty. She didn't mean to suggest that Miss Palmer wasn't much good as an actress. It's just that the old gossip was more interesting to her. I'm sorry if she upset you.'

Amy shakes her head, smiling. Philip nods in the direction of the old people who are slowly clattering towards the dining room. 'I expect a good many of them will remember her. Although most of them are younger than she was.'

Prudence says, 'Eighty-seven.'

Vic says, solemnly, 'A good age.'

Prudence says, 'I meant, I was thinking, Mrs Farrell is eighty-seven, too. It must be unbelievable to her, losing her twin sister after all those years together. Like an amputation. I thought, when I was with her, that she understood what had happened. Granny thought she did, too, and she's probably a better judge than I am. But now I'm not sure.'

Philip puts his hand on her arm. To reassure her, to comfort himself? 'Perhaps she slips between knowing and not-knowing. I would guess it must seem like a dream.'

Portia says, 'I lost a good friend not so long ago. Sometimes I can't really believe that he's dead. It's as if he's playing a game with me, lurking just round the corner, or in the next room.'

Beryl says, 'Well, she's at peace now, poor lady. Though I expect all hell will break out for the rest of us once the newspapers find out about it. I'd better go and warn Daddy.'

She clops off, making a noise like a horse in her high platformed sandals. For a minute those left behind look at each other with a strange, awkward shyness as if they are suddenly fearful they may not have accorded this sad, sudden death its proper weight, its due gravity. Then Amy says, 'What did she mean, *warning Daddy*?'

She laughs. Philip understands this is not a real question, but one of those English jokes about class: she is laughing at Beryl because she calls her husband Daddy. Philip finds this habit quaint, but not comic.

159

Portia says, 'Presumably they've all had the obit filed and waiting for years. Is she still news, do you think? How many twenty- to thirty-year-olds will have heard of her? They're the readers my paper believes it is aiming at. God knows why, you'd think people that age might have better things to do with their time. And though the agencies will have the police report by now, it will only be that a British tourist has drowned, they won't know *who* it is, will they? I mean, they'll have the name, but would anyone immediately translate Laetitia as Tish? Unless . . .'

Portia has met her newspaper's Athens correspondent at a contributors' party in London, at the new British Library. A lovely man, dark eyed and soft skinned; she had meant to look him up anyway. It would make a good story.

But she wants nothing to do with it.

Amy says, suddenly, 'Her mother was Edith. Edith Palmer. I remember that from the book. There was a photograph of her with them, such a little woman standing between her twin daughters. They were wearing those straight shifts girls wore in the twenties, and looked tall as trees.' She sighs with satisfaction. 'I suppose that's why Tish called herself Edith.'

'Undoubtedly,' Portia says drily. Amy blushes and Portia relents. Poor Horsey has had a rough enough time from the Court Correspondent. 'Sorry,' Portia says. 'That was childish. I just couldn't resist it, do please forgive me.'

And is rewarded by a look of such glowing gratitude that she is shamed into wishing she had meant this formal apology.

To everyone's amazement Jane Farrell walks into the dining room that evening, tall and straight-backed in a grey silk

160

dress, her only concession to age and frailty a silver-capped ebony stick with which she thumps on the marble floor for attention as soon as she reaches her table.

Mrs Honey, Prudence and Amy all hurry towards her, but she waves them aside. 'Thank you, my dears, I am managing perfectly.' Her voice is gentle, but carrying; she breathes from her diaphragm, like a singer. 'My thanks to you all for your care and concern. Especially, of course, to Mr Jones for saving my life, and for trying so gallantly to save my poor sister's. I know she would wish me to apologise to you for disturbing the peace of your holidays. There should be no further disruption. I have spoken to my son who will arrive some time tomorrow, so you can all be assured that I am in no further need of practical help.'

And she smiles round the room with great sweetness before she sits down. And picks up the menu.

'Great performance!' Portia whispers to Vic, who frowns and shakes his head.

Portia shrugs. She has already decided to set off with Vic tomorrow (as long as he doesn't change his mind) but rather wishes that he shared her feeling that today's drama should not end so tamely. She objects to sitting in silence with her eyes on her plate as Vic seems to think she should do. As if normal life had come to a stop.

She keeps her voice low, all the same. 'I suppose I ought to have rung the paper. It's a bit of a scoop, isn't it? Heroic Attempt by British MP to Save Elderly Hollywood Queen. Dashing Rescue Of Drowned Film Star's Sister. But it's not as if I were on the staff. I don't owe them.'

'What do you want to do? Or do you want an excuse to do nothing? Like, you've made arrangements to go on this trip and you know I'd be disappointed if you had to cancel?'

Vic's eyes are watching her steadily, with amusement, and Portia is suddenly overwhelmed with relief. 'I'd like to clear out of here soon as possible. You knew that, didn't you?'

She thinks, *but not why*. She hopes not, anyway. She says, 'Of course, if you want to stay, or feel you ought to stay. To support Tom?'

Vic shakes his head. 'Tom doesn't need his dad to look out for him. Never did. Whatever he's done, he's done on his own. Of course, to begin with, it was his mother who made sure he stuck to his schooling. All I did was take him fishing sometimes. What do you want to drink, pet? Or shall we wait on Tom and Amy?'

They come in then as if on cue. Amy looks at Portia, raises her eyebrows, and smiles. As if they have become best friends suddenly, Portia thinks rather sourly. But instead of joining Vic and Portia, they go straight to Jane Farrell's table. Jane stretches out one hand to Tom, one hand to Amy: they each kiss her on both cheeks, then sit down with her.

Vic says, 'Well, that's right and proper.'

Whatever he means by this, the other members of the group appear to concur. Philip, sharing a table with Prudence and her grandmother, catches Portia's eye and smiles; the Boots, who have been looking stiff and embarrassed since Jane Farrell made her regal entrance and declaration, examine the menu, begin to talk to each other. Beryl laughs.

Vic beckons to the waiter and embarks on an optimistic discussion of the pretentiously lengthy wine list. Portia

162

decides to let him discover the actual limitations of the Hotel Parthenon's meagre cellar for himself. All at once, she finds herself terrified. What has she let herself in for? How much is it reasonable to suppose she would know about Tom? Can she survive several days alone with Vic without giving herself away? Why does she care, anyway? Oh, she knows why.

Vic is watching her. The waiter has gone. He says, 'What are you thinking?'

And she replies, flustered, 'That you must be very proud of your son.'

By the time they have finished dinner this evening she has heard enough about Tom from Tom's father to provide some insurance against slips of the tongue. (She practises saying to Tom, should Amy and/or Vic be present, 'I *think* that's what your father told me.')

She has also discovered how much, and how humbly, Vic loves his son.

'He was always a clever boy, of course, he got that from his mother, she was the one with the brains. He was a bit lazy, too, I dare say he got that from me! It was his mother who kept him at it, kept him all weekend if he hadn't finished his homework. I thought that was a bit hard sometimes, especially if I'd had the idea I might take him off fishing. That was about the only thing we did together, all there seemed to be time for. But she was right, I was just being selfish. The way you start a boy off with the habit of work is more important than fishing.

'Tom owes it all to his mother. She started him up in politics, too, she'd always been active, and she got Tom delivering leaflets for the Labour Party when he was barely tall enough to reach up to the doorbells. That was in Cwmgarw, before we moved up to London. When we left, early sixties that was, Tom would have been going on ten. It was a bit of luck that my cousin wanted to stay on in the house, we might have got rid of it otherwise. Tom's mother wanted to sell it, as a matter of fact, so that's one thing I did for him! When he was looking for the nomination, it was a help to have a house in the constituency. The one he'd been born in. And his mother's family still local, you see; both his aunties on the council and an uncle the chairman.'

Portia knows that house in Cwmgarw. A cousin from Tom's own generation lives there now, the daughter of one of the 'aunties', and Tom keeps a room for when he goes down for his weekend surgery and doesn't feel like catching the last train. Or, if he has driven down, is too tired to drive back. There had been a time, a few years ago, when Portia drove him occasionally. They would get off the motorway on the way back to London and find an hotel and Tom would ring Amy and promise to be home Sunday lunchtime.

She wonders if Vic has always called his dead wife 'Tom's mother'. There must have been a time, if only before Tom was born, when the woman had a name of her own. Portia could ask Vic; it is a quite natural question. But something inhibits her: an unusual delicacy on her part, or perhaps an unconscious wish to keep Vic's first wife's identity at arm's length from Vic. She thinks, *first wife*! A telling slip, surely.

Vic says, 'I've told you Tom's mother was a very bright lady? It lay a bit heavy on me that she felt her talents were wasted being a wife and a mother. I know Tom thought at one time that I'd hampered her. I can see there's some truth in it, but only with hindsight. Once I'd finished my

164

National Service, she had the boy to look after, and it seemed perfectly natural, my getting a job, her looking after the house and the baby. That's what all the young wives were doing with their men coming back from the Army.'

He says, 'Though if she hadn't been behind Tom all the way he might not have got into Parliament. And that was the proudest day in her life. Her own town, where she'd been born and reared, everyone knowing her, knowing their new MP was her son. I never saw her so happy. Nineteen eighty-three. A big year for Tom's mother.'

Portia waits for him to say that he only wishes Tom's mother could have lived to see Tom in government. At the very least, a cabinet minister in a big second-tier depart-ment like Education. It was Education he had hoped for this last time when he had failed to be voted on to the Shadow Cabinet.

Vic says, 'I'd never have said it to her, but I doubt he'll go all that much further in politics. He's a good lad but too decent. No killer instinct. I had a friend like that, a good boxer, but he could never bring himself to finish the other chap off. You like a man for that but you wonder if he's chosen the right profession.'

Portia nods her head gravely.

Vic says, 'I wonder if there will be anything in the news-papers? I really shouldn't think of it, with the poor lady drowned, but it might be the right kind of publicity for Tom. Ordinary people read that sort of thing and say to themselves, that man's got guts. If you were a senior politi-cian, up in the hierarchy, say, would it affect you? I ask because you might know, working in the House. You must meet all types, from the bosses to the rank and file.'

Portia says, 'I can't answer you, Vic darling, I simply don't know. If there was a general election next week, rescuing an old lady from drowning would be worth a few hundred votes. The whips would certainly notice. It's certainly better publicity than the sort of thing Members of Parliament generally go in for – selling arms to our enemies, secrets to chums on the Stock Exchange, patronage and pork-barrelling and cheating on their wives. Though not Labour MPs, as you rightly observed.'

She looks at Vic, very straight, and smiles.

🌸 11 🌸

A LETTER ARRIVES THE NEXT MORNING from Amy's mother, to
Tom.

My dear Tom,
Dick and I hope you are both having a wonderfully
recuperative holiday. I remember Nauplion and the
Hotel Parthenon as the most peaceful place on earth.
Day after gentle day with no worries except which
beach to swim from and where to eat in the evening.
I wonder if what they call the Night Flower is scent-
ing the air? Such an insignificant plant in the daylight,
but walking through those romantic old streets in the
evening with my darling Amy, I felt transported to a
richly perfumed Heaven.

My reason for writing this letter is this. Amy will
have told you about the financial arrangements I am
making to protect my sweet Dick and his children,

and why. So I won't go into that. I am, of course, leaving small legacies to Bill and Kate, and Amy will have my mother's jewellery, some of it quite valuable, not that the value will matter to Amy. And I know she doesn't often wear jewellery but you may be able to persuade her to wear some of the pieces: my mother's pinchbeck brooch, and the ruby and diamond earrings are particularly dear to me. My mother always wore them for great occasions; you may remember her wearing them for your wedding? She was getting a little vague by then and we had to keep a sharp watch in case she took the earrings off and forgot where she'd put them.

Now, *revenons à nos moutons*! My dear Tom, I have wanted so much to leave something to you that is absolutely pertinent and personal. As you will remember, when my poor darling parents died six years ago, so happily for them (though sadly for me) within a month of each other, I was too busy nursing my first husband to do more than dispose of the house and the furniture. There was an absolute mountain of papers in my father's library. The accountant and the solicitor dealt with much of it but there was such a pile of family stuff, old letters and diaries and so on, that after a quite *desperate* week (as darling Amy will perhaps remember) we just heaved the lot into a couple of tin trunks we dragged down from the attic (one of them went back to my father's days in the Navy, can you imagine?) and they went into store with some of the best pieces of furniture. And there they have stayed – until two months ago when I had a perfectly shocking bill from the storage company and decided to do something about them. So with darling Dick's skilled assistance (clever of me to marry a librarian, wasn't it?) they are all sorted out, ticketed, docketed, and may be of some family interest.

The furniture is remaining in storage until you and Amy (and perhaps Bill and Kate) have had a chance to take a peek at it. But there is one little legacy that I hope you will be happy to accept for yourself, with my very best love. It is my grandfather's Diary – six volumes, all written on thick linen paper in his beautiful copperplate hand, and nicely bound; hand sewn, with handsome endpapers. Dick and I have glanced through it and we both feel it should be of particular interest to you. As you know, my grandfather went into Parliament when he left the Army in 1919 and served for seventeen years until *his* father died and he resigned to take over the family breweries. He was a loyal and hardworking member of the Liberal Party and although he never achieved office, he did a lot of good work on the back benches. You will know, dearest Tom, how exacting that can be! It was said that he was a protégé of Lloyd George, but not much came of it!!! All the same, you may find he has some interesting insights into that wicked old man!

I hope the diaries will amuse you and that you will accept them in the spirit in which they are wholeheartedly given; that is, *not just* in gratitude for your being such a good husband to my dear Amy, and a wonderful father to my dear grandchildren, but as a loving and *very personal* gift from your devoted mother-in-law.

Nothing more to be said – except, once again, take

full advantage of this lovely peaceful time together; breathe in the heavenly scents of the land, and enjoy the beautiful and healing sea.

She has signed herself 'Me/Granny/Harriet'. Like her daughter, Amy's mother has her uncertainties, and how to refer to herself when writing to her son-in-law is one of them. Tom has always had the feeling she would have liked it if he had called her 'Mummy' as Amy did, but he could never get his tongue around that particular diminutive. Mentioning her to his children, or when they are present, he calls her 'Granny'; talking to Amy, 'your mother', or 'Harriet', or 'old Harriet'. When forced to address her face to face, or to attract her attention, he will usually call her by name because there seems no alternative. But he senses that she wishes he would think of one.

Tom says to Amy now, 'Your mother has given me a very special legacy.'

'I wondered what she was writing to you about.'

Amy had collected the letter from the desk as she came back from her morning swim. Now she has just stepped out of the shower. She flaps her wet fingers at Tom and he waits patiently until she has dried her hands.

She cannot guess from his straight face, his fixed, bland, half-smile, what might be in the letter. She takes it to the balcony to read it. (Amy has only recently been prescribed glasses and is still in the stage of forgetting or resenting them. One of the minor pleasures of Greece is that the light is good enough to read quite small print, even her mother's scribbly handwriting, without these loathsome objects that hurt her nose and make her feel old.)

Tom knows how she feels. He is usually maddened when

she screws up her eyes and goes to the window rather than finding her glasses and putting them on, but today he is not even mildly irritated. He gets out of bed cautiously and experimentally, tightening the muscles of his legs and his buttocks in anticipation of pain, but to his amazed relief he feels nothing except a quite pleasant ache in his calves and upper arms, a healthy reminder of his unexpected exercise yesterday. He turns sideways to the mirror, pulls in his stomach and pats his waist encouragingly. He could be imagining it, but he fancies he looks slightly trimmer.

This makes him cheerful. He calls out, 'Finished yet?'

But the helicopter is clattering over the sea as it has been doing since first light, and she hasn't heard him. When he follows her on to the balcony she turns from the rail, one hand clasping the white towel to her breast, the other holding the letter out, handing it back to him. Her expression is tragic.

She says, 'Oh! Tom!'

'What's the matter?'

'Tom! You know!'

'I'm not sure that I do.'

'Don't pretend, darling. The only thing I would say in her defence is that she didn't mean to hurt you. She just wanted to give you something, as she said, something personal. And she was *fond* of her grandfather.'

'I am not in the least hurt,' Tom says. 'Why should I be?'

Amy frowns. He knows he is tormenting her. He tells himself, *only teasing.* A little bit of getting his own back for the news she gave him late last night, when he had been too exhausted to take it in properly. Dinner with Jane Farrell had been a social and moral necessity. He had been seized by the romantic notion that having saved her life he

171

had taken on some responsibility for her, at least to the extent of eating a meal with her. But he hadn't bargained for her stamina. The remote and distinguished elderly lady she had appeared to be in the company of her famous sister, had vanished entirely. Alone, Mrs Jane Farrell turned out to be a garrulous old party whose sole topic after dinner was limited to the talents and virtues of her son, Max, who was a merchant banker like his dead father but could have been anything he chose, a violinist, a poet, a great mathematician.

A praise-singer was what Amy had called her when they finally reached the haven of their room, and when Tom questioned her, went on to explain that it was someone employed to sing the praises of an African chieftain. Although Tom was well aware that Amy had only meant to make a gentle joke, he had kept pace with Mrs Farrell for two hours, matching her brandy for brandy, and was in a mood to pick on the doorpost. He had disputed Amy's use of this term as being not only unfamiliar to him, but demonstrably inapplicable to a doting old woman and her middle-aged son until she had burst into tears, thumped him on the chest, said she was almost certainly pregnant, how could he be such a pig, and fled to the bathroom.

Tom had got into bed, grateful that he had already cleaned his teeth and emptied his bladder. Amy couldn't be pregnant, surely? Nothing of that sort had gone on for at least four weeks before his operation, he had been much too uncomfortable and dispirited and he had come out of hospital over two weeks ago, more than six weeks altogether; if she had thought there was any chance, she would have surely told him much earlier? Convinced and comforted, he lay back and closed his eyes. He had not been asleep when

172

she had switched off the bedside light and crept into bed, but he had thought it sensible to pretend to be.

Waking, slowly remembering the events of the previous night, he had felt himself to be more in the wrong than he cared for. The idea of a baby was plainly absurd. The silly girl had probably missed a couple of periods, that was normal enough at her age, but she had jumped to another conclusion. Or (though this would not be like Amy) she had made use of a distant possibility as a weapon in what had been a stupid, drunken argument, only partly of his making.

Tom has always found it hard to apologise. In the circumstances, Amy's mother's letter has made things much easier for him. He knows precisely why Amy expects him to be hurt and, indeed, it is true: he *is* hurt that old Harriet should be so certain that he is untalented, unsuccessful, and so generally useless that he will never be offered even a junior ministerial post. But he is no more hurt than he can bear.

In fact, Harriet's letter had made him smile, if a touch wryly. He had laughed out loud at the way she was always so determined to point out that Dick was such a *useful* chap, able to catalogue family letters! What a big deal! Of course, he wouldn't dream of pointing that out to Amy in any case. But to make up for last night, he will be especially magnanimous.

He says, 'Darling, I thought that was a thoroughly sweet if somewhat dotty letter. I love your mother for it. Mind you, it was all right for your grandad! He had the brewery to retreat to. But never mind that. You don't really think you might be having a baby?'

*

Encountering Tom Jones at the breakfast buffet, helping himself to yoghurt and prunes, Prudence thinks he looks much too red in the face. She wonders, professionally, if he should have his blood pressure taken. Sedentary, middle-aged men with broken veins on their nose are entering the danger zone; sudden and violent exertion can trigger a heart attack.

But she is a fellow guest, not his doctor. She says, as she waits her turn at the yoghurt bowl, 'How are you feeling after yesterday? That was a good long swim!'

Tom smiles. His eyes light up. He looks fifteen years younger, and Prudence revises her opinion of his health prospects.

He says, 'What really exhausted me was the subsequent evening. I'd no idea being snatched from the jaws of death could make someone so talkative! Do you know if she's all right this morning?'

'My grandmother spent the night with her. I told her I didn't think there was any need once she was safely tucked up in bed, but Granny insisted. I think she thought it might be fun to spend a night in one of those grand suites. As well, of course, as wanting to be helpful. She says Mrs Farrell slept like a baby and had a simply huge breakfast brought up this morning. I think she just needs someone to talk to, or just to be with her, until her son gets here. Philip, that is, Philip Mann, you know, the American, says once she's up and about, he'll take the morning shift. He says he's good with old ladies.'

Remembering the circumstances in which Philip had offered this information, Prudence feels her face start to flame. But, mercifully, Tom isn't looking at her. He hasn't really been listening either. He is moving away, bowl in one hand, plate of cheese and rolls in another. Realising, perhaps, that they haven't quite finished their conversation, he glances back over his shoulder, leaving her with a quick nod, a perfunctory smile, and advances with a determined stride towards the table where Beryl is sitting.

Tom is vaguely conscious of having been abrupt with that pretty girl. *Chatter, chatter*, he thinks, *bloody women*. But this is only to steel himself for the coming ordeal.

He smiles at Beryl, his best smile, honest and open, and says, in his most sincere voice, 'I owe you an apology, Mrs Boot. I was quite appallingly rude to you yesterday. The fact is, I was beside myself with terror. That's no excuse, of course, just an explanation, but I hope you can forgive me.'

'I never learned to swim,' Beryl says. 'I had TB when I was a child and I wasn't allowed to go to the baths with the others at school.'

Tom wishes he could hurl his plates of food on the floor, stretch his arms to the skies and howl like a wolf. Or utter some dramatic, ancient curse that would bring the walls of the Hotel Parthenon tumbling around them.

He says, with absolute truth now, 'I'm so very sorry.'

'Thank you.'

Recognising this apology as genuine, Beryl accepts it graciously, bowing her head. She dabs her mouth with her napkin, picks up her handbag, and rises. She is dressed in a safari suit made of pale yellow silk and a pretty, matching cap. Tom says, 'You're not going to the beach this morning, I take it?'

'Oh, dear, no. Could *you*, Mr Jones? I don't think I even want to *look* at the sea ever again. It's really upset me. I'm like that, I don't get over things easily. And they don't let us forget it, do they! That noisy helicopter, though of course you can't complain when you know what it's doing. Daddy thinks we should clear off, out of the way for a day or two. Until the fuss has died down. And he wants to look at a few properties round and about . . .'

She looks at her watch and lets out a sharp cry. 'Oh, look at the time! Sorry, Mr Jones, I must love you and leave you.'

She tittups off on her delicate sandals and Philip, entering the dining room, stands back to hold the door open for her.

Philip is happier (so he feels at this moment) than he has ever been in his life. He tells himself that this cannot be true; that he must have experienced this airy sensation before, this wonderful combination of pure, singing joy and bodily pleasure. When he had married Matilda? When his children were born? Oh, he remembers happiness, certainly, but happiness earthbound, weighed down by his own youthful solemnity, sense of commitment, responsibility. The first time he had held Matilda in his arms he had felt love, but he had also felt terror.

He sees Prudence at the buffet and his head spins, his legs weaken. He is not sure he can manage to go near her in public without making his glorious folly apparent to everyone. Or not until he has composed himself, anyway. He is old enough, and old-fashioned enough, to think of a girl's 'reputation'. He thinks, *That'll make her laugh when I tell her*.

He notices that Beryl has picked up a suitcase from the reception and is lugging it towards the entrance to the hotel. He strides across the marble foyer and takes it from her, just as Mr Boot emerges from the lift, carrying two more bags, one in each hand. He nods curtly at Philip, either thanking him for helping his wife, or issuing some kind of masculine challenge: Philip finds Mr Boot's physical gestures, facial tics, hard to decipher. He must remember to tell Prudence this. He loves it when she laughs.

Outside the hotel, Amy is standing by a small blue car, talking to Vic, who is sitting in the driving seat. Portia, beside him, waves at Philip through the open window.

She says, 'Ciao! I'm off for a couple of days. As you see, I've acquired a driver!'

Philip wants to laugh at this. Instead he says, 'Good for you', with what he immediately fears may be seen as a wolfish leer. He adds, attempting a redeeming severity, 'Give my love to Pylos, nice little town on Navarino Bay', but Portia has already lifted a reproving eyebrow and, to his further mortification, he blushes very slightly.

She says, out of the window to Philip, as Vic drives off, 'Takes one to know one.'

Amy looks at Philip enquiringly and he shrugs his shoulders and says, with a laugh to show he is not being serious, 'I seem to have joined some kind of secret society.'

Amy gives him a puzzled glance, and turns to the Boots with the air of a hostess who has just spotted some guests who seem to be left out of the party. 'Are you going somewhere nice?'

Mr Boot's cold blue eyes regard her reflectively but Amy's sweet, tentative smile is disarming.

He answers grudgingly all the same, 'Wasteful to come all this way just to sit on your haunches and look at the same patch of sea. And I think it's likely to get unpleasantly crowded round here the next couple of days. Reporters nosing about, making trouble for innocent people, you know what newspapers are nowadays! Dregs of humanity! So I asked the hotel to rustle up a comfortable car. With an English-speaking driver.' He shoots his wrist out of his white linen sleeve and looks at his watch. 'Late,' he says. 'Typical.'

The black Mercedes swoops into the hotel entrance, wheels with a spurt of stones, and squeals to a halt. A young man, whose long pigtail is tied with a glossy red rib-bon, leaps from the driver's seat and runs round the car to seize Mr Boot's hand and shake it up and down, hard and enthusiastically. 'I am your driver, Mister Bottis. My name is Irakles. In English, you say Hercules. The strong man, the lion killer! We will discuss the old legends together, while I am driving you. We will become good friends, Mister Bottis, I can assure you.'

Mr Boot is seen to wince. But he shows no other emo-tion and, ignoring his wife, marches around the car, flings open the rear door and climbs in. Hercules opens the near-side door for Beryl who flutters her hand at Philip and Amy and says, 'Cheery-bye.' Hercules picks up the suit-cases, all three together as if they weigh no more than egg-boxes, hurls them higgledy-piggledy into the boot and leaps into the driving seat.

He is gone in a cloud of dust, in a screaming of tyres. Amy and Philip look at each other.

Amy says, 'I want to laugh. Isn't that awful? I mean, so soon after. Do you think they will find her? I know I should be thinking more about poor Mrs Farrell, one should always think more of those left behind. But she was so lovely, Tish Palmer. All that talent, all that grace . . .'

'Come to dust,' Philip says. 'Yes, I know.'

But happiness insulates: he cannot at this moment feel a proper grief for the drowned woman, the mourning sister. To make amends he says, gravely, 'Do you think there will be much newspaper interest? Apart, I mean, from the *Athens News*? They told me at the desk that the local television station would like an interview with Mrs Farrell. I said they must ask her. Would she agree, do you think?'

'I should think nothing would please her more,' Amy says, feelingly. 'Tom and I discovered last night how much she likes to talk. On and on like a waterfall. I tried to feel sorry but I ended up just terribly tired.'

'I'm sorry, I hadn't realised. I saw she was dining with you. I went to my room after dinner. Sat on the balcony, looked at the moon, that sort of thing. It was such a beautiful night.'

To Philip's ear this sounds like a confession. But Amy has only heard the words he has used; she is deaf to the implications behind them. She says, 'Tom thinks, once they know who she was, one or two of the Athens correspondents of the English press will be likely to come. It depends what else is going on. Trouble with Turkey or a scandal about the CIA will wipe anything else off the map! But unless one of the editors is a major fan, they're unlikely to run anything beyond the agency reports. And the obituaries. But of course, as I said, this is what Tom thinks. I really don't know at all. Have you had breakfast?'

Walking into the dining room, Philip keeps a few steps behind Amy, self-consciously using her as a shield, shyly peering around him. Although a remote part of his mind registers that something unusual appears to be happening on the terrace beyond the dining room, nothing matters to him except finding Prudence. Then, to his inexpressible joy she is suddenly there, eager, excited and loving.

She says, 'Darling Philip, you must come, Mrs Farrell is putting on a really tremendous show . . .'

And she takes his left arm and places it round her waist, as if this is the most natural thing in the world, and walks him towards the terrace and the blue blaze of artificial light.

🌸 12 🌸

THE LIGHT IS VERY BRIGHT. IN its glare, Jane Farrell sits on a white plastic chair, wearing a white dress, a gold cross on a thin chain round her neck, but no other jewellery. Her pale hair is brushed back from her fine, bony face. She looks very old, very calm, very beautiful.

A young man hefts a heavy camera on his shoulder. An older man, on one knee beside her, holds out the microphone. If he has been asking questions, he is no longer doing so. She is talking, he is listening. Also watching and listening are Tom Jones, standing behind the light, shoulders hunched, hands in his pockets, Mrs Honey beside him, and a small group of old people who have been dragooned, or persuaded, to keep their distance from the star performer. Some of them are settled on chairs they have arranged in a semicircle, automatically composing themselves into an impromptu television studio audience.

It occurs to Philip that this is a concept they are all so familiar with that none of them feel this behaviour is in the

181

least voyeuristic, or remember there had been a time, not so long ago either, when civilised men and women shrank from intruding on grief. He would like to say this to Prudence. He no longer fears she will think him prudish and old-fashioned; indeed, he has been slightly alarmed (though, of course, gratified) by the deference with which she appears to regard his every utterance, as if it had come from a god. But she is pulling him forward, her fingers laced with his, holding his hand at her warm waist. And he is helpless.

Jane is saying, '. . . the better swimmer, that is one thing I do not understand. She wanted to swim to the island. She had set her heart on it. She knew it was too far for me, but Tish always did what she wanted. I think she thought that while we were together, nothing could happen. We had been born together, we would die together. When we were girls, that was what we imagined. Of course we had no idea how differently life was going to treat us . . .'

She bows her head and sighs. Perhaps there is a tear on her cheek? She takes a handkerchief from her sleeve and touches it to her eyes. Then she lifts her chin bravely.

'My poor Tish longed to marry, longed for children! Instead she became famous and, oh, what emptiness! But so much is due to Lady Luck. We had organised a Dramatic Society for the poor children in my father's parish, and the Lady sent a young friend of Mr George Bernard Shaw to stay with a gentleman who belonged to our church on the night we performed a play about the Round Table. I had written the play. Tish played Guinevere. I married Mr Shaw's friend and Mr Shaw got Tish her first part on the London stage. I can't remember the name of the play. I never saw it. My dear son was born on the first night. But

Louis B. Mayer was in the audience and he signed her up. Oh, this is all ancient history, isn't it?'

She looks at the perspiring man holding the microphone and giggles, sweetly and lightly.

Appalled, Philip whispers to Prudence, 'Should we stop this?' But Prudence shakes her head. There is no way they can interfere without treating this proud old woman as if she is incompetent, even verging on senile.

And she seems in control, perfectly clear and unworried.

She leans forward a little and speaks directly to the camera. 'Tish went to Hollywood because I had Max and she wanted a baby. She was all twisted up, tormented, by jealousy. She was in love with my husband. She even put it about that Max was really her child and she had been persuaded to give him to me because Metro Goldwyn Mayer wanted to cast her as a young virgin. She told other tales, too, she was always a terrible liar. But that was her unhappiness. Oh, how I did pity her!'

Philip looks at her audience. Is this real to them? He cannot tell from their polite, guarded faces.

She looks at them now, widening her eyes as if she has only just noticed them. She says, confidentially, 'Of course you will all know about the career. She got to Hollywood when actresses like Garbo had just passed their peak. Nothing much to begin with, then the war came and she played Doris in *The Nice Girl and the Soldier* . . .'

Behind Philip, a voice. 'Oh, for Christ's sake.'

He is a small, round man, bald on the top of his head with a fringe of longish grey hair surrounding the baldness like the skirt of a hovercraft. He wears heavy-lensed glasses and a crumpled dark suit. He has removed his tie and one end of it trails from his jacket pocket. He says, to Philip,

183

'D'you speak English? Can you tell me what's going on? I thought I'd get here in time. God, I should have known better. What *is* this outfit?'

Philip detaches himself from Prudence. In his new happiness, he is not embarrassed to be seen entwined with such a young woman, but it seems disrespectful in front of a man even older than he is.

He holds out his hand. 'Max Farrell? We spoke on the phone. Before I put you on to your mother. I don't think these people can do much harm. It's the local TV operation. Neighbourhood news. Unlikely to go any further.'

Max Farrell takes off his glasses and wipes the sweat from his eyes. 'OK. OK. Better deal with it.'

And he pushes past Philip, past the man with the microphone, deliberately knocking it out of his hand. He puts his short, stout arms round Jane Farrell and lifts her up from her chair. He shouts at the young man with the camera, 'Turn that bloody thing off, the bloody light, too.'

And, in a quieter voice, but loud enough for Philip and Prudence to hear, 'Come along, Auntie Tish. The show's over.'

'I should have known,' he groans an hour later, sitting in the dark of the foyer bar. 'Not that I could have stopped it, but I could have tried to warn you. Mind you, when she told me Mother was dead, I thought, her *twin* – even Tish'll be too upset to get up to her tricks! Not that it was just Tish, you know. Mother was as bad, they played merry hell with just about everyone. Doctors, dentists, well you can just imagine! *Isn't it funny, dear Doctor So-and-so, that old scar seems to have vanished!* No way of telling one from the other except that Mother could never do the Voice. Tish

184

was the better mimic; she picked up her version of cockney from the nanny they'd had when their monstrous old father was preaching about the nobility of poverty to the poor in the East End of London. But they'd change around just like kids, turn and turn about, not much harm done most of the time, just a bit of mischief really, kept them amused. But I never thought Tish would try to swap coffins.'

Amy says, 'I'm so very sorry about your mother. It's terrible that you should have this to cope with as well.'

'I've rehearsed it often enough. Never went out without leaving a telephone number on the answerphone.' Max has a warm, friendly smile. It doesn't make him less plain but it makes him more likeable. 'What I had underestimated was the purgatory of having to get to wherever it was when one of them popped her clogs.' He nods at Philip. 'When you got me last night, I was at a city dinner. I got my man to fix up a flight and he said Gatwick was the earliest possible. I got there as fast as I could. And I was disgusted!'

He glares around the bar. He, Tom and Philip are drinking ouzo, Amy and Mrs Honey have ordered coffee. Max Farrell says, with shuddering emphasis, 'Have any of you ever been on a *charter flight*?'

At this unexpectedly angry question, they look at each other uncertainly. Mrs Honey says, 'Not for a long time. But I am sure Prudence has. She would know how . . . If you wanted . . . Do you want me to get her? I could stay with your – with Miss Palmer.'

'No, no. I merely wanted someone else to confirm the sheer horror of the experience. But if none of you has suffered recently, I am even happier to be able to tell you how fortunate you are! I am not exaggerating when I tell you that the scenes at Gatwick were like something out of a flourishing Old Testament Hell. Except perhaps for the burning! Bodies shuffling in queues to get on the plane, and once aboard, those same half-dressed, unwashed bodies crushed in such frightful proximity one can only wonder that they didn't start biting each other. Some of these people, I told myself, have almost certainly protested noisily about the discomfort of the trucks in which cattle are dispatched abroad without once making the obvious equation. I rang for the steward, just in case, you know, there had been some fearful calamity which would explain the condition of this particular hell hole, but he said no, it was a full plane, their planes usually were full at this time of year and very few people complained. They must all be mad in that case, I said, no one but a lunatic would take such a journey a second time. Then I saw that he thought I was mad, so I shut up. And endured.'

Mrs Honey clicks her tongue sympathetically. Tom looks at Amy, relying on her to respond suitably. Amy says, 'You must be very tired. Up all night. Was it difficult getting a taxi from Athens?'

'Philip here – I think we're on first-name terms, aren't we? – arranged a taxi to meet all the planes landing from London. I am deeply indebted for that.' Max yawns suddenly. 'Maybe I better try to sleep. I must warn you, there may be the odd journalist turning up some time today or tomorrow. I rang *The Times*, and the *Guardian*. I thought, you see, there might be a bit of a mix-up this end, knowing my wicked old auntie. Though I didn't know quite what she would devise for us, I guessed she would devise something. Of course, the papers won't be covering the death of my poor mother, or only incidentally. Nor just Aunt Tish's survival, unless one of the colour supplements, or that chap, whatshisname, on the telly wants to do a piece on the old bat. It's a case of Labour MP rescues Legend, I fear. So if you want to clear out, Tom, any of you, best get going. I can stand guard. I've done it before.'

He finishes his ouzo and stands up. He smiles his friendly smile. 'I can't thank you enough. When I think you're all strangers, to me, to each other, it restores my faith in humanity. If there's anything I can do for you, apart from apologising for disrupting your holiday, I'd be glad if you'd tell me.'

Mrs Honey clears her throat. Tom and Philip exchange a horrified glance. Amy closes her eyes. Mrs Honey says, 'There is something I *would* like to know, Mr Farrell. I hope you don't think me indelicate but it was common gossip, you must have been asked before . . .'

She pauses – even Mrs Honey has some sense of shame. But she rallies fast. 'There was a rumour,' she says, gabbling, flushing, 'that the Prince of Wales was your father.'

Max Farrell laughs. Tired as he is, he laughs so hard that his shoulders shake, and the plump jowls of his neck. 'No, my dear,' he says, at last. 'My father was short, fat, bald and half blind, just like me.'

'How d'you think he usually travels?'

'Concorde? Private jet? Camel? Actually, I found that outburst refreshing. Rather as if a Minister for Transport who's never used the Underground in his life had suddenly found himself stuck on the Northern Line at rush hour. Something you may have been told about but never experienced at first hand! A revelation! Like when we first saw the Taj Mahal with our own eyes. No words could do justice.'

187

Amy laughs, as Tom means her to, but she is in the grip of a painful uncertainty. He has been so kind. Too kind. Unnaturally kind. No, that's not fair. Oh, but she does hope he is not *making an effort*.

They have fled from the hotel, to lunch at the fish taverna on the sea that Amy remembers as being so good when she came with her mother. Tom has ordered a lobster. While they wait, they are picking at a tomato and cucumber salad, and sipping a sharp, resinated wine, the taverna's own wine, from the barrel. They sit at a table covered with a sheet of clean paper, facing a wide stretch of sea, a great bay; the mountains beyond, range upon range, snow on the higher peaks, clearly visible in this dry, sparkling weather.

Tom says, 'You do remember the Taj Mahal, don't you?'

He puts his hand out, across the table, and she takes it gratefully. 'Yes, I do. I remember thinking at the time it was so like the Northern Line . . . Oh, Tom. Is it really all right? I mean, it's my *fault*. I stopped using that thingummy. I thought, I mean, I honestly thought, that I was past that stage of my life. I'm so sorry.'

'Shut up. Please. Darling. All right, I didn't throw my hat in the air when you told me. I think now I may be quite pleased, and I will probably find I am very pleased in a day or so. There's been a lot going on, if you'll pardon the understatement. Besides, you're not exactly over the moon yourself, are you?'

'I don't know. I suppose I think I'm too old. Then I think, Bill and Kate will be pleased. And Mummy, of course. But it's you it depends upon, really.'

'Oh, God!' But Tom is grinning at her. He squeezes her hand. 'Then I am delighted. That suit you? Now you tell me something. That film, the one you've always told me she is remembered for. *The Nice Girl* . . . I never saw it, you know, though you've taken me to some of the later ones.'

'It was on television once, I persuaded you to watch and you went to sleep. But you've seen *Mrs Miniver*? Tish's film was sentimental tosh too, but at least it was about a working-class girl, not a lady. The munitions factory where she works has been bombed and she goes on a holiday to the country. She stays on a farm and meets her soldier. Only he is an *Italian* soldier, a prisoner-of-war who is working and living on the farm. That was a very young Laurence Olivier. And of course they fall in love.'

Although Amy laughs at this banality, she feels a sudden rush of sweetly painful nostalgia. She had first seen this old black and white film with her mother. They had both wept throughout the last half-hour and emerged sad, but uplifted, to comfort themselves with cream cakes for tea in the cinema café.

Amy's throat is suddenly creaky with tears for happy times past. She says, to distance herself from this silliness, 'Of course, it was the song, "All the nice girls love a sailor", that gave them the title.'

Tom has been told the plot of this famous film several times before. He has also been told (by Amy's mother as well as Amy) that it was one of the factors that conditioned the people of the United States to the moral necessity of the Second World War. Although Pearl Harbor was important, of course, *The Nice Girl and the Soldier*, along with *Mrs Miniver*, helped to persuade ordinary Americans that there was an emotional as well as a military reason for backing the British in their fight against Hitler.

Another reason why Tish's film had made cinema history

was the famous nude scene: Tish and her Italian prisoner in the hay loft.

Tom (who had not slept absolutely all the time *Nice Girl* was on television) remembers this sequence as fairly un-titillating, being shot through what appeared to be a dense fog, but he knows better than to say this, either to Amy, or to her mother. Experience has taught him that any criticism of this sort is likely to involve him in a passionate discussion (passionate on their part) of an art form that he finds overrated and more or less boring. (He doesn't much care for theatre either, or novels, seeing no point in the fictional representation of life.) But he doesn't mind sitting quiet while Amy tells him the story of some film or play that excites her. He doesn't have to listen, after all.

He wishes he could explain to Amy why he is apparently so lukewarm about the baby. At first he had been rigid with horror. Amy may feel she's too old: he *knows* he's too old. Now he can see that he may, later on, feel somewhat differently. There is a kind of flattery implicit in late fatherhood: mixing with much younger dads in the park, pushing swings, playing football . . .

But that is far in the future, light years away. Meanwhile, he has to keep Amy happy. And ignorant. She will want to tell Vic. Is there any way he can stop her? A woman of Amy's age will need to have tests to check that the child is normal. Down's syndrome. Could he persuade her to keep the good news from Vic until they know all is well? She wouldn't want to disappoint poor old Grandad, would she?

Vic is hardly poor, or old. If he puts this to Amy, she will think him deranged.

Perhaps he can persuade her to tell Vic privately. Explain that he doesn't want it *bruited abroad*. Not as yet. If the press do turn up, does she really want Vic to pass on the glad tidings?

On the other hand, if he tries to keep it a secret from Vic, if Amy ever finds out about Portia, it will look to her as if what he really intended was to keep it a secret from his ex-lover.

Which, of course, is what he is hoping to do.

Perhaps they can clear out before Vic and Portia come back to the Hotel Parthenon. No reason why they shouldn't hire a car, do a bit of exploring on their own. After all, Vic went off without a backward glance, didn't he? Driving a rattly hired car might not be quite the physically healing holiday he had hoped for, but that went out of the window on the first day! Or they could fly home tomorrow. Though Amy would rightly object to the waste of money. The air ticket home is already paid, part of the package deal, and they would have to pay full price for a one-way fare . . .

The lobster has come, is set down between them. Amy watches Tom lovingly while he picks out the delicious white meat from the shell and puts one whole, perfect piece on her plate. 'Oh,' she says. 'What a treat!'

Philip and Prudence are spending this lunchtime in bed, in Philip's room at the Parthenon. Philip speaks into Prudence's ear, buried in her forest of hair. 'You must be hungry after all that. Shall I get you chocolate from the minibar? Or a packet of nuts?'

'Don't you dare move.' Prudence stretches like a cat, arching her back. She wraps her long legs and long arms around Philip, locking him close to her. 'Though I ought to go and find Granny.'

'I thought she was happily lunching with Max and his auntie.'

'She'll wonder what I'm doing when she's stopped eating. Don't laugh. She likes to be entertained. I can't just run out on her. Don't want to, either. But I want to spend the night with you, don't I? So I have to explain my absence from my chaste maiden couch. If I'd known beforehand I might have got her to make different arrangements. But she booked this double room because she likes a gossip last thing. I can't palm her off on old Tish again.'

'Is that what you did last night?' Philip asks, interested: he has never met, let alone made love to, anyone so straightforward and innocently ruthless before. He wants to look after Prudence, of course he does, he feels at this moment that he never wants to let her out of his sight. But he doesn't have to worry about her. He feels he has discovered a freedom he didn't know existed before.

'Oh, not really. I would have looked in on her from time to time if Granny hadn't offered to stay with her. But there's no need for anyone to keep watch tonight.' She sighs, histrionically, and rolls over, on top of him. 'I suppose I'll just have to tell her.'

'No!' Philip laughs. He feels he is hanging on by a thread to his old life, to the rules he has lived by, even to sanity. 'No, you can't, darling. Darling Prue. Of course you can't tell her. She's an old woman. A different generation.' Closer in age to him, than he is to Prue. He says, heartfelt, 'Believe me, I know.'

Prudence is kissing him with her eyelashes. Butterfly kisses. She says, her breath warm on his mouth, 'And you believe *me*. All Granny will worry about is my getting pregnant. As long as she knows that's taken care of, she'll be delighted it's you, and not some handsome Greek waiter.'

Mrs Honey may not be sure what Prudence is up to at this precise moment, but she is moderately certain she knows what she will be up to quite soon, and with whom. Look at the way she had wrapped herself around Philip this morning, like a climbing plant round a tree! The girl was longing for sex, you'd have to be blind not to notice! Anyone would do, almost anyone, anyway! She won't care that he's all those years older! Of course, old men have better luck than old women that way, but Mrs Honey is only mildly resentful: Prudence works so hard, she deserves a bit of fun on her holiday. Mrs Honey has even resigned herself to spending more time on her own than she had reckoned on. And because of all the excitement she minds this prospect less than she might have done.

She is enjoying sharing a table with Tish Palmer and her nephew. Mrs Honey likes her wine, and Max has been able to persuade the waiter to produce a good bottle; a Greek wine that has actually won an award in Bordeaux. Max had known what to ask for, the year, the name of the vineyard. 'That's always the trick,' he tells Mrs Honey and his Aunt Tish. 'Get hold of the name of something. A vineyard. The name of the head waiter. The local football team – just about anything. You'll get better service. If I have to go somewhere in a hurry, my man always makes a few notes of that sort when he gets the tickets.'

'You always get your priorities so absolutely right, Max my darling,' Tish Palmer murmurs.

'Now Aunt Tish, don't be catty. Drinking vinegary wine won't bring Mother back.'

Max winks at Mrs Honey, who is torn. She likes good service herself, and is impressed by a man who knows how to get it. On the other hand, she doesn't want to offend Tish who has enviable, if distant, connections with royalty. She may not have produced a royal child, but she had known the Prince of Wales before he became Edward VIII and married Mrs Simpson.

She says, 'No one feels much like eating or drinking when they've had a bereavement. But you have to keep your strength up, so there's no harm in tickling the palate with something tasty if you can get it. Red wine is good for you, that's now accepted medical opinion. But in my experience, and I have been a trained nurse for longer than I like to admit to, bad wine can give you really nasty indigestion.'

Tish Palmer looks at Mrs Honey rather (so Mrs Honey feels) as she would look at a beetle. A creature almost beneath notice except that it might suddenly scuttle alarmingly. She turns to Max and says, in a fretful voice, 'There were always the two of us. And we could each change around, be the other if we got bored with ourselves. I don't think I can bear being alone with myself. Oh, Max, dear Max, what in Heaven's name shall I do?'

And Max says, wearily gentle, a man who has spent too many years of his life caretaking two dominant, impossible women, 'You can go on playing games if you want to, Aunt Tish. No one can stop you.'

Vic and Portia are pleased with themselves, with each other. They have both lived alone long enough to find it astonishing that another person could be so neatly complementary. What is delighting them at the moment is the remarkable discovery that Vic enjoys driving but hates reading maps, while Portia prefers, and is skilled at, map reading.

'You get the scale right,' she explains. 'Learn the symbols, get your bearings in your head, tell yourself that the map's only a guide to the real world out there. If you don't do that, you start all that silliness of turning the map upside down to match the way you are going.'

'Tom's mother used to do that,' Vic says. 'For all she was so clever.'

Portia says, hastily, 'I think it's probably some mechanism in the brain. You either have a good sense of direction or you don't. It's nothing to do with cleverness. Just the luck you were born with.'

Vic doesn't take his eyes off the winding, mountain road or a hand off the wheel, but his voice is a caress. He says, 'You are a nice lady, you know that?'

And Portia is so pleased by this unaffected compliment that she feels her throat constrict.

Vic says, 'And a hungry one by now? Any hope before nightfall?'

'*After* Orchomenos, don't you think?'

They have been to Epidaurus, where Vic barely spoke. He sat halfway up the great theatre auditorium, stunned and silent. Portia left him alone, as she assumed he wanted to be, and fell in with a bearded Swedish archaeologist who told her about another theatre, a treasure, small and unvisited, not far from Tripolis. The journey looked easy enough on the map but it is taking longer than Portia expected. They have taken the old road over the mountains, precipitous and beautiful and almost empty of traffic, but slow and difficult driving. Vic has not stopped for three hours.

195

'Unless you are starving,' Portia says, conscience stricken, 'we should turn off this road before we get to Tripolis, but we can drive on, into the town. Or there may be somewhere at Orchomenos. In the village.'

'Orchomenos it is, my lady.'

Vic mimes touching the peak of a uniformed cap and, for a fraction of a second, turns and winks at her. And then catches his breath.

The road is climbing towards the top of the pass. The precipice is on their right, sheer rock on the left. A black BMW is coming round the steep bend, on their side of the road, the wrong side, the precipice side, and travelling fast. Vic grunts and swerves towards the rock, in front of the oncoming car. Portia closes her eyes. There is a *thump*, a heart-stopping, giddying jolt, then a surprisingly delicate tinkling of metal, before she is thrown forward and jerked back by the seat belt. *Head on*, she thinks – and wonders why she is still alive.

She opens her eyes. The little car is facing neatly down-hill, turned around, on what is now the right side of the road. She is covered in pieces of glass. Vic is picking them off her legs, off her lap, off her breasts. He is saying, 'All right, my lovely. Just made it. Thought we weren't going to for a second.'

'You drove *in front* of that car!' This is all Portia can think of.

'Didn't fancy the alternative, to be honest. That's a heavy vehicle. She'd have had us over the edge, my darling, and I didn't fancy losing you quite so soon.'

Portia's door is jammed, bent inwards. Vic helps her crawl out across the driver's seat. 'There, not a scratch on you – how's that for a miracle.'

There is blood on his hands, however, and on the side of his face.

Portia says, 'Let me see, Vic.'

There is a cut, quite a deep cut, at the corner of his eye.

She says, 'There must be a first-aid kit.'

But the woman who was driving the black BMW is coming up the road towards them, staggering, weeping. She is younger than Portia, so Portia judges: younger and thinner. Richer, too, if the gold round her neck and dangling from her ears is any guide. She is wearing the kind of jacket and skirt Portia has never dreamed of affording.

'Oh, I am so very sorry,' this rich young woman cries. She speaks English prettily. 'There is never anyone on this road since they built the new motorway. My husband will kill me.'

Portia observes that her huge dark eyes are beautifully melting with tears. She has a smooth white complexion that will coarsen, not wrinkle, with age. But she will not be old for a long time.

Vic goes up to her, puts an arm round her. 'Hey,' he says, 'it can't be so bad. Might have been much worse, after all. I'll take a look . . .' He fishes a handkerchief from his pocket. 'Don't cry, now. Can't be all that much damage to your car, you just clipped our back wheel. It was our tin can got the worst of it.'

She wails and collapses against him, burying her face in his neck. He pats her tenderly. Portia decides that she hates her. As Vic walks her down to the BMW that she has left dangerously parked on the bend, Portia stalks behind them, her body trembling. Shock, she tells herself. But it feels like anger.

The BMW has a dent in the bumper, a scrape on one wing, and a smashed headlamp.

'The headlamp'll cost you,' Vic says. 'The other bits aren't too bad unless you want to replace the bumper. But the insurance will pay, if you have comprehensive that is, and I rather assume that you do!'

She starts crying again. Tears pour down her white cheeks in a waterfall. 'Oh, no, no, no. You don't understand. I can't tell my husband, I will have to take it to the garage and get it mended before he comes back from Cairo. I will have to pay for it, and it will cost more to do quickly. I don't know about the insurance, only that it is impossible for me to tell him. If you will give me the money for the repair, then I will say nothing about it.'

Portia cannot believe what she is hearing. 'But you came round the bend on our side of the road. You could have killed us!'

She gives a hiccup and stops crying. She looks at Portia now, not at Vic. 'Your husband drove across the road just in front of me. That is what happened. Anyone can see it is what has happened.'

'But you were driving straight at us! You were going to knock us over the edge.'

She turns from Portia to Vic, hands out, appealing. 'Please, oh please help me. It is not a lie I am telling you. He will kill me. Give me the money and I will go straight home and ring someone to come here and help you. If you don't, I will go to the police. You are a foreigner, they will believe what I tell them.'

Portia says, to Vic, 'The woman's mad.' But she is inexplicably afraid suddenly. She moves closer to Vic.

'About forty thousand drachmas should fix it.' Vic takes his wallet out of his pocket and counts the notes carefully. He hands them over, his face impassive. He says, 'If you send someone, you will hear no more about it. If you don't, we shall see. But you must go now, before someone comes round that bend and kills all three of us.'

And he marches to the BMW, and holds open the driver's door.

Before she gets in, she puts her hands either side of his face and kisses him, quite lingeringly, on the mouth. Portia growls under her breath. But when Vic turns, she is smiling. She even waves at the departing car before she says, 'You know what I think? She wasn't supposed to be in that car, on this road, at this time. That's what all the fuss was about.'

'Some men are obsessed by their cars,' Vic says. 'That's a new BMW.'

'Off to see her lover,' Portia says confidently. 'Or on the way back. Either way she takes a road where she's not likely to meet anyone. She'll get caught sooner or later if that's the way she usually drives. She was lucky this time to run into a soft-hearted gent. Easily bamboozled.'

'I didn't take to her,' Vic says. 'But there's always the chance people may be telling the truth, even if they aren't your cup of tea. And I got the feeling you were scared of her. So I thought, get rid of her as quickly as possible!'

'I wasn't scared of her. Well, yes, I was for a minute. I can't think why.'

'Crazy, wasn't she? At least marching to a different drum. That's always frightening.'

'So you didn't fancy her?'

Portia is surprised to hear herself saying this and mortified to feel herself blushing.

Vic laughs.

'Look,' he says. 'We'll have all the time in the world to

discuss that sort of thing very shortly. My guess is we'll have to sit here and wait until someone comes by on a donkey, but first things first, we've got to see to the car.'

The back wing is bent inwards, crushed against the back wheel. It is obvious, even to Portia, that they cannot move this hired car, let alone drive it. The lid of the boot is jammed tight. Even if there is a red triangle inside, as there should be, they cannot get at it. At least the accident has placed them, fortuitously, on the correct side of the road, tucked well in to the rock, and anyone coming up the hill will have a clear view of the crashed car, time to take action. But it is dangerously close to the top of the pass.

They walk up to the bend, holding hands. At the top, a merciful providence has provided a shrine, a tree, a patch of shade, and a clear view of the empty white road winding down to the plain.

🌸 13 🌸

Portia and Vic return to the Hotel Parthenon the next morning. Apart from one early bather in the pool, swimming laps with a noisy display of honking and huffing, the hotel appears to be sleeping as soundly as the night porter behind the reception desk.

This to Portia's relief. Until she observes her reflection as they approach the glass doors of the entrance, she has been feeling as serene as she has ever felt in her life, healthy, slender and young, comfortable inside her own skin. Seeing her true, ghostly image, stocky, overweight, hair flying wild, is a humiliation. Her immediate impulse is to hide – at least to get to her room without being seen by anyone less besotted than Vic. He, to her chagrined eyes, looks much the same as he did before their long night began: competent and composed, hair neatly slicked from the sea instead of matted and stiff with sticky grey sand. *Undignified, she groans inwardly, at your age, silly cow, rolling about on a beach . . .*

Tom, coming out of the lift, raises his hands in dramatic amazement. 'Hey, what happened to you?'

Then he stops laughing. 'My God, *Dad*! Have you been in an accident?'

Portia says, stiffly, 'What makes you think that? Your father and I have been dancing the night away. A ball at Buckingham Palace. Of course we had an accident, you bloody fool!'

Tom frowns, warning her not to be so revealingly intimate. But she has already seen her mistake. She says, archly, 'I can tell you one thing, Tom Jones! Your father is a good man to stand back to back with on a stricken field. Let him tell you about it while I put myself back together.'

And she sweeps past him into the lift, turning to smile with devastating sweetness at Vic before the door closes behind her.

'You're up early,' Vic says, to his son. 'And I'm hungry. So why don't we go and have breakfast?'

Until this moment, Tom had not intended to breakfast. Eating three times a day is only habit, he has been telling himself. In pursuit of his new health regime, he has risen in order to take a walk around the town, up and down the marble staircases, tautening his thigh and stomach muscles and filling his lungs with clean air. But it would be unkind to abandon his father when he has a story to tell. And, as Tom reminds himself now, breakfast is by far the best and most sustaining meal at the Parthenon: white cheese, figs, eggs that are usually bullet hard and lukewarm but wonderfully tasty, and small, sweet, brownish grapes, fresh off the vine.

'Good idea, Dad,' Tom says. 'I find myself peckish suddenly. What have you been up to?'

He has no premonitions. Nothing much can have hap
pened. A minor accident, not much harm done. Portia may
have looked as if she'd had a hard night but she's not as
young as she used to be. Indeed, he reminds himself, she is
at least two years older than he is, which is old enough to
be sensible. He can barely remember why he had been so
agitated yesterday. Things fall into place if you wait calmly
and quietly. The wild idea that he and Amy might fold
their tents and flee from the scene had been kiboshed late
last night by a call from London: the Chief Whip informing
him that the Leader of Her Majesty's Opposition would be
ringing him today, eight o'clock, Greek time, this evening.

Tom has no intention of telling his father this dis-
turbingly interesting piece of news. He has not told Amy,
who was asleep when the telephone call came through. He
feels safer this way; protected against uncertainty, disappointment.

Though he might, once, have told Portia . . .

His father is saying, 'She was magnificent. Mind you,
she's quite a toughie, young Portia! But not a word of complaint, not at any point. Took it all in her stride. You have
to hand it to her.'

Tom nods agreement. Although his attention has wan-
dered, he has taken in enough of his father's adventures to
agree that Portia's behaviour has been exemplary. After the
accident, they had waited several hours by the side of the
mountain road, stopping all that passed: rickety lorries saving the toll on the motorway, farm trucks, farmers on
donkeys, before the recovery service finally found them. It
was dark before they reached the coast at Myloi, on the far
side of the bay from the town and the Parthenon, and the
ELPA driver was tired.

'You can see his point,' Vic said. 'He lives in that village, pparently, and he'd been on the road most of the day. At least, that's what we thought he said, there was a bit of a language difficulty you might say. We decided he was trying to tell us his cousin had a friend with a taxi, but we thought, well, we're hungry, so we stopped in a taverna. Nice fresh fish and a lot of wine from the barrel, and we could see this town, not so far away it seemed, just over the water, all the lights twinkling, and Portia said, why don't we just leave our traps and walk back round the bay? I said, don't be silly, girl, but then I thought, why not, you're only young once.'

Looking up from buttering his bread, Vic shakes his head in delighted amazement.

Tom growls, 'It's quite a way, but not all that far, is it? How long did it take you, for God's sake?'

'We took it nice and easy. She had a fancy for a midnight swim. Then a four o'clock in the morning swim.'

Vic has an idiotic grin on his face. Tom clenches his fists. But the grin vanishes of its own accord and Vic says, shining-eyed, shyly, 'This has been the most wonderful night of my life, Tom lad. I'm still pinching myself to see if I'm dreaming.'

Tom says, 'You can't do it to him, Portia. What the hell – he's an *innocent*! I don't expect you to give a damn how I feel, OK, I don't blame you, but my poor old dad is another matter! If you're doing it to get your own back on me, and I can see that might enter into it, then, please, *please* think it through, try to look at it from his point of view. He's a decent man, very straight, very *simple*.'

'Too good for a devious hussy?'

204

Portia is sitting on the bed, wrapped in hotel towe. one knotted above her breasts, another turbaned aroun her head. She had ordered coffee from room service, left the door on the latch, and been in the bath when Tom had burst in; his furious face materialising like a genie above her; an apparently bodiless head, shrouded in steam.

'Oh, God, no, *idiot*! You know I don't mean that!' Tom claps the back of his hand to his forehead and groans. 'He's not in the least sophisticated, don't you understand that? I don't suppose he's ever met anyone like you in his life. He's bowled over!'

Portia raises an eyebrow. 'What do you mean, anyone like *me*? I'm not a member of your chattering classes. I left school at seventeen and worked as a typist. OK, I married my boss, but that just put me off the boss class for ever. And what makes you think your father isn't sophisticated? He's a normally complex, civilised man. Not some kind of rude mechanical who has only just emerged from the Stone Age. He's sensitive to people's feelings and that makes him mannerly. It also makes him an exceptionally satisfactory lover, but that's not your concern. One thing he would never do is crash in on *anyone* in the bath. Certainly not without knocking.'

'All right. All right! I'm sorry. OK? Though I would have thought we'd seen each other naked enough not to be fussy. But of course you're right. I should have made an appointment. Thing is, I was *desperate*. He thinks he's in love with you. He thinks you're in love with him. For Christ's sake, he's talking about getting *married* '

Portia gets up from the bed, one hand steadying her now toppling turban, the other tightening the towel round her body. She says firmly, with dignity, lifting her chin, 'I think would prefer to discuss this with my clothes on. You may think our previous relationship entitles you to insult me but I beg to differ. Perhaps you would be good enough to wait on the balcony?'

Tom doesn't know whether to laugh or to cry. He splutters, 'You always were absurd! Oh, Portia!'

He advances towards her, arms open, hungry, but she nips round him neatly and darts into the bathroom, slamming the door shut. But he thinks she was smiling.

She says, through the closed door, 'Your father and I suit each other admirably. Neither of us is burdened with too great a conceit of ourselves for one thing. And I think we could be happy together. He would be happiest if we got married. That's all you're entitled to know. Everything else is between him and me.'

Tom hisses through his teeth. 'You know I can stop it. I've only to tell him.'

'Wait,' Portia says. 'You just wait. I'll tell *you*.'

Tom retreats to the balcony. It is now nearly nine o'clock. Amy is still safely in bed. He has ordered her breakfast in the room at nine-thirty. Vic would not come to Portia's room without ringing her first. (Tom reminds himself that he must not answer the telephone.) And his first appointment is with the Greek correspondent of the *Daily Chronicle* who is coming from Athens. Ten o'clock on the terrace.

He settles in one of the two big balcony chairs, drumming his fingers on the wooden arms, glowering sullenly at the flat sea. He feels let down by life, by its serpentine ways. Why can't it be more straightforward? There was Portia in the bath, sweetly pink, roundly naked. The natural thing would have been to heave her out, cart her over

206

to the bed. She was a bit heavy to carry far, perhaps, but tumble on the marble floor of the bathroom would have been a touch chilly.

Could he have lifted her? He was out of condition after the operation. Not that he had ever been all that much *in* condition, to be honest. Would she have been willing? She had been, often enough. Why not once more? Just a last quickie. Vic was an *exceptionally satisfactory lover*, that's what she'd said. What the hell did she mean? Can't imagine the old man had had all that much practice during his marriage. Made up for it since, that was obvious. Just hope he hasn't picked up anything nasty along the way . . .

Behind him, Portia says, 'The coffee has come. Would you like a cup?'

Tom shakes his head. She sits in the chair opposite. She has a cup of coffee in one hand, a fattish red book in the other.

She is smiling steadily. A thin cotton dress clings to her still slightly damp body and shows the outline of a brief pair of knickers and a rather more substantial bra underneath. Her feet are bare.

She says, 'Listen, Tom Jones. I am extremely fond of Vic. I have no intention of hurting him. So I'm never going to tell him that you and I had a flutter back in the Dark Ages. Nor will you tell him. I'll rephrase that. If you tell him, you'll be sorry. I don't want to blackmail you. It would just be pleasanter all round if you'd accept gracefully that I might be quite a nice mother-in-law.'

'Blackmail?'

Tom is watching her intently. This is just a game, presumably. Oh, well. Let her have her fun.

She clears her throat. She is not finding this easy, he is

ad to see. She gives him a ghost of a smile, the corners of her wide mouth turning down. 'You wouldn't want the press to know, would you? Labour MP on holiday with wife and ex-mistress. The Eternal Triangle.'

'I thought you were hoping to keep it from Vic?'

Her smile becomes broader. 'I didn't expect you to fall for it. But it was worth a try. The real thing, the other thing, is likely to be more effective.' She taps the fat red book on the arm of her chair. 'Bumpy's Diaries.'

She is looking slyly sorrowful and Tom feels, for the first time, a stab of unease.

She says, with a sigh, 'He left them to me. I've been asked if I'd like to write his biography. I don't think I will. I asked Philip, you know, that nice American, he's a publisher, so I asked him if it would sell in the States. He said, no, probably not, it might be part of the dumbing down of America, but there wasn't much interest around in European politics. Unless it was something, some new scandal, or angle, on Churchill, perhaps for a while yet on Thatcher. So as I wasn't all that keen, really, I decided to let myself off the hook.'

'It would have been quite an undertaking,' Tom says cautiously.

'A long haul for a flutter-brain like me?'

Tom raises his eyes to the ceiling and disdains to answer.

Portia giggles.

Tom looks at her, and sighs. 'All right. You could pick out the salacious bits and publish them in the *Sun*. But that's not what you're on about, is it?'

'There are no salacious bits,' Portia says indignantly. 'You know Bumpy!'

'Not as well as I thought I did, it would seem.'

Tom thrusts his fists deep in his pockets, stretches o
his legs, crosses his ankles, stifles a yawn with a smile. H
hopes by this display of comfortable nonchalance to con-
vince Portia that he is absolutely unworried, a man who
knows more or less everything there is to know about more
or less everything, and is unlikely to be perturbed by anything she might have to tell him.

He fancies that Portia is looking slightly less confident.
She fishes in the pocket of her cotton shift and brings out
her sunglasses.

'Let's be having it, then!' he says, amused, jocular.
'Straight from the shoulder!'

She puts her glasses on, pushing them up on the bridge
of her nose and then takes them off again. She says slowly,
'You must know that he didn't rate you particularly? Didn't
exactly hold you in high regard?'

Tom shrugs his shoulders. 'If you say so. I suppose it
shouldn't surprise me. That the old man might harbour a
few unkind thoughts about his predecessor, I mean. In fact,
once or twice, I found myself a touch jealous of him.'
Portia's eyebrows shoot up, and he adds, hastily, 'Not, of
course, recently.'

'Bumpy wasn't *jealous*! Honestly, Tom. That's a thoroughly coarse thing to say! Typical of you, if you don't
mind my saying so!'

'I do mind it! Look, you make these mysterious utter-
ances, nudge, nudge, hint, hint, come on, let me look at the
blasted thing.'

She seizes the red book and holds it against her. To his
surprise her eyes are suddenly wet, tat tears spilling out
from the corners, dribbling down her face. She rocks from
side to side, sobbing. 'No, no – I can't do it, can I? Anything

at hurt you would hurt Vic and you're right about him, he sort of good man he is, I'd rather never see him again, just walk *out* of here, rather than hurt him . . .'

'Twaddle!' Tom shouts, incensed. 'Total, soppy, tosh and twaddle. I thought you had a *mind*, Portia, not a deliquescent mush of sentiment.'

He starts to rise from his chair. She gives a sharp cry of what sounds like real terror and scrambles up clumsily, shrinking away from him, clutching the diary. She turns to escape, run into the bedroom, and crashes into the sliding glass door. She screams and collapses backwards, her hands over her face.

Tom is in time to catch her. He lowers her gently into the chair she was sitting in, crooning softly. 'Oh, Lord, that must have hurt. Darling, you are an idiot. What did you think I was going to do? Come on, now, let me look, see the damage . . .'

She moans, but allows him to remove her hands from her face. He makes a nannyish clicking sound but she doesn't laugh. He says, 'Skin isn't broken, that's something. You haven't got any arnica by any wondrous chance? Hang about. I'll get something cold from the minibar.'

There is no ice. He removes four miniature bottles and wraps them in a face towel from the bathroom.

'A bit clumsy, but better than nothing,' he coaxes her. 'Speed's the important thing. Just hold it there, perhaps you'd better lie on the bed. I'm afraid, whatever we do, you're going to look like a punch-drunk prize fighter. Oh, I *am* sorry.'

'Bloody hell you are,' Portia says indistinctly. She is obviously in more pain than she can easily bear, but she pushes him violently enough in the chest to send him staggering.

She says, 'Go, go. Get *out*, can't you?' She gives a strangled snarl of rage and hurls the miniature bottles and their towelling wrapping away from her. A couple break on the marble floor of the balcony. Glass splinters everywhere.

'That was bright, wasn't it?' Tom roars. 'Cut your feet to ribbons, too, *what* a good idea!' He storms past her into the bedroom and returns, his face a mask of fury, to throw a pair of leather sandals in her lap. 'Put those on,' he orders. 'Get into the bathroom and bathe your face with cold water. I'll ring down and get them to send someone to clear up the mess. Then I'll clear out.'

To his surprise, she is suddenly laughing. Little whoops and whistles; deliberately mock-hysterical. 'You better behave, Tom Jones,' she splutters, 'or I'll tell your father you gave me a black eye.'

Only joking, he knows that. Or is almost sure that he knows it. On the terrace, talking to the man from the *Chronicle*, watching for, and dreading, Portia's appearance, his mind wanders. The journalist has a sad, gentle face, a domed, egg-like forehead and although his English is excellent, he is softly spoken for a Greek, which gives Tom an excuse to ask if he would mind repeating his last question.

'I am a little deaf,' he explains, miming this condition, leaning forward and cupping an ear.

'I asked if you are confident, Sir, that your party will form the next government. I ask this for my own information, off the record, you understand, not for publication in the newspaper.'

He has already switched off the tape recorder he has been using but Tom is unwilling to be drawn all the same. Before he embarked on this interview, the only other per-

211

on on the terrace had been Philip Mann, sitting at a discreet distance and reading a manuscript; since then, the terrace has been invaded by elderly holidaymakers, their number suggesting that most of their group has decided to abandon whatever cultural excursion has been planned for today and hang around the Hotel Parthenon in case there should be further excitements. Tom allows that after yesterday's television dramatics, the appearance of a single, sober, print journalist must be disappointing, but he senses a kind of impatient greed among the waiting ancients that makes him uncomfortable.

He says, 'Well, of course, nothing is ever certain in politics, but I would think the odds are fairly clearly on us at the moment,' and begins to shift in his chair.

He catches Philip's eye. Philip raises an enquiring eyebrow and Tom crinkles his eyes at the corners and gives a quick nod of assent. Philip gathers the pages of his manuscript and comes to the rescue. He is polite to the newspaperman, introducing himself in Greek, apologising for intruding. Then, in English, to Tom, 'Sorry, there's something we must . . . That is, when you're ready.'

Together they walk the journalist to the hotel entrance. He shakes Tom's hand and thanks him. A waiting photographer takes several pictures of Tom, posed against the sea. Tom apologises to Philip. 'They were hoping for a photograph of Miss Palmer but Max won't let them see her.'

Philip shakes his head, smiling. He leans his lanky body against a pillar and prepares to wait patiently.

'Sorry,' Tom says, when the men have gone finally. 'And thank you. Funny feeling, suddenly, back there on the terrace. As if I was in some sort of circus. Part of the spectacle.'

'People don't look away any more. That struck me yesterday. Though maybe it was only ever Anglo-Saxons who did. I remember breaking down in France once, and cars slowing, not to stop and help, only yelling out of the windows, *Combien des morts?*'

They smile at each other. Tom says, 'At least they're not all perched on the shore waiting for the body to be dragged out of the sea. Like a line of vultures. Have they stopped trying to find her? I haven't heard the helicopter lately.'

'Prue says . . .' Philip clears his throat fussily. 'You know our young doctor? She says the body won't surface before six days at least. Between six and fourteen days. I asked the police – Max wanted to know, of course – and if the coastguards haven't found her by then, they will recall the helicopter.'

'What's he going to do? Max Farrell. Lord, what a business!'

Tom thinks, *mother drowned, auntie daft as a brush, oh, the poor devil*, and feels his lips twitching. There is always a point when tragedy becomes comedy. And vice versa. But Philip, like Amy, is too grave a character to share these thoughts with.

Philip says, 'He hopes to take Miss Palmer home, tomorrow, if possible. Get her safely out of the way. He asked me if I thought Mrs Honey would mind going with them. Prudence says there's nothing her grandmother would enjoy more. I assume he's anxious to have someone else around in case they find his mother's body. He'll have to see to all that. I can't say I envy him.'

He seems to hesitate, then says quickly, with no change of tone, 'Matilda – my wife – she died four weeks ago. She

213

killed herself.' Then, apologetically, 'So you see, I can sympathise with the problems of death and disposal.'

'I'm so sorry,' Tom says.

Absurdly, he feels he should offer some confidence in return. His operation? Portia's unexpected presence? Amy's – equally unexpected – pregnancy? None of them quite measures up.

He says, it is all he can think of to say, 'These last few days haven't given you much of a chance for rest and recovery.'

'We came here together, some years ago. I thought . . . Well, never mind.'

Philip is looking painfully embarrassed now. Clearly wishing he had never spoken.

Tom says, heartily, 'Holidays seldom turn out the way you expect, not in my experience, anyway. I'd thought we, that is, Amy and I, might take off for a few days, see something of the country. Instead of which, it turns out I'm stuck here, waiting for a call from our House of Commons, from my political masters. The Leader of my Party wants to speak to me. No idea what it's about, but it's the sort of thing puts up the blood pressure!'

Tom laughs, to show this is a light-hearted remark, and adds, seriously, 'I haven't told my wife, by the way. Thought I'd wait and see.'

'I won't tell her,' Philip says.

To Tom's surprise, he is smiling quite broadly.

Philip cannot imagine why he told Tom about Matilda, blurting it out like that, without thinking. He has always judged himself a cautious man, careful with confidences. He tells himself, *stingy* might be a better word.

214

He wonders briefly about Amy. Prue had said thought she might be pregnant. He could have asked To But it appears that this is a couple who keep secrets fro each other.

As he has kept secrets from Prudence. She knows his wife is dead, but not how she died, nor how recently. At the beginning there had been no reason to burden her with the entire, terrible story, even if he had felt able to tell it. But if he tells her now, will she feel he has cheated her?

He is waiting for her now, on the terrace. This is their last day together. They have one more day, one more night.

Philip tells himself: this is something they have both known all along. That he has to fly back to the States as she will have to fly back to her hospital. What he has kept from her are the other duties that wait for him: the arrangements to be made about the apartment, about Matilda's possessions, her clothes, her papers (a trunk full of letters, the daily journals she had kept from a schoolgirl), pieces of jewellery which must be divided between her daughter, her sister. His children will need him. Matthew, particularly. Above all, there is his guilt to be purged, his knowledge of failure. And there is no point in encumbering Prudence with all these shabby necessities. It is not as if they could have any future together. Whatever he may have said, last night, in her arms . . .

Although Philip has been brought up not to blow his nose in public, he does so now, to hide his tears.

Prudence says, 'All right. I'll go home and you'll go home. Fair enough. I can see that from your point of view it wouldn't exactly be tactful to turn up with a bimbo like me quite so soon after. I mean, when your children are still

rning their mother. You need time, too, you've had
te a battering. Why don't we give it six months?'

She is white-faced, but determinedly smiling. They have
aken a taxi along the coast to a shack on a mud flat
halfway around the great bay, run by one old man and
guarded by a ferocious grey dog, a hound of hell on a rattling chain. Having passed this Cerberus, they are sitting
under a canopy of dried tobacco leaves, drinking ouzo and
eating stale bread stuck on toothpicks with lumps of feta
cheese and tomato.

Philip puts his head in his hands.

Prudence says, sharply, 'If you don't love me enough for
that, then just say so.'

Philip groans. 'OK. You go back to Daniel and see how
you feel. But give him a proper chance. Give yourself a
proper chance. Don't think about me.'

'Six months,' Prudence says. 'You'll find some nice older
woman with an expensive facelift and a healthy bank bal-
ance. I'll marry Daniel and have a baby. Or have a baby and
then marry Daniel. Or marry some other man. I don't care.
Don't you think it's just possible that I might rather wait to
see if you still wanted me?'

'Oh, Prue,' Philip says. 'Oh, my darling.'

He doesn't think he can bear this.

She says, 'Listen. D'you know the old story? The one
about the French king and his jester? It goes something
like this. The jester annoys the king. The king says he will
chop his head off. The jester begs for his life. He says, look,
you have a favourite horse. Give me a year and I will teach
your horse to talk. All right, the king says, I'll give you a
year. He puts his crown straight and sweeps out and the
other courtiers say, what's the point? Twelve months is the

216

point, he says. In that time I may die anyway. Or the
may die . . .'

She looks at Philip questioningly. 'Yes,' he says. 'I will
enamoured of this lady with the facelift, or you will hav
married Daniel.'

'Right,' Prudence says. 'Right, my friend. There is a third
possibility, isn't there?'

He puts out his hand to her. But he is sitting with his
back to the sea, looking inland. And down the dirt track
that leads to this remote and dusty ouzerie that Philip paid
the taxi driver to find for them (somewhere quiet, he had
said, not a tourist place, away from the town, by the sea) a
grey car is bumping, raising clouds of red dust, causing the
tethered dog to leap to the end of its rattling chain, yelping
wildly and dangerously. Out of it, when it stops, two familiar figures emerge.

Portia is wearing her enormous sunglasses. Her right cheek
is a patchwork of muslin and plaster. She throws up her
hands, miming surprise and mock-horror.

'Heavens,' she cries – bustling forwards, since there is a
clearly no turning back – 'I didn't think anyone else would
be here.'

Sitting down at an adjacent table, she beams cheerfully
at Prudence, at Philip. She says, 'There's a kind of battered
sign on the road, looking as if it leads nowhere, but Vic
said, let's go and investigate. Is that what happened to you?'

Philip says, gratefully, 'Someone said this was a good
place to watch birds.' He flaps his hand at a solitary egret,
stalking by the muddy edge of the sea. 'So we got a taxi.'

'We can take you back if you like,' Vic offers immediately. He glances at Portia for guidance.

n, of course,' she says brightly. 'Though I must warn
, we're not staying any longer than it takes to knock
k a huge, healthy drink. My face I don't mind it, but I
n behind it. Vic's done his best to patch me up, rushed off
o the kitchen for bags of crushed ice, but I feel such a fool,
that's why I was hoping to avoid civilised company. So
when Vic pointed out the sign, I said, that looks a good
hideaway. But what is it they say? If you wait long enough
at Piccadilly Circus the whole world will come by.'

Portia waits for one of them to say something. Anything.
But it seems they have been struck dumb. Portia has never
seen two such miserable faces. She would like to knock
their heads together.

She says, 'Unfunny joke. Sorry. Did you know we had a
crash yesterday? A fool of a woman tried to drive us over
the edge of the mountain. Luckily, the car hire people gave
us another one without fuss.'

Prudence makes a visible effort; her face shudders like
the sea when a cloud passes over it. 'That's how you hurt
your cheek?'

'I'm afraid not. If it had been the car crash, I wouldn't
feel quite so silly!'

She smiles at them blandly. 'I just slipped on a piece of
soap in the bathroom, would you believe it?'

🌸 14 🌸

In Greece, the Orthodox dead are buried swiftly: in the afternoon or evening if they die before noon, the following morning if they die after midday. In general, the same ruling applies to other religions out of hygienic necessity: outside Athens there is no refrigeration and except for a brief spell in winter the weather is usually warm. Cremation, which might seem to be an answer in these circumstances, is illegal.

So Mrs Honey has discovered this morning. She is visiting the florist who is also the undertaker for the town, a useful combination of trades that delights her practical mind, as does the mission Max Farrell has given her. There will be different arrangements, of course, for a corpse taken out of the sea, but Max Farrell likes to have what he calls *the whole picture*, and has delegated Mrs Honey to fill in minor details of the landscape.

She is in her element. The florist is a charming man who has set a chair for her on the pavement, sent for coffee, and given her a strongly scented gardenia. He cannot help her with the decisions that will have to be made should her friend's body be recovered, but he is a good listener and gives Mrs Honey the comfortable feeling that he has all the time in the world for her.

'They were devoted to each other. More than devoted, of course, being identical. Even if identical twins are separated at birth, their lives will usually follow the same patterns; they will catch the same illnesses, marry the same sorts of men. Nature is very wonderful . . .'

Mrs Honey is not absolutely sure that the florist is understanding her. She hesitates, but his dark eyes, brimming with kindness and sympathy, are definitely encouraging her to continue.

'In the ordinary way it would be more sensible to bury her in Greece, and it would be *possible*, wouldn't it? She is an Anglican, and the Anglican are in communion with the Orthodox Church. But I expect her sister would want her brought back to England so that when the time comes, they can share the same grave. Or the same casket . . .'

She wonders if it is tactless to mention caskets. She has understood from this understanding and attentive Greek that the reason the Orthodox Church forbids the burning of bodies is their resurrection at the Last Trump. Though if the Lord can recreate a person's body out of bones, why not out of ashes? It shouldn't be beyond Him, in Mrs Honey's opinion.

She says – hastily, in case this irreverent thought should somehow linger in the air and give offence – 'Her son will have to make the decision, of course. But her sister, that is, *his* aunt, Miss Tish Palmer, is a strong-minded person, if a little confused at the moment. But as I said to Mr Farrell,

he can't rely on her *staying* confused. She has had a sl.
and in my experience with old people, the confusion n
pass all of a sudden, and *then*, if she doesn't like wha
been done, she'll create merry hell. So we have to mov.
carefully.'

Mrs Honey relishes that 'we'. She has had a happy life
since her husband died, busybodying away, a bit of nursing
here, a bit of Conservative Party committee work there,
plenty of money for travel and a good game of bridge most
weekends, but although she loves her daughter and granddaughter neither of them have needed her, in the way she
would have liked to be needed. For the moment Max
Farrell needs her, not for ever, perhaps not even for long,
but it will be interesting while it lasts, and something to
talk about after. There is always the *possibility*, however
remote, that there may be more in the royal connection
than Max is prepared to admit to . . .

Miss Palmer may turn out to be more forthcoming. In
Mrs Honey's experience it sometimes takes time to win an
old person over. Tish is not particularly friendly to her at
the moment, but that will change, Mrs Honey is confident.
Max has told her of the excellent housekeeper who has
always looked after the sisters in their flat in Eaton Square,
but she is not a nurse, and in Mrs Honey's judgement, Tish
will need nursing care.

In fact, it is only decent to offer! In her mind, Mrs Honey
hears herself saying to Max, 'I don't know why, but I feel so
responsible for your poor, dear aunt. Such a dreadful thing
to happen on holiday. I suppose, in a funny way, it's
brought us all closer together. We're no longer just a bunch
of strangers who happen to be staying in the same hotel
and can just wave goodbye at the end. Speaking for myself,

221

a busy woman, but not so busy that I haven't time to
p out a friend . . .'

Satisfied with this speech, Mrs Honey is keen to deliver
.. Rising from her chair, she says, 'Well, I really mustn't
hold you up any longer, you've been more than kind.'

Graciously, she holds out her hand, half expecting this
nice foreigner to raise it to his lips, but perhaps that is not
the custom in Greece because he says, 'A minute, wait,
please,' and calls out to someone in the dark of the shop. A
dark, pretty girl, smiling, brings out a large sheaf of white
roses, wrapped in figured plastic and tied with white ribbon.

The florist says, 'Take, please. For the *Kyria* Palmer.'

'What lovely roses.'

'They come from the florist's. He gave them to me to give
to poor Tish. He is the undertaker as well. Isn't that quaint?'

Amy wonders why she dislikes Mrs Honey quite as
much as she does. Oh, she knows why. *Poor Tish*! How pre-
sumptuous! But she feels she is being intemperate, all the
same.

She says, 'How is Miss Palmer? Have you seen her
today?'

Is it pregnancy making her irritable? It would comfort
her to know that the urge towards physical violence that
has suddenly seized her is the result of hormonal disturbance. Or perhaps it is only proximity, trapped as she is in
the lift from the town with this relentlessly confident, self-
satisfied woman. Once they are released into the outer air
she will become less intolerant.

The lift whines, lurches, and stops. The door shudders
open. Amy says, 'I hope Miss Palmer enjoys her beautiful
roses.'

Mrs Honey turns the corners of her mouth down. matter of coals to Newcastle, I fear. Max has filled room, waste of money, in my opinion, since they're fly. off tomorrow. Though there may be somewhere, a hospit. an old people's home, that would like them. I thought I'c ask Philip if he would deal with that. I'd sort it out myself, only I've decided I must offer to travel home with poor Tish. Take a bit of the burden off Max. It means cutting my holiday short but it's a sad old world if you can't put yourself out for others occasionally.'

Amy nods and smiles agreement. There is nothing wrong in any of this. Perfectly reasonable sentiments, even if they are not expressed all that elegantly. So why does she still feel so hostile?

Mrs Honey says, 'I've nothing to keep me here, now Prudence has fixed herself up, if you get my meaning!'

And she rolls her eyes and winks in a way that Amy finds quite disgusting.

Amy has been to the town to buy stamps and postcards. She has a list of names and addresses, printed out from her computer and stuck, every year, in the back of her diary. Although she has intended to sit on the terrace with her pen and her postcards, as she crosses the lobby she is growing irresolute. How can she possibly write ordinary holiday postcards? *The weather is lovely. We are having a nice, restful time. And an old lady has drowned in the sea.*

She does not have to mention this tragedy. She has no intention of mentioning her pregnancy. But to leave out Jane Farrell's death would seem to dismiss it. Would be somehow irreverent.

Amy hesitates. A voice in her head rebukes her. 'My, my,

e sensitive, aren't we?' She decides to ignore it. Her
es are usually craven. She will write letters instead; a
er is more dignified than a picture postcard, more
spectful to the dead. There are desks provided with
eaded hotel writing paper on the mezzanine floor but no
one seems to use them; although the lift door opens at the
mezzanine automatically, no one ever comes in or goes
out. She will be private there.

And at first it seems that she will be. The floor is car-
peted, the solid furniture gleaming with polish, sofas and
chairs plumply upholstered in shiny material, the harsh
light from the windows softened with blinds. Amy thinks –
only conspirators would come here, to whisper in secret.
Or, perhaps, castaways.

It is then she sees Beryl Boot, crouched in the corner of
an over-stuffed sofa, staring at her like a hypnotised rabbit.
As Amy moves towards her, she starts to sob, stuffing a
handkerchief into her mouth, her whole body shaking.

Amy puts a tentative arm round her shoulders. Beryl
collapses, limp as a weeping child, her face hot and wet
against Amy's breast. Amy holds her more tightly, rocks
gently. 'Ssh, *there*, don't worry, cry all you want . . .'

And she continues to make soothing noises until Beryl
detaches herself, sits up, blows her nose. 'Oh, I'm so sorry.
What will you think of me? It's just, Daddy doesn't like to
see me upset and I thought I'd be all right, hiding here.'

'Then it's I who should be sorry, isn't it? Bursting in on
you?'

She is hoping to coax a smile, but Beryl only sighs and
pats her hair. 'I must look dreadful.'

Amy assumes this is not a serious remark. 'Is there anything I can do?'

Beryl shakes her head and sighs again. 'They've arres
the boys. It's not Daddy's fault. The boys went too far.'

A memory flicks across Amy's mind, a darting fish, va
ishing. No point in chasing it. She says, 'Would you like t
tell me?'

'I don't mind,' Beryl says – as if she is doing Amy a
favour. But this is not what she means, apparently. She corrects herself. 'I don't mind *for myself*. I worry about Daddy.
It's so unfair. He's been a good father. And he's never over-
stepped the line himself. Legally, I mean. You couldn't
expect him not to be a bit careful and make sure he got his
rent, can you? And someone has to take in all those poor
people turning up at the airport with nowhere to go and no
money. Daddy did his best for them, not exactly the Ritz
Hotel I grant you, but no one else took the trouble. At least
they weren't sleeping in doorways. And all he gets for it is
insults. Welfare millionaire, that's what the newspapers
called him. All right, he's made money but he's worked for
it, let me tell you!'

Beryl looks at Amy as if throwing down a challenge.
Amy is struck by how much more intelligent she looks
and sounds when she is fired up and indignant. And now,
of course, she remembers what Daddy's boys have been up
to! Claiming housing benefit, often for fictional tenants,
defrauding the Department of Social Security, defrauding
the taxpayer. Not to mention the genuine claimants who
have found themselves living in squalor.

Amy says, cautiously, 'I think I know what it's about. I
suppose, if your husband wasn't directly involved, he may
still be required to give evidence. Is that worrying you?'

'Oh, we're not taking the risk! Daddy's made up his mind
to stay out of the country until it's blown over. Though

dy says if the police really want him they can get hold
him, so maybe we should go somewhere else. Daddy
nks northern Cyprus. That was what was upsetting me,
ally. I'd got over Mother. As Daddy says, Gavin can take
care of her. And the girls can always fly out to see us. But I
like it here. I'd found a house . . .'

Tears are welling up again. Although it seems more than
likely to Amy that Daddy Boot is as liable as his sons for his
firm's illegal behaviour, she finds herself suddenly – and
surprisingly – sorry. Amy is a conscientious lawyer. She
works hard for her legal aid clients, who are frequently
petty criminals, but although she pities them sometimes,
thugs and thieves are not social victims to her, still less
social heroes. So it seems strange to her that she should feel
sympathetic to Beryl.

She says, reluctantly, 'I shouldn't really advise you. You
should ask your own solicitor. Though she'd say the same
thing. All anyone can really tell you is that although
England does have an extradition treaty with Greece the
system is so expensive and clumsy that it's not often used.
You'd need to be wanted for a major crime, terrorism, a ser-
ial killer, something like that. But if your husband wanted
to get to northern Cyprus, he would have to go from
Turkey. And the Turks could simply refuse him entry and
deport him straight back to England. So if the police are
likely to want to – to speak to your husband, if I were you
I'd stay here.'

'I don't even like her much,' Amy says.

She is lying in the bath; Tom is shaving at the basin. He
is watching her in the glass.

She says, 'I think I felt *responsible* for her. Something

226

like that. I don't know. Mysterious. Maybe it's that woman drowning, it's as if we'd all been shipwrec together and have to look out for each other. I though them being stopped at the airport in Turkey and put on flight straight to London and just felt that I really mus warn her. And she's found a house in the town that she wants to buy and do up. I don't know why that should have touched me, but it did. Or pregnancy has softened my brain.'

'It's made you remarkably cheerful.' Tom pats his face dry and looks at his watch. 'How much longer are you going to stay in that bath?'

'What's the time?'

'Just after seven. I told Vic you'd be down for a drink well before eight. I thought I might follow you later on. I don't think I can stand another celebratory session. You do your bit, I thought, then I'll join you.'

'Are you really so upset? Don't you like Portia? Or would it be the same whoever she was? Someone taking your mother's place?'

Tom is not sure how to reply to this. He senses traps set for him everywhere. He says, carefully, 'I can't really answer that, can I? Portia is the only candidate we've been offered. And I'm not *upset* Just uncertain.'

'I think she's a good thing.' Amy stands up and steps out of the bath. Tom wraps her towel round her and kisses her forehead. Amy says, 'She's intelligent, and she's jolly, but she's ordinary, too. I mean by that, she's not going to have any grand expectations. I wouldn't think she's a particularly ambitious woman, would you? Either socially, or intellectually. And she's pretty, but she's not *marvellous* looking, and she's the right sort of age. I mean she must be older

you. There can't be much more than sixteen or sev-
en years between them. So she's old enough to be glad
have a nice man like Vic to look after her.'

'What patronising bunkum!'

Tom is taken aback by the wave of anger that seizes him.
He prevaricates hastily. 'Sorry, darling, but that was rather
de haut en bas, wasn't it? Not like you, either.'

Amy is sitting on the side of the bath, drying carefully
between her toes. She doesn't look up, but her face is crimson. She says, 'I like Portia. I didn't mean to put her down.'

'Ordinary!' Tom says, as lightly as he can manage.
'Humble origins! Low expectations!' A more telling reproof
seizes his mind. 'Come to think of it, you were more patronising towards Vic! A good enough match for the old man.
Not too sophisticated! Not too demanding, intellectually or
socially! Pretty enough, but not so striking that she's likely
to be besieged by younger men. And old enough to be
grateful!'

Amy is staring at him, her mouth slightly open. She says,
'Oh, *Tom*!'

Watch it, Tomkins! He can hear Portia saying this and it
brings him a curious comfort that he refuses to analyse. He
will have to be wary.

Amy is wearing her black dress with the purple roses. She
doesn't much care for this garment, feeling it makes her
look like a maypole, but she believes that Tom likes her in
full-skirted dresses and Vic has admired it.

Although she was puzzled by Tom's outburst in the bathroom, it has not upset her. She thinks now she knows what
has caused it. Portia is so unlike his mother, so clearly better suited to Vic's easy temperament that Tom must be

228

terribly torn: on the one hand, glad for his father, a
the other, resentful and sad on behalf of his mother. A
rather proud of her own careful craftiness, slightly d
grading Portia instead of lauding her to the skies and t.
underlining her own joy in the prospect of Vic's seco
marriage turning out less of a purgatory than his first.
Tom feels she has been unfair to Portia, it may dispose him
to look upon his new stepmother more favourably.
Meanwhile she is delighted to have the chance to congratulate them without Tom's inhibiting presence looming and
glooming beside her.

They are waiting for her, a bottle of already opened
champagne in a bucket. Except for Portia and Vic, the terrace is empty. The old people's tour have a video showing
in the television room, a silent film and a live lecturer. Max
Farrell is taking his famous aunt and Mrs Honey out to dinner: one meal in the Hotel Parthenon was enough for him.
Both Portia and Amy would prefer to dine in the town but
neither of them has suggested it; Portia because of her battered face, Amy because they have paid for full pension and
she is frugal by nature. Vic eats what is put in front of him.
And Tom is waiting for a telephone call.

Portia's bruises have developed magnificently. She turns
to Amy, displaying her purple cheek, the colour of an arch-
bishop's robe, and holds up a warning hand. *'Don't ask!'*

'It's all right, Amy love, I haven't been knocking her
about. After all, we're not married yet!' Vic enjoys this joke,
laughing as he gets up to kiss Amy, fuss over seating her.

Amy wonders if she should have kissed Portia before
she sat down. Too late now. Never mind. The important
thing is to show Portia how delighted she is without overdoing it and perhaps betraying to Vic how dreary she has

thought his first wife, his first marriage. She puts
_nd on Portia's arm.

_m has just told me. We are both enormously pleased.
_n't say I hope you'll be wonderfully happy because I'm
sure you will. For myself, I shall enjoy having you as my
_other-in-law as well as my friend. And I know the chil-
dren will be delighted to acquire such a lovely young
grandmother.'

To Amy's nervously critical ear this stiff speech sounds
(as indeed it is) over-rehearsed. Something else is needed,
something spontaneous, to make Portia feel she is properly
welcomed as one of the family. Something personal.

She says, 'And I'm sure our new baby will be pleased,
too! We were going to keep it a secret until we got home,
but this is such a special occasion!'

Portia takes this news calmly. Odd of Tom not to have mentioned it, but that's all. It is the throbbing sincerity in
Horsey's voice that makes her uneasy. She has not really
considered before that Horse-Face might develop into a
problem. Although she has accepted that she will have to
tread carefully if Vic is to be happy (and Vic's happiness is
important to Portia) she has been finding the prospect
exhilarating rather than threatening. She has finished with
Tom, after all; she will only have to guard against slips of
the tongue. But if Amy is going to be so demandingly loving, that may turn out harder to handle.

Portia looks into Amy's moist, shining eyes, and reminds
herself that, barring accidents, she and Vic should be safely
out of here by this time tomorrow, the two of them on
their own in Monemvasia, or in Pylos, or Delphi, depending upon where fancy takes them. She says, sedately,

'Thank you, Amy. I have never really wanted chi..
myself, but I have often thought I might enjoy beir
grandmother.'

Vic has embraced his daughter-in-law, patted her, kisse
the top of her head. He says, 'Now we have two things tc
celebrate. I am a lucky man.'

Portia watches him, pouring champagne. He is both a
dear friend, and a stranger. Nice eyes, nice hands, nice
mouth. The skin round his lips is soft and smooth and
warm. He is looking at her now, she feels the blood pump
in her cheeks, her throat constrict, sensations that she
identifies as a happy mix of affection and lust. Oh, well, call
it love if you must, she concedes grudgingly. And to distract herself from the inconvenient surge of emotion that
has swept over her, she smiles dazzlingly beyond him, at
Philip and Prudence who have just appeared on the terrace,
arms linked, hands tightly laced, as if they are trying (so
Portia thinks) to grow into each other.

Philip doesn't realise Portia is smiling. In the last few
days, he has given up wearing his spectacles unless he is
reading. This is not because he has heard somewhere
that bifocals are ageing. (Or not consciously, anyway.)
He has told himself he doesn't really need glasses for distance; in the clear Greek light he might not even need
them for driving. But although he can recognise Portia
and Amy and Vic, he cannot be certain of their facial
expressions.

Prudence whispers, 'We'd better just say good evening,'
and steers him towards them. She says, to Portia, 'I'm so
sorry about your face. I ought to have been more sympathetic this morning. But you seemed so cheerful about it. Is

nful? Can I do anything?' She looks at Portia, and
_hs. 'Or would you rather I didn't mention it?'

_low sensitive she is, Philip is thinking. Dearest Prue.
_e must be an excellent doctor. He imagines himself, next
_me he comes to London, knocked down in the street,
carried unconscious into the nearest hospital, waking to
see Prudence's sweet, concerned face above him, her cool
fingers on his wrist. Would she recognise him? Next year,
perhaps. But in five years? In ten years?

Portia says, 'I can hardly expect anyone to ignore it. I
know I look hideous. Don't all rush to deny it. But I really
would rather it wasn't mentioned. Or not above once an
hour, say. And, if you don't mind, I'll stop smiling. It hurts
to smile. As long as no one asks me what's wrong, why am
I looking so miserable.'

Philip thinks, nice woman, sensible woman, it might
have been better if . . . But he refuses to allow himself to
drift further along this particular speculative road. His habit
of second-guessing alternatives is a foolish one. Besides, he
loves Prudence. And they have so little time left. He grips
her fingers even more fiercely. 'Prue is kindly taking me for
a last look at the town. I'm off to Athens tomorrow, early
start, dropping in on one of our more elderly authors along
the way. She has a house not far from Nemea.'

He is surprised at his fulsomeness. He has not felt so
awkward since he was adolescent, sweating over the agony
of entering or leaving a room full of people. At least he
knows now that no one else notices.

Except perhaps Portia. In spite of the pain, she is smiling
a little. Like a kindly aunt, she comes to his rescue. 'We'll
all be up early, there'll be time to say goodbye then.'

*

Tom says, 'Well, you'll be off in the morning, Da
may not be here when you get back. I can't remer
when's your flight, Portia? We've got another few a
haven't we, Amy darling?'

He knows the answers to these questions already. F
and Amy are staying in the Hotel Parthenon for anothe.
four days. Portia is booked for a fortnight. Vic has yet to
arrange his ticket but presumably he will want to fly back
with Portia. Tom is not really interested in these tedious
travel plans. He is filling in time.

He is waiting until the last minute. After dinner, over a
last drink in the town, in the square, on the harbour? He
cannot guess what their reactions will be, what he wants
them to be. Nor what he feels himself.

He says, finally, when he has told them, 'You could look
on it as an insult. Shoved upstairs, conveniently out of the
way, to make way for someone more successful. More useful, anyway. It seems pretty clear that this renegade Tory
will expect more than just my safe seat but he didn't go into
that. None of my business, presumably. There was a deal of
flattery, naturally. All the good work I could do in the
Lords, what a marvellously reliable committee man I have
always been. And so remorselessly on . . .'

He is half afraid to stop talking. They are sitting round a
small marble table, on uncomfortable chairs. There is no
moon, and no stars; there is a black sky, a black sea. It is a
warm night with no wind.

Tom laughs. 'I must say, it's a great turn-up for the books,
isn't it? What the hell does that mean, anyway? You never
know what's lurking round the next corner. The best-laid
plans of mice and men.'

Portia says, 'You did tell him you wanted a government

he Lords if you gave up your seat in the Commons?
n, you did strike a *bargain*?'

ar as I could. I can't hold him to it though, can I?'

You could be bloody awkward if he doesn't stick to it.
wmgarw is one of the biggest Labour majorities in the
country. They may not be exactly over the moon at having
a turncoat Tory dumped on them, even if he is a junior
minister.'

'He'll keep his word for precisely that reason!'

Tom is smiling at Portia. He is annoyed with her. Does
she think him so stupid?

Vic says, 'I understand why the top brass want Tom's
seat. There's this Tory defector, the first important one to
cross the floor of the House. They'll need to find him a seat
with a big majority because a lot of Labour voters won't
vote for him. They'll vote another way or they'll just stay at
home. But I'm not absolutely . . .'

He is looking at Portia. What he isn't absolutely sure
about is what Tom wants, how Tom is feeling. But if that's
what he wants to know, he should be looking at Amy.

Portia turns to her enthusiastically. 'What do you think?
How do you feel? You haven't said anything. Shall you like
being m'lady? I tell you one thing it's useful for. Booking
tables in busy restaurants.'

Tom says quickly, 'Amy doesn't care for titles. Anyone we
know who's got a handle, she does her best to avoid using
it. A Quakerish attitude.'

He thinks, *of course* he should have told Amy first! On
their own, privately. He says, 'In this case, darling, it would
just go with the job. But if you feel terribly strongly . . .'

Amy shakes her head. She puts out her hand and he
takes it. She says, smiling at Portia, 'I knew you'd be a

marvellous person to have in the family! You've worke
the House of Lords! It'll be a huge help to Tom if he can a
your advice if he needs it. You can guide his faltering step
I know he'll be grateful.'

Tom looks at Portia, too. She returns his gaze calmly, not
the tiniest flicker of amused recognition.

Tom thinks, good girl. Will she manage to keep it up?
He says, gravely, 'It's a funny old world.'

Vic says, 'I'll tell you one thing, my lad. Your mother
would have been a proud woman this day.'

Max Farrell's party is the first to leave. Mrs Honey has
helped Tish Palmer to dress: her wardrobe has yielded a
black dress and a black lace mantilla she has chosen to
wear as a veil. Perhaps she is hoping for photographers at
the airport. If so, she will be disappointed. Max has
arranged for Mrs Honey's ticket to be upgraded to first
class and for the three of them to be driven straight to the
plane. He has organised this through a Pasok politician
who is a friend of his and owes him a number of favours to
do with his banking arrangements in Switzerland.

He is glad to be leaving. Like Amy, he cannot understand
why anyone should want to do nothing on holiday, though
unlike Amy he has no wish to go walking or bicycling or
sailing or mountaineering: work is his recreation. His
mother's death will not distract him for long. Her affairs are
in order – he knows this, because he has ordered them. His
Aunt Tish is a responsibility but it is one he is long accustomed to, and Mrs Honey (or Florence, as she has asked
him to call her) is turning out to be another useful subor-
dinate in a long line of useful subordinates. He intends to
cherish her for as long as he needs her.

rudence is at the hotel entrance to say goodbye to her
ndmother. Before she gets into the back of the car the
vo women embrace. Prudence murmurs a half-hearted
pology for not spending enough time with her, and
Florence Honey pinches her cheek and laughs in a sugges-
tive way that Amy would doubtless find vulgar but sounds,
to Prudence, understanding and loving and generous.

She waves until the car is out of sight and says, to Philip
who has been standing back until the farewells were over,
'I do hope she had *quite* a nice time.'

Philip says, tenderly, 'You do love her, don't you?'
Prudence's capacity for love seems wonderful to him. He
had loved, and still loves, his good foster parents, all his
kind, foster family, but he feels that he has never understood the visceral love that binds blood relations until he
had seen Prudence with her grandmother. It amazes, and
awes, him that she has so much love left over for him.

He is feeling wonderfully happy this morning. There has
been a stay of execution. Only one more day, but the hours
stretching before him seem limitless. Prudence is coming
with him to Athens. A taxi to Nemea, where he will see his
old author, and a bus from there to the airport. They will
find a room in an airport hotel. His plane does not leave
until midnight.

Portia and Vic, breakfasting in the dining room, are
ready to leave; they have handed in their keys, paid their
bills, packed the hired car.

Portia says, as Philip and Prudence stop by the table,
'Always more baggage at the end than you started out with.
I never understand it.' She laughs then, as if she understands it only too well, and says, hastily, 'I think I am just
being defensive. Vic is so neat.'

'Then we are complementary,' Vic says. And looks smile at his son.

Tom is yawning. He has left Amy resting (retrea perhaps, behind the safe excuse of her pregnancy?) a come to say goodbye to his father and prospective ste, mother. Still widely yawning, indeed, acting up hi exhaustion, rubbing his eyes and rolling his shoulders (as if being tired might be a form of protection, not unlike having a baby) Tom prowls the length of the buffet, helping himself to hard-boiled eggs, cheese, several slices of pale pink generic meat, three puffy white rolls. This is more than he had intended to take. On the other hand, he needs to keep his strength up. And he owes himself a treat, to celebrate his new place in society. He would never say so (except perhaps in a weak moment to Portia) but he is pretty chuffed at the thought of it. Besides, the Lords is a more tranquil place than the Commons. Oh, he intends to put his back into it, be a dutiful working peer, but it will be less of a scrum. He will have time to think, time to spend with his new son or daughter.

He is aware that little Beryl Boot is beside him. 'If you please, Mr Jones, would you mind getting one of those peaches down for me? My silly little arm isn't long enough.'

There is a pyramid of fruit on a stand at the back of the buffet. They are almost out of Tom's reach, which makes him suspect they are for display, not consumption. Certainly, the beautiful peach he selects has the solid feel of an uncooked potato. 'I don't think . . .' he begins.

But Beryl thanks him effusively. 'It's for Daddy, he'll be so pleased when he sees it. He does like a nice peach and they don't bring you fruit when you order your breakfast in bed.'

smiles politely and she flushes softly. 'He's ever so
ul, too, for the advice your wife gave us. I know he'll
to say thank you *in person*, so perhaps we can have a
ak together some time.'

Her blush deepens. 'They're most of them going, aren't
ney, all our little lot? There'll be just the four of us left, you
and me and your nice wife and Daddy. So we'll have lots of
time to spare for each other.'

Tom has settled his father and Portia into their car, check-
ing, like a good son, that they have the right maps, the
right guides, an English/Greek phrase book and a plastic
bottle of drinking water.

The green hotel minibus is parked behind their car, and
behind the minibus, an elderly taxi that has a large, dangling crucifix almost obscuring the windscreen. As Vic
drives off, Prudence and Philip emerge from the hotel in
time to wave at him. The taxi is theirs. They shake hands
with Tom while a hotel porter wheels out a baggage trolley
and passengers appear for the minibus. Tom watches them
idly. Two women, three men. A fairly obvious mother and
son; a single woman, perhaps in her thirties, very composed, very pretty; a handsome male couple. He has seen
none of these people before. He catches Philip's eye and
nods in their direction, raising an eyebrow. Philip looks;
shakes his head. Prudence puts her hand to her mouth. She
whispers, 'Perhaps they've just been here for the night.'

Philip turns to speak to the porter, who shrugs his
shoulders and laughs as he answers. Philip interprets. They
have all been guests in the hotel for a week. Prudence says,
'It's not possible. How can we have missed them?'

They look at each other. Perhaps these strangers kept to

their rooms. Perhaps they never ate in the hotel, ne
on the terrace, never drank at the bar, never swam i
pool . . .

Prudence says, 'They didn't even seem to notice ea
other.'

She looks shocked, almost frightened. Tom says, 'Don
worry about it. Just tell yourself it's a mystery. I know I can
live with that!'

'I hate not knowing.' Prudence slips her hand under
Philip's arm.

Tom says, because it suddenly seems important to him,
'There are a lot of things you have to learn to live without
knowing. Or not knowing for certain. More and more as
you get older. Most things are contingent, approximate.
What d'you think you are going to do, next month, for
example? Next year? The year after?'

Philip and Prudence look at each other. Prudence says,
uncertainly, speaking to Philip rather than Tom, 'We might
die, I suppose. You might die. I might die.'

'Or the horse may talk.'

Philip's answer is incomprehensible to Tom, who doesn't
know the story. But it makes Prudence laugh.

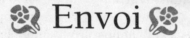 Envoi

IN SPITE OF HER NEPHEW'S PRIVILEGED arrangements, there are television cameras at Athens airport to record Tish Palmer's departure; a tall, tragic, veiled figure tottering between the hired car and the plane, supported – hustled along – by Mrs Honey and Max. This is her last public appearance. On her return home, in spite of Mrs Honey's attempts to divert her, Tish opens the envelope from her cutting agency to be faced with her own obituaries, published after her presumed death by drowning. These are distressingly perfunctory; only *The Times* and *The Telegraph* give her more than half a column. But it is the hideous photographs both these papers have chosen to accompany their premature valedictories that cause the fatal heart attack, which in its turn, inspired by the comedy-tragedy of the double death, produces longer and more respectful accounts of her life and times. Too late, alas, for her *amour propre*.

Tish Palmer dies in Florence Honey's arms. Max, who

has other things on his mind, including the dispo.
mother's body which is washed up on the beach a
three days after his aunt's death, accepts her offer t
charge of the funeral arrangements. Mrs Honey cons
that Highgate Cemetery would be an appropriately rom.
tic resting place for a famous actress connected with roya
and decides, indeed, during the course of the ceremon
that she would like to be buried there herself, close to Karl
Marx.

It is a dank, dark day. Max, returning precipitately from
organising his mother's internment in an Athens cemetery
(since her twin sister is dead, he sees no point in going to
the expense of flying her body home) catches a nasty cold
which turns, owing to the damp air and his weakened
state, into bronchial pneumonia. Mrs Honey nurses him
efficiently and relentlessly and cooks infinitely better meals
for him than his housekeeper. While he is too ill to care,
she sends the curtains in his study and living room to be
cleaned, washes the delicate nets herself, in the bath, and
generally brings the whole flat to a level of polish and
spruceness that astonishes him when he rises from his bed.
By the time he has recovered his strength, the housekeeper
has departed indignantly and Mrs Honey has so inextrica-
bly wound her life around his that he cannot see how to
break free of her. Nor, in truth, does he want to. He has
come to pride himself on his skill with elderly ladies and he
misses his aunt and his mother. A little to his annoyance
Florence Honey refuses to move in with him, turning down
the generous offer of his old housekeeper's very comfortable and quite separate apartment, but she occupies his
spare room on her increasingly frequent visits to London to
see her daughter, her granddaughter, and, eventually, her

ndson; keeps a sharp eye on the help she hires and
him, and expects him to look after her stocks and
, speak to the bank for her, and fill out her tax return.
ᴐes not like her all that much, nor she him, but they
fulfil a need in the other: he would have no personal
without an awkward old person to nurture, and she is
eased to be taken out to dinner by a man who knows
about wine and commands respect in a restaurant. Without
each other, in fact, they would both be lonely.

As Beryl Boot is to be for almost a year. Daddy's boys,
Alan and Eric, play a last nasty trick on their sorely tried
father. They put a stop on transfers of money from the
firm's bank account, leaving Stanley Winston Boot (Daddy
was named after two British Prime Ministers) with no
option but to go home. At least he has made sure that Beryl
is safely out of the way. He has put enough money in her
account in the National Bank of Greece to rebuild the
house of her dreams and keep her in at least moderate
comfort until he can return to take care of her.

Taking care of his family has always been Stanley Boot's
first concern. Alan and Eric have been a heavy burden to
carry, but if he was careless in not questioning the suddenly
improved cash flow into the business, it is largely due to a
father's natural wish to believe that his sons have at last
chosen to go straight, work hard and do well. It is only
partly the need to sort out his finances that sends Daddy
Boot back to London. He has a weary affection for his wild
boys, and perhaps some guilt to do with their sad, murdered mother.

So he goes back to 'face the music' – this is how he
explains it to Beryl. The trial lasts nine months; at the end,
Daddy Boot is found technically innocent but ordered to

pay his own costs. Alan is sent to prison for five years a
Eric for seven. 'At least you'll know where they are for
while,' Beryl says when she meets Daddy at Athens air
port. She has bought herself a pretty white trouser suit for
this occasion and had her hair dyed a slightly darker shade
of blonde. She has also acquired a dog, a small, white,
woolly bitch called Delilah.

Tom and Amy and Vic all follow the case in the newspapers. Tom thinks the man is a fool to have come back to
London. Amy is sorry for Beryl. Vic says, to Portia, 'I expect
the poor devil got drawn in, step by step, not really meaning to, just finding himself out of his depth all of a sudden.'
And Portia, who doesn't give a damn about Daddy Boot one
way or the other, just answers, 'Darling Vic, you are just the
nicest man in the whole bloody world, you know that?'

Vic sells his flat in the Barbican and moves into Portia's
pretty terrace house in Islington which he enjoys doing
up to his own high standards, painting with good, National
Trust colours, putting in a power shower, and strengthen-
ing the floors so that they will take the weight of Bumpy's
books in the bookshelves he plans to build for them.
Praised by Portia, who is constantly amazed at her luck in
finding this paragon, this good, funny, kind man who
seems to be able to fix just about anything, Vic shrugs,
points at the photograph he took at Epidaurus which he
has enlarged and hung on the wall and says, with a deep,
deep sigh, 'That's the best any man could ever do.' And,
with a grin, 'I put it there to keep me in my place! In case
I get above myself.'

Portia is happy with Vic. She feels safe with him. She had
felt safe with Bumpy, but Vic is the first man she feels she
can trust to look after her in the way she once trusted her

...er when she was a little girl, riding high on his shoulders. Sometimes, with Tom, she feels a faint, stirring ...elleity but only for the excitement of intrigue, a spot of sly secrecy. She enjoys watching him growing into a certain pomposity, a member of the House of Lords. And the father of twins. He pushes them through St James's Park, side by side in their buggy and is becoming one of the most photographed and most popular government ministers. He is putting on weight but he does nothing about it although he sometimes suggests to Amy that they should both go on a diet.

Amy would do what he asks if she thought he would stick to it. Sometimes she wonders if she should ask Portia to speak to him, suggest he should stop eating those huge slabs of chocolate, and perhaps take some exercise. Tom listens to Portia. Amy can see how much she amuses him; she knows he thinks she is pretty, and clever. Sometimes, watching them, particularly on occasions when they sit side by side on the sofa each holding a gurgling twin, Amy is conscious of a kind of nudge in her mind, a gentle shove, as if she knows more than she thinks she knows and if she only stopped still for a minute, paid close attention, she would know what it was. But she is too busy: her job, and entertaining for Tom, and the twins, of course . . .

Who would have thought of *twins*, at her age? She remembers that nice American buying the pregnancy test for her in that Greek pharmacy and sometimes dreams, fleetingly, of meeting him again, by chance, on a bus, on the Underground, and feels an unexpected flush of sexual longing. She remembers thinking he looked like James Stewart. But he lives in the States, of course . . .

Amy is wrong about that. Philip and Prudence and their

baby son have a house in Montague Square. Philip is
ing a small publishing house and Prudence is hoping f
consultancy in geriatric medicine. It is fairly safe to assu.
that they will live happily ever after.

Also by Nina Bawden

IN MY OWN TIME
Almost an Autobiography

'A joy' – David Holloway

'A born story-teller, a gift as evident in this autobiography as in her novels' – *Independent*

Nina Bawden's acclaimed career spans twenty adult novels and seventeen for children. Hugely admired as a novelist who unravels the complex emotions that simmer beneath family life, she now turns to her own story. In deceptively simple vignettes she takes us through her life and, fascinatingly, reveals the origins and inspirations of her many books. We learn about her childhood evacuation to Suffolk and Wales, and of her years at Oxford where she met Richard Burton and Margaret Thatcher. Perhaps most moving of all is the courageous account of her oldest son Niki, who was diagnosed a schizophrenic. In My Own Time is a tribute to the great talent and quiet heroism of a very special woman.

A WOMAN OF MY AGE

'Rarely have the workings of a woman's mind
been revealed with such clarity' – *Daily Telegraph*

Elizabeth and Richard, eighteen years married, have come
to Morocco on holiday, journeying from its fertile coast to
the barren uplands beyond the Atlas mountains. As the
adventures and disasters of their travels unfold, so too does
Elizabeth's account of the desert her life has become. Her
grievances and frustrations are credible and sympathetically told, yet, simultaneously and subversively, Nina
Bawden demonstrates the inevitable ambivalences and
deceptions within marriage. These tragic, comic tensions
are highlighted by the unexpected arrival of a friend travelling with a much younger lover and by the potentially
oppressive companionship of the garrulous Mrs Hobbs
with her considerate, quietly literary husband.

As the story moves towards a shocking catastrophe and an
extremely surprising coda, Nina Bawden deploys her
themes – marriage, families, expectations and betrayals –
with poise, wit and charm, and proves once again that
there is no more subtle chronicler of the human heart.

Now you can order superb titles directly from Virago

☐ Woman of my Age	Nina Bawden	£6.99
☐ Tortoise By Candlelight	Nina Bawden	£5.99
☐ Little Love, A Little Learning	Nina Bawden	£5.99
☐ Birds On Trees	Nina Bawden	£4.99
☐ George Beneath Paper Moon	Nina Bawden	£6.99
☐ Familiar Passions	Nina Bawden	£5.99
☐ Grain Of Truth	Nina Bawden	£5.99
☐ Ice House	Nina Bawden	£6.99
☐ Walking Naked	Nina Bawden	£5.99
☐ Family Money	Nina Bawden	£5.99
☐ Devil By The Sea	Nina Bawden	£6.99
☐ Anna Apparent	Nina Bawden	£6.99
☐ In My Own Time	Nina Bawden	£7.99

Please allow for postage and packing: **Free UK delivery.**
Europe: add 25% of retail price; Rest of World: 45% of retail price.

To order any of the above or any other Virago titles, please call our
credit card orderline or fill in this coupon and send/fax it to:

Virago, 250 Western Avenue, London, W3 6XZ, UK.
Fax 0181 324 5678   Telephone 0181 324 5516

☐ I enclose a UK bank cheque made payable to Virago for £ . . . .
☐ Please charge £ . . . . . . to my Access, Visa, Delta, Switch Card No.

Expiry Date ☐☐☐☐   Switch Issue No. ☐☐

NAME (Block letters please) . . . .

ADDRESS . . . .

Postcode . . . . Telephone . . . .

Signature . . . .

Please allow 28 days for delivery within the UK. Offer subject to price and availability.

Please do not send any further mailings from companies carefully selected by Virago ☐